A Summer Place

ARIEL TACHNA

Published by
Dreamspinner Press
http://www.dreamspinnerpress.com/

A Summer Place

Cover Design by Mara McKennen

ISBN: 978-0-9795048-4-6

Printed in the United States of America
First Edition
July, 2007

eBook edition available
eBook ISBN: 978-0-9795048-5-3

Acknowledgments

To Dawn, the first of my adopted sisters, who befriended me when I had no one else and encouraged my writing when no one else cared. She's read everything I've ever written, even when she disagrees with me over the content.

To Glynda, without whom I would never have resumed this journey into writing. Only she could manage to wring 689 pages out of a two page set piece.

To Emmet and George who ate lunch with me, brainstormed with me (called me a serial killer) and generally made me believe I could do this. Slash me up, baby!

To Jean, who held my hand through the mystery part of this story, making sure my sheriff and my villain both were believable and that I stayed as true as possible to lawmen of the time.

To my other adopted sisters, Nancy, Holly, Connie, Cat, Carol, Madeleine, Gwen, and Julianne, who read and reread and edit and encourage. Without you, this dream would never have come to pass.

Chapter 1

Bar Harbor, Maine, 1884

FOG.

That was all they had seen for days, a solid bank of unrelenting white, broken neither by sunlight nor moonlight as they inched their way north toward Bar Harbor. A ship had come in to Boston from the north, so they knew the harbor had thawed from the winter, but project overseer Nicolas Wells had begun to wonder if he should have waited another few weeks before heading up to resume construction on the summer homes his employer, the architect William Randolph Emerson, had designed for the moguls of American industry. They were all there: Pulitzer, Rockefeller, Dorr, Morgan, Vanderbilt and all the rest, building elaborate 'cottages' with forty to fifty rooms, heedless of the cost of transporting the granite, marble and gold by schooner up the coast to Mount Desert Island. Money was no object to these men, only being in the right quarters.

Pacing toward the bow of the four-masted schooner, Nicolas frowned as he heard a sailor's cry, warning the captain of rocks ahead. At their slow pace, they could avoid them easily, but the thought that their continued safety depended on the sharp eyes of a boy hanging off the front spar made him increasingly nervous.

A foghorn sounded in the distance, the noise eerie in the blanketing whiteness. Even at night, it was white, a ghostly soup that reflected the light but gave no visibility. He would be incredibly glad to get back ashore and begin work. Anything to relieve the tedium of this trip.

"You shouldn't be on deck in this weather, Mr. Wells," the first mate, Mr. Worth, said softly so as not to interfere with the calls fore and aft.

"I can't breathe belowdecks," Nicolas admitted. "Even in good weather, it's hard, but knowing it's like this… I'd rather be up here."

Mr. Worth nodded his understanding. He spent as little time in his quarters as possible for the very same reason. "Very well. Just stay out of the way of the crew in case they need to move quickly."

Nicolas agreed, settling on one of the hatches leading to the cargo hold. As near as it was to the front mast, whose sails were down to slow the speed of the ship in the fog, he would be out of the way of the boom, the block and tackle, and the crew.

They had left Boston two weeks earlier and should have arrived already, but the fog had drawn out the trip. He hoped they were getting close, because he was far beyond restless now, ready to arrive and get started, just to be off this damnable ship. Sailing had never been his favorite way to travel, but with the current conditions added to the equation, he liked it even less. The entire amalgam led to a nebulous sense of dread that had never before accompanied his trip to Bar Harbor. He shivered in the cold wind that sprayed the condensation from the mast and lines across his face. Mr. Worth was right. He would probably be more comfortable below, certainly he would be warmer, but he could not face the dank gloom.

The sound of metal scraping on rock sent chills up Nicolas's spine. Even he knew that was not a good sound. The cursing of the crew as they surged up on deck provided a confirmation he neither wanted nor needed. Shouted orders traveled back and forth along the ship as sailors loosened the sheet to let the sail luff, ending their forward propulsion. Others pulled on lines at the two center masts in response to an order to raise the centerboards halfway. Near the bow, still others pushed the schooner back off the rocks with long poles. Nicolas watched their focused industry helplessly, wanting to contribute in some way, but knowing that he would only interfere if he tried. He cursed silently, wondering what had possessed him to take the first ship, rather than waiting another week or two; wondering, too, if he would make it to Bar Harbor or if this was to be his end. *Please, God, no*, he prayed. He could face many things, but the thought of a watery grave froze the blood in his veins.

"There!" a sailor shouted. "Harbor light off the starboard bow!"

Nicolas peered into the fog in the indicated direction, trying to make out what the man had seen, but either the sailor had sharper eyes or Nicolas did not know what to look for, because all he saw was the unrelenting wall of white.

With the bow pointing in the right direction, the sails were trimmed again and the centerboards lowered partially. They continued their halting progress forward, every eye on deck searching for the lighthouse beam to guide them away from the rocks and into the harbor.

"Rocks fine on the starboard bow!" one sailor shouted.

"Rocks fine on the larboard bow!" another added.

Nicolas tensed, sure they were going to shipwreck. His hands gripped the mast as if that could somehow steady him or the ship.

"On the starboard beam!"

"On the larboard beam!"

It seemed, impossibly, that they were passing between the rocks without hitting them.

"On the starboard quarter!"

"On the larboard quarter!"

"Clear!"

"Clear!"

Nicolas let out a sigh of relief, sagging against the mast. When his legs stopped trembling, he pushed back to standing and walked unsteadily toward the hold.

"Good news!" Mr. Worth said when Nicolas walked by him. "We're inside the harbor. We should dock in an hour or so and you'll be safely ashore a few minutes after that."

"That is good news," Nicolas agreed, feeling some of his fear ease.

SHERIFF Shawn Parnell loved two things in life: his job and his island. It was his job to make sure no one threatened his island, and right now, someone was. He did not know who or exactly why, but he did know how: murder. And he also knew, much as he would have hated to admit it, that it would not be an isolated case. He only hoped he was fast enough to outsmart the murderer and keep the likely next target alive. To that end, he stood on the pier, despite the cold and the fog, awaiting the arrival of the schooner which had been sighted entering the harbor, hoping that Mr. Wells would follow his usual pattern and arrive aboard the first ship from Boston. If not, Shawn had no idea what he was going to do to protect the island's young blacksmith. They could not afford to lose him now that old Mr. Gibson, the former blacksmith, had retired and left the island for warmer climes. Shawn did not want to lose any of his residents, but the community could not survive without someone to do the metal work during the winter. Fortunately, Wells made a habit of hiring locally on his construction site before sending for more laborers from the south. Shawn's young friend had resented the idea at first, but the sheriff had insisted. Now it remained only to gain the overseer's cooperation.

Through the fog, Shawn could hear the shouts and curses of the sailors as they tried to dock. He gripped the rail of the wooden structure tightly. Docking was a delicate enough procedure in the light of day. With the fog obscuring objects only a few feet away, it was downright precarious. After several fraught minutes, he heard the shout signaling a line being thrown and another that it had been caught. Moving forward, he offered his brawn to help the men on the shore pull the heavy vessel into its berth. The harbor men knew the sheriff well enough to accept his help, heaving hard on the thick lines until the ship finally drifted into view. A few minutes more to secure the ship and arrange the gangplank, and the passengers were able to disembark. This early in the season, they were few in number and Shawn was relieved to see Wells's blond head among them.

He hailed the overseer as soon as he set foot on the dock.

Nicolas looked up, surprised to hear his name called. He recognized the local sheriff, but that only surprised him more. The two men knew each other to speak on the street, but they had never socialized during previous summers. Nicolas wondered what Parnell wanted with him.

"Sheriff," he acknowledged, touching the brim of his hat respectfully.

"Welcome back," Shawn said with a hearty clap on the other man's back. "Let's get out of this damned fog. I'll buy you dinner and a drink."

Nicolas tensed as he always did in unfamiliar situations, especially in situations like this where his body's unconscious reactions could give away his most closely guarded secret. In Boston, where he was mostly anonymous and relatively unimportant, it did not matter so much, but Nicolas had come to the island enough times to know better than to reveal it here. Still, he could think of no good reason to refuse, and his belly craved a hot meal after the days of hardtack at sea.

"Since you asked so nicely," he agreed, "though I will have to do something with my trunks."

"I'll have them seen to," Shawn assured the other man. "You'll be staying in the caretaker's cabin by Cleftstone Manor again, I assume."

Nicolas nodded, more than a little discomfited to realize the sheriff seemed so focused on his actions. In his experience, people only paid that much attention to relative strangers when they wanted something. He did not know if Parnell's wants were personal or professional, and that made him nervous. Had he given himself away somehow? Had something in his behavior, as circumspect as he had always tried to be, made the sheriff deduce

Nicolas's preference for his own gender? And if so, what did that mean for his future here on the island?

Taking a deep breath, the builder reminded himself that he was jumping to conclusions, that Parnell had given no indication, in word or action, that he had guessed Nicolas's secret, or that it mattered if he had. He would continue to act circumspectly, as he always had, and wait to see what transpired.

Shawn thought he sensed a certain tension in Wells that he had never noticed before, but he dismissed it as a normal reaction to an officer of the law. Even honest citizens were not always comfortable with him, as if afraid he was looking for fault. "Let's go. I'll have someone take your trunks out to your cabin."

"Let me just get my satchel," Nicolas requested.

Shawn waited patiently while the overseer went to his trunks and removed a battered leather pouch. He could not tell what was inside, but he could tell the contents were important to the other man by the way Wells held the bag.

Feeling self-conscious, Nicolas turned back, his satchel tucked under his arm. He trusted the sheriff, as much as he trusted anyone on the island, but he would not risk his secret in the hands of whomever Parnell found to transport his belongings. Some of the drawings in his sketchbook could be explained as artistic studies, but others were far too… intimate to be anything other than the sketches of a lover of men, and if that became public knowledge, he could say good-bye to his career. No crew would agree to work for him if they knew, and with no crew, he would have no job.

The two men left the wharf for a local tavern that also served meals. Parnell took a table away from the handful of other patrons, adding to Nicolas's sense that the sheriff wanted something. They sat in silence, though, until after their food and ale were served.

"We had a murder last week," Shawn began casually when he was sure they would not be disturbed. "I'm sure you'll hear about it as you start to assemble a crew. A young man who moved here a few years ago from New York."

"Really?" Nicolas asked disinterestedly. "Someone I know?"

"I don't think so," the sheriff replied. "James Reed. He was a clerk at the bank. Thin, blond, green eyes. He wore glasses when he worked, but never outside the bank."

Nicolas remembered the young man in question. He had been attractive in a pretty sort of way, an almost girlish beauty that held a certain appeal, though the overseer generally preferred a more masculine appearance. "Why was he killed?"

"He made a poor choice of lovers," Shawn replied diplomatically.

"A married woman?" Nicolas suggested. "Or did he despoil someone's daughter?"

"It's not quite that simple," Shawn stalled. "You strike me as an open-minded man."

"I try to be," Nicolas agreed, not sure where this was leading.

"Reed's lover, well, ex-lover, was a young man, and without revealing details you don't need to know, it was obvious he was killed because he was a sodomite."

Nicolas flinched at the word, though he could detect no condemnation in the sheriff's voice. "And what does that have to do with me?" he asked coldly.

"The relationship between the two men came to light a few days before the murder when Reed and his former lover split rather publicly, and I'm afraid the other man is also at risk. I know he isn't the murderer. He was here in the tavern when the murder took place and was clearly shocked at the news. My only concern is keeping the boy alive."

"Boy?" Nicolas asked, concerned now as well.

Shawn shook his head. "No, not really. He's well past being of age, but I remember him in short pants."

"You still haven't said how this concerns me."

"The man is the island's blacksmith. I know you'll need one on your site, and I'm hoping you'll agree to hire him. He doesn't need the job, but your site is closed to outsiders. He'd be safer there than anywhere else on the island, except maybe in my jail, but I'm not really equipped to hold prisoners for more than a day or two, and he's done nothing to warrant being locked up. Will you help me, Mr. Wells?"

Nicolas knew as soon as the sheriff asked that he would say yes, for only his own discretion had kept him from facing the same hate that now threatened the blacksmith, but he did not want to appear too lackadaisical about what should have been a shocking situation. "He does quality work?"

"The best," Shawn assured the overseer. "His master, old Mr. Gibson, said he hadn't seen such talent but a few times in his life. In a larger city, he could probably make a living as a sculptor, such is his artistry. Here, there's not enough demand and so he makes barrel staves and horseshoes. And hopefully, the metalwork for your cottages."

"Very well," Nicolas agreed, "but I expect him to be discreet and pull his weight on the job site. It won't just be forge work. We all have chores at the camp as well."

"He understands he'll have the same responsibility as anyone else on your team."

"I'll start hiring the local crew over the next few days. He can come whenever he wants, but it'll be rough living until we have a cook and get a camp established for the off-island workers," Nicolas warned. He knew there was an extra cot in his cabin, but he did not offer it. One man might share lodgings with another without censure, but not if one was a known sodomite and the other was supposedly not. He could not open himself to speculation that way. "I don't even know if the tents we used last summer survived the winter. He wouldn't be able to return home like the other locals if the point of being there is to protect him."

"It's not a perfect plan," Shawn agreed, "but it's the only one I have. And there may be a bit of a camp already established. We've had a couple of ships come in from closer than Boston with some of your crew from previous summers."

"Then I would do well to get out to the site and make sure all is as it should be. Thank you for dinner, Sheriff. I'll look for you and the blacksmith tomorrow."

"You're welcome," Shawn replied, "but I'll be bringing Philip out tonight. I don't want him in his house alone even one more night."

THE shadows protect me as the sheriff leaves the tavern in the direction of the sodomite's house. He has never shown any sign of the moral abomination it is my task to end, but I will have to watch him closely. I will eradicate this pestilence from the island before it spreads further, corrupting other god-fearing youths. Reed was the first, for his faithlessness as well as his sodomy. I have yet to decide who will be next: the blacksmith or the dead man's other lover. It will depend on their actions and on what opportunities arise. Either way, I will prevail and rid my home of this godlessness. I dare not linger to see what has brought the sheriff to Hall's house, even under the cover of darkness, but I will know the truth before long.

Chapter 2

"No, damn it! I already told you I didn't want to do this."

Shawn looked at his friend, the local blacksmith, and shook his head. "And I told you, Philip, that I wasn't giving you a choice," he retorted. They had discussed this already, multiple times. He had not relented before. He would not relent now.

"What are you going to do if I refuse?" the young man challenged. "Lock me up? I haven't done anything wrong, Shawn, and you know it."

Shawn sighed. Philip was right, of course. Half the town had been sitting in the tavern with him that night when Reed was killed. There was no question of Philip's guilt or innocence. However, Shawn was not risking so much as a hair on that head of dark brown hair. "I may know it," he agreed, "but having to prove it before a court of law would be time-consuming and expensive. You had the best motive, after all," he pointed out. "He was cheating on you."

The words carried no heat, no condemnation, but Philip felt them like a blow. "I *loved* him, Shawn," he whispered, "or thought I did. Even after what he did, if I could have believed he would stay faithful, I would have taken him back. Now I'll never know what might have happened, what we could have been. Haven't I suffered enough?"

Shawn's menacing façade shattered at the sight of Philip's genuine distress. There was a time when he would have pulled the boy into his arms to comfort him, a time when the boy truly was a boy. Shawn could remember clearly the first time he had seen the lad, a stowaway who was trying to sneak off the schooner he had snuck onto a week earlier to get out of New York. The captain of the ship had been livid when he caught the boy, dragging him to the sheriff and demanding justice. What a twelve year old boy could offer the captain was beyond Shawn, and rather than see the lad in more trouble, he had paid the captain himself and informed Philip that he could pay Shawn back by doing odd jobs around his office. Vernon Gibson, the local blacksmith, had agreed to take Philip on as an apprentice a few months later, when the boy had proved his dedication in Shawn's office. Now, fifteen years later, Shawn saw not the boy but a man, grieving the loss of his lover. That, too, held Shawn back. He did not condemn Philip for his choice, but he was no longer completely sure how to interact with his longtime friend. Would the embrace he offered in comfort be viewed as more than Shawn was willing to give?

If he forced his mind to look at the blacksmith objectively, the sheriff could see the younger man's profligate beauty, could understand why a woman would desire him. Philip had the face of an angel, high, delicate cheekbones that belied the brawn that came with his choice of profession, a curved bow of a mouth, the lower lip barely plump enough to form an irresistible pout. He had heard the young women exclaiming over the breadth of the blacksmith's chest, the strength of his arms if they happened to see him working in his shirtsleeves. Yes, he could see it when he looked at Philip objectively, but the moment he abandoned that objectivity, he saw the man again, and that was the end of Shawn's interest.

"Yes," he replied, answering Philip's question. "That's why I need you to take this job. I don't want you going through what Reed went through. I don't want to find you stripped and strangled and violated."

Philip's head jerked up. This was news Shawn had not shared with him before. "V... violated?" he stuttered, his heart breaking all over again as he finally understood that Shawn was not simply worrying for nothing.

Shawn nodded. He had not wanted to tell Philip, but it had clearly become necessary. "They, whoever they are, used a broom handle," he said softly, "and left it inside him. He died from having his throat slit, but he had bled, and badly, before they killed him."

"They killed him because of me," Philip whispered, stricken.

"No," Shawn insisted. "They killed him because they're narrow-minded bigots who have no place on this island. It's my job to find them before they kill again. And since they know about you and James thanks to the lovely scene the two of you enacted, you're their next likely target. I can spend all my time here, watching you, or I can put you the safest place on the island besides my jail and spend my time tracking them down. Which do you prefer?"

Philip did not hesitate. "Find the bastards," he declared. "I'll go to this construction site and do their pretty metalworking if you think that'll keep me safe. But find them, Shawn. I want to do to them what they did to James."

"You know that's not an option," Shawn reminded him.

"I know," Philip replied, "but I can dream." He took a deep breath and locked away the grief and anger he still felt at James's death. "I don't think I've ever talked with this overseer. What's he like?"

Shawn smiled. "Quiet," he began. "Reserved, but reliable. He's agreed to hire you and help keep you safe. Now all we have to do is get you out there and settled."

"I guess I'll need to take some things with me, won't I?" Philip asked, looking around his small house. "I probably won't be coming back here for a while."

"Not until I catch the bastards," Shawn agreed, "but if you forget anything, let me know and I'll bring it out to the camp for you. For now, let's just get the basics."

Philip nodded and started to prepare a pack. He had a bedroll he used when he hiked up into the mountains on the far side of the island. He pulled that out of a cupboard and added several changes of clothing and a shaving kit. A towel and a set of metal dishes completed his gear. "That should do it for now," he declared. "I'll need my tools, but I won't be able to carry those. I'll see what this Mr. Wells has on site and bring a wagon back for the rest, duly escorted, I promise."

Shawn nodded. "I know you think I'm being overprotective, and maybe I am, but I'd rather be that way and have you alive than find you dead somewhere."

Philip grimaced. "As you say." He cast one last glance around his little house, trying to make sure he had not forgotten anything important. He hated to leave, which was why he had argued so long with Shawn over the necessity of it. All his life, he had lived under someone else's roof. First his parents', then Widow Taylor's as Shawn's ward, then Gibson's. Finally, he had his own place, his own space, only to have to leave it not six months later. He knew what life would be like in the camp, living in tents, probably with several other men, no privacy, nowhere to go to be alone for a few minutes to tend to his personal needs. And the other men would have heard about James, about the argument he and Philip had before James's death. They would know Philip preferred male company to female and they would look at him askance, wondering if it was catching or if he would try something while they slept. He would not, of course, as he preferred his lovers willing and eager, but it would take weeks or more to convince the other workers of that, and for that time, he would, once again, be the outsider, the outcast. Just once, he thought, he would like to be welcomed for who he was rather than judged for it.

THE sheriff's comment about workers already being at the site had Nicolas more than a little concerned. Though far from finished, the manor and storage sheds already contained valuable materials and tools. If any damage had been done, if anything had been taken, that would put them behind schedule, and ultimately, he would have to answer for that. Emerson trusted him to get the building done right and on time, without exceeding the agreed-upon price. So far, Nicolas had delivered. He had no intention of failing now. That meant getting to the site and seeing what was going on as quickly as possible.

Fortunately, the owner of the tavern had a nag he was willing to rent Nicolas until the overseer could make arrangements for the summer. Swinging aboard the horse, Nicolas headed for Cleftstone Manor.

To his relief, he recognized the voice that challenged him when he drew near the site. Even better, when the owner of that voice stepped out of the shadows, Nicolas could see a long-barreled shotgun in his hands. "It's all right, Sullivan," he called. "It's Wells."

"Mr. Wells!" Eric exclaimed with a sigh of relief, lowering his weapon. "We're glad you've made it."

The sheriff had not said who or how many had already come, but if Sullivan was here, Nicolas had no doubt that Johnny West and Carl Malone were somewhere in the camp. The three of them had been his crew bosses since his first year as overseer, three very different men with three very different personalities, yet together they had helped him create some of the finest architecture on Mount Desert Island. "I'm glad I made it, too," he admitted. "The journey up was… harrowing."

Sullivan nodded sagely. A native of the Maine coast, though further south, he knew all about the fogs that settled in for days, or weeks at times. "It's like that in the spring sometimes," he agreed. "If this is the first time you've encountered it, you're a lucky man."

"I've had a day or two of fog before, but never weeks like we had on this trip. I'm not sure I've seen sun or moon since we left Boston."

"It has been thicker than usual this year," Eric observed. He started back toward the camp. "Have you eaten? I know you'll be wanting something hot after the long trip. Johnny's got enough in the pot for one more, I'm sure."

"Thank you for the offer, but I ate in town," Nicolas replied, keeping his horse's gait slow to match the big man's pace afoot. He could still remember his awe the first time he had seen

Eric, towering over the other men, shoulders almost half again as wide. More than once, the simple presence of the crew boss had stopped a fight before it could start. Though Nicolas had reason to know he was as gentle as a lamb, Eric looked like he could tear a man apart with his bare hands. "The sheriff met me at the pier. It seems there's been some excitement in town."

"So I heard," Eric agreed. "A boy got himself killed."

"And the sheriff seems to think the killer's not done yet," Nicolas continued. He paused to greet the other two men when they reached the tents set up in what would eventually be the gardens of Cleftstone Manor.

"Talking about that poor bugger Reed?" Johnny drawled from his seat by the fire. Johnny was the oldest of the three, though he did not look it. A widower with two young children who spent the summers with their grandparents, he relied on his job with Nicolas to tide him through the long winter since he did not have enough property to support himself farming. He had told Nicolas in a rare moment of complete honesty that he needed the time away as well to keep from losing his mind over his wife's death.

"Yes," Nicolas replied. "Did you know him?"

"A little," Johnny answered. "It's not every day someone moves onto the island from so far away. He was a bit of a curiosity from the start."

"I don't think I know him... knew him," Carl inserted. Nicolas smiled at the youngest of his three crew bosses. Carl had shown up that first summer looking for work, heartbroken because his fiancée had left him for another man. Nicolas had taken pity on him until he had seen the man work stone. He had not pitied him since, not with a talent like Carl possessed.

"He was the bank clerk," Johnny said. "You know, the flamboyant one, the one whose mannerisms always seemed just a little... too much."

Carl frowned, trying to figure out who Johnny was describing. Finally, he pulled up the image of the young blond clerk who always had a brightly colored kerchief in his breast pocket. He nodded. "I know the one you're talking about."

"But what's that got to do with us, Mr. Wells?" Eric asked. "Why would the sheriff want to talk to you about the murder? You weren't even on the island when it happened. He can't think you know anything."

"No, he doesn't," Nicolas assured his crew. He debated what to tell the three men, not sure what their reaction would be to the revelations the sheriff had shared with him. "He wants me to hire the local blacksmith for the summer."

"You always hire local when you can," Johnny commented with a frown. "Why was that worth meeting you at the ship?"

Deciding there was no way around it, Nicolas replied, "Because he thinks the blacksmith will be the murderer's next target. He wants the young man – Philip, I think he called him – to stay on the site here since we control who comes in."

Nicolas watched in silence as the three men digested that information, watched as the coin dropped and they figured out what it must mean that the sheriff wanted to protect the young man. The other men looked at each other silently for some time before Eric nodded.

"I can't say I agree with the choices the blacksmith seems to be making," he said slowly, "but he doesn't deserve to be killed for them."

The other two signaled their agreement as well.

"Glad to hear that," the sheriff's voice came from the darkness. "And I know Philip will be, too."

Chapter 3

ALL four men looked up in surprise, Eric's hand lifting the shotgun he held. They relaxed when the sheriff stepped into the circle of firelight and lamplight by which they were talking.

"Don't scare me that way, Sheriff," Eric scolded. "I might have shot you before I realized who you were."

Shawn had the good grace to look embarrassed. "I didn't mean to startle you, but I couldn't help overhearing your conversation. I take it Mr. Wells has filled you boys in. Can I count on your help in keeping Philip safe?"

"If Mr. Wells has decided to hire him, then he's one of the men," Johnny offered, clearly speaking for all three of them. "We look out for our own."

"Good," Shawn declared. "The island could survive without a lot of things, but we wouldn't make it through the first winter without a blacksmith. We can't afford to lose the one we have."

"So where is this irreplaceable wonder?" Nicolas asked, curious now. The sheriff had said he would bring the young man out to the site. The sheriff was here, but Nicolas had yet to see anyone else.

"Philip!" Shawn called. "Come on."

The man who stepped from the shadows was undeniably young, but he was also obviously a man, despite the sheriff's reference to a boy. His broad chest and thick shoulders spoke clearly of his chosen profession. The shadows cast by the firelight hid the details of his features, but Nicolas had the impression of a strong silhouette and serious face. Knowing what he did of Philip, knowing the blacksmith's preferences so matched his own, he studied the shadowed face, taking in the hint of a beard, the longish hair. The firelight gave a reddish cast to the dark locks and an eerie glow to his skin, capturing the overseer's attention.

Philip eyed the four men around the campfire with a mixture of anxiety, disdain, and hope. They knew the truth about him – everyone on the island did, of course, but they were outlanders. If they scorned him for his affections toward James, he would lose any chance of being accepted by the rest of the crew. Mr. Wells had agreed to hire him, though Philip did not know how much persuading Shawn had done. Even so, that meant he, at least, was willing to accept Philip as he was. The other three men were saying the right things now, but Philip wondered if that would still hold true when Shawn and the overseer were absent. He hoped so. He could hold his own in a fair fight, but he would never stand a chance against Sullivan. The man was a mountain, to rival Cadillac Mountain behind them on the island. The other two were smaller than Sullivan, but hardly small. He might take one of them, but certainly not all at once.

Deciding to end the stalemate, Johnny rose from his seat, offering his hand to the blacksmith. "Welcome to the crew," he said. "I'm Johnny West. This is Carl Malone and Eric Sullivan."

Surprised and pleased, Philip took the outstretched hand, grasping it firmly. "Philip Hall."

"We only have a couple of tents pitched," Johnny told the blacksmith. "We'll pitch you one in the morning, but for tonight, you can bunk with me if you'd like. It's still a little chilly to sleep outside at night, even for an island native like yourself."

Philip wanted to believe the sincerity of the offer, to trust the kindness he heard in the other man's voice, but he had seen even long-time friends turn away these past two weeks since his fight with James and his lover's subsequent murder, not because they thought he was guilty of murder but because they knew he was guilty of sodomy. "You're not afraid I'll try something… unnatural during the night?" he asked bitterly.

"No," Johnny replied with perfect honesty. "You wouldn't be a respected member of the community here if you went around indiscriminately accosting people. But I'm more than capable of defending myself if you did."

"Philip," Shawn scolded. "That's hardly the way to make friends."

"I'm here to work, aren't I?" Philip retorted. "You'll excuse me if I'm a little testy about being dragged out of my home in the middle of the night. I'll do my job because that's what I've been hired to do, but that doesn't mean I'm happy about it."

Nicolas frowned, rising to his feet, drawing the eyes of the others there. Sensing his boss's displeasure, Johnny stepped back to let the overseer handle the situation.

Nicolas stepped forward so that he stood where Johnny had, toe to toe and nose to nose with the blacksmith. "I agreed to hire you on the sheriff's recommendation," he began, "and I'm a man of my word, but I run a tight ship and there's no place here for that kind of attitude. I understand that you've just suffered a grievous loss, so I'll excuse your insinuations with West and your ill will this time. That won't last forever, though."

Philip felt his breath catch in his throat when he got his first good look at his new employer. He had seen Wells from a distance over the past ten years as the overseer came to the island to work. Vernon, Philip's mentor, had always turned down the offer of employment for the summer, saying he had enough to do keeping up with the island's inhabitants' needs to take on more work, thus depriving Philip of the chance to see the man up close. The firelight muted the older man's aquiline features, but even the flickering shadows could not hide the chiseled planes of Wells's high cheekbones and wide smooth forehead. Dropping his eyes to the mouth currently set in a tight line, his eyes settled on a tiny scar bisecting the overseer's upper lip. He had the ridiculous urge to flick his tongue over the small imperfection, as if he could somehow ease the pain of a wound long healed. Giving himself a mental shake, he looked up again and met the project manager's eyes. "I apologize," he said softly. "I was out of line. It won't happen again."

Nicolas nodded shortly, turning his attention back to the others. "I hope this goes without saying, but I don't have time for any stupidity on my job site. If there is any and I find out who started it, it won't matter how much or how little experience he has, I'll fire him."

"That won't be necessary," Johnny assured him. "Hall's just a little out of sorts because of everything that's happening. He'll get to know us and realize we're decent men and we'll do the same with him. By the time you hire the rest of the crew, there won't be any question of foolishness. You can count on us to make sure of it."

"That's definitely part of it," Shawn agreed, inserting himself into the conversation, "but it's more than just that. If I'm right and Philip is the next target, it will also mean protecting yourselves and him against a madman. I know Mr. Wells keeps a closed site, so that will help, but our murderer isn't likely to come in through the front gate. He's more the kind to jump the fence."

"That was going to be my first order of business in the morning," Nicolas explained. "We'll need to set a night patrol rather than just someone at the gate, but with just the five of us, that's a little complicated, especially since having Hall on watch alone defeats the purpose."

"You're probably safe tonight," Shawn reminded him. "No one knows Philip's here."

"That's not an excuse to be lax," Nicolas disagreed. "I take my responsibilities seriously."

"I'm not a responsibility," Philip interjected hotly. "I am perfectly capable of taking care of myself."

Nicolas did not respond in words, pivoting instead and taking the blacksmith to the ground with the force of his weight. The younger man struggled, but the overseer caught him in an implacable grip, pinning Hall beneath him. "If I were the murderer, you would be at my mercy now if you weren't already dead."

Releasing the islander, he pushed back to his feet. "As I was saying, we'll need to set a watch and make sure Mr. Hall is never left alone. Anyone can be caught off guard, and I have no intention of having a murder on my job site."

From his place on the ground, Philip frowned. He had not expected the overseer's move and had, as the man said, been caught off guard. That was bad enough, but his reaction to being tumbled was even worse. Despite the situation, despite the clearly non-sexual tone of the man's actions, despite being surrounded by men whom he barely knew, the feeling of Wells's strong body atop his sent tendrils of lust curling through Philip's body. He knew better than to let the reaction show, but that meant staying where he was for the moment. He feared otherwise that even the shadows would not hide the evidence of his arousal. He tried to think, to remember if he had ever reacted to anyone the way he reacted to his new employer. Certainly, James had been attractive and Philip had enjoyed their time as lovers, but the feelings had not been this instantaneous, this… all-encompassing. To his mind, that was the scariest part. He could deal with being attracted to the overseer. He had come to terms with his sexuality years ago, when his fumbling attempts with the local whore had come to naught. He could even deal with feeling this attraction so soon on the heels of James's death. After all, they had separated bitterly before the murder, James's betrayal having killed all emotions but lust for his erstwhile lover. He found it much harder to deal with the intensity of the attraction, the desire to forget about everything else, even his own safety, in favor of basking in the magnificence of the golden god of a man before him.

Realizing that he was staring, Philip forced his eyes away from his new obsession, looking around instead to see what reaction the others had to Nicolas's display. The three crew bosses appeared engrossed in the discussion of watches and security, leaving Philip relieved at not having lost their respect. He knew their good will was essential to his success at the job site, to say nothing of his safety. Reminding himself that this conversation concerned his well-being even more than theirs, he focused in on the words, catching the tail end of Johnny's comment. "…share my tent tonight until we can come up with a more workable solution. I'm a light sleeper. I would hear any commotion."

"That's fine with me," Philip commented. "I know having me here is an imposition. I'll do what I can to minimize it."

Nicolas looked down at the blacksmith. "Yes, you will," he agreed, "and you'll do it by following my instructions instead of asserting your independence. Unless it's a legal matter, my word is law here. That's the first thing you need to learn. After that, everything else is easy."

Philip had the feeling the overseer only added his qualification in deference to Shawn's presence. It was quite obvious to him that Mr. Wells was used to ruling the roost, so to speak. He had no problem with that. He enjoyed a strong man. Being one himself, finding someone strong enough to make him bend was a rare treat, for it was more than simply physical. Mr. Wells had proven the strength of his body already, and now his mental strength was coming to the fore, only adding to his attractiveness in Philip's eyes.

Nicolas felt the blacksmith's dark eyes linger on him, assessing him. He knew the look, the one that conveyed interest, even desire, and it tempted him on an incredibly deep level, but he could not give in to it. Too much stood in the way: their ages, their relationship as employer and employee, the need for Philip to stay on the island, the threat that hung over the younger man's head. No, as attractive as the blacksmith was, as satisfying as it could be to indulge for the summer, Nicolas had never engaged in casual flings. His affairs, while they lasted, were monogamous and intense. He doubted Hall, recovering from his lover's death, was ready for the intensity, even if he was willing to commit to the monogamy. More than anything else, though, Nicolas knew what would happen at the end of the summer. The days would grow too short and too cold to work on the cottage and so he would catch a schooner south again, to wile away the winter on his earnings from the summer and prepare for the next season's work. For ten years now, he had followed this pattern. It was one he could not alter.

"Let's get settled for the night," he declared, tearing his thoughts away from his dour musings. "We're sitting ducks here around the fire with no one on watch."

Johnny, Carl, and Eric rose willingly enough, Eric offering to take first watch. The other two agreed, Johnny leading Philip to his tent while Carl returned to his. Nicolas turned back to Shawn. "Good to see you again, Sheriff."

"Welcome back to the island," Shawn replied, "and thank you for your help."

Nicolas inclined his head in acknowledgement. "I should get some sleep. We have work to do tomorrow."

Shawn nodded and left the construction site, heading back into town. It was almost too late to return to the boarding house he called home, but perhaps the lovely widow Taylor would still be up, finishing the preparations for the next day's meals. If so, he might even persuade her to share a cup of coffee with him before they each retired for the night.

Back at the camp, the five men were each lost in their own thoughts as they settled in for the night. Johnny's mind was full of images of his son and daughter as he had last seen them, playing joyfully at his parents' house before he slipped away, knowing that was easier than saying goodbye. His eyes closed as he called up the image of his dead wife. Virginia had been an earthbound angel and he could not blame God for wanting her back. His tears welled again as they always did when he thought of her. He let them fall unchecked, his tribute to the depth of their love.

In the tent next door, Carl's thoughts, too, were with a loved one far away. He had told Nicolas the truth when he first arrived, his fiancée having left him. What he had not told Nicolas, or anyone else since, was that he had found someone to replace the faithless bitch. He had met Kevin Frost when he returned home that fall. It had taken him some time to grow used to the idea of loving another man, but Kevin had persuaded him and Carl had not looked back since. He thought briefly of the young blacksmith, wondering how he would feel if he were in Philip's shoes and Kevin dead at the hands of a madman. That did not even bear thinking about, he decided, not wanting to imagine a life without his lover.

Eric paced the perimeter of the small camp, shotgun in hand. He was not completely comfortable, to be perfectly honest, with having the blacksmith on site, both for the issues of security and because he had always been taught to condemn the sodomite. His heart, though, was too gentle to allow someone to be threatened without moving to help. He would just have to find a way to accept this and move on.

Alone in his cabin, Nicolas closed his eyes and remembered what it felt like to have Philip beneath him, the blacksmith's powerful muscles bunching under his touch. He had absolutely no intention of acting on the lust shooting through him, but he was honest enough with himself to admit that it was there. Knowing he had to get it out of his system, he slid his hand into his trousers, determined to burn this attraction out of himself. There would be enough worries without adding his libido to the mix.

On his bedroll in the tent he now shared with West – Johnny, the man had insisted Philip call him – Philip tried not to toss and turn. He could hear the muffled sound of weeping from the other side of the tent. He almost asked what the matter was, but an invitation to share his tent for a night, an invitation even to use the other man's first name, was not an invitation to that level of intimacy. He held the silence, giving Johnny that much privacy with his grief. The blacksmith's thoughts wandered unerringly back to the overseer, specifically to the feel of Wells's body pressing down on his. He ached to feel that again, to relive the glorious weight above him, for more than a few seconds as a lesson. He would never speak of it, for he knew such advances would be unwelcome, but he wanted Nicolas Wells as his lover. His body reacted predictably to the thought and he shifted uncomfortably in his bedroll, wishing for the privacy to tend to his erection. That would have to wait until morning, though, because Johnny showed no sign of falling asleep. With a sigh, he closed his eyes and tried to will away the throbbing desire.

Chapter 4

THE next morning, Philip did what he always did when he needed to think: he worked the forge. The one there on site was rudimentary at best, and he resolved to fetch his own tools or have Mr. Wells send for them at the first possible opportunity. The overseer's reputation made it clear he demanded quality work. Philip was perfectly capable of providing that level of work, but only with the proper tools. The ones here would not suffice. Even so, he fired the forge and worked the bellows, shedding his jacket and vest despite the frost on the ground. The heat of the coals and the softening metal was more than enough to keep him warm. Were it not for the occasional gust of glacial wind that tore through the open shelter, he probably would have shed his shirt as well, despite the risk of sparks. He was skilled enough that he no longer worried about burning himself on the metal he was working and a few stray sparks were not enough to deter him when the heat of the forge combined with the heat of the day.

The rhythmic pounding of hammer on steel soothed his thoughts, subsuming all his passion into the creation of something new, in this case a ploughshare he had promised to a local farmer. He would replace the metal from his own stores, and he hoped Mr.

Wells would understand and accept that. If he did not, Philip would have to tell Shawn to find another way to protect him.

From his vantage point beside a nearby shed, Nicolas watched the blacksmith at work. He was familiar with the process, had even wielded a hammer and tongs once or twice himself. It was a point of pride with him that he knew every task he asked his crew to perform, even if he was not skilled at all of them. He would never be an artist with metal, but he knew how to heat and shape iron into the simple braces and spars they needed. He was surprised to see Hall in his shirtsleeves, for Nicolas was bundled up against the chill, but the smith was an island native, more used to the extremes of temperature, and he had the fire to provide some heat.

Privately, he would admit to himself that he was glad of the opportunity to study the other man in the light of day, although the distance between them still made it difficult to make out the details of the man's features. The thin shirt, though, let Nicolas's eyes follow the movement of powerful muscles as Hall's hammer struck repeatedly, imagining the flex and bend of olive skin beneath the material. The blacksmith paused in his task to return the fagot to the fire and work the bellows, heating the metal to white-hot before removing it and taking up the mallet again. Nicolas felt bad about interrupting, but they had things to discuss and he could not put that off all day for the guilty pleasure of watching the younger man. Steeling himself to ignore the shivers of attraction he dared not acknowledge, he moved from the shadows, striding purposefully into the forge.

Movement on the edge of his vision broke Philip's concentration, but he forced himself to finish the last few strikes before plunging the heated metal into a bucket of icy water to cool. "Morning," he said with a curt nod, grabbing a rag and wiping his hands and face free of the soot and sweat of his work.

"Good morning," Nicolas replied, summoning a smile. "We didn't discuss your salary or your responsibilities last night. I wanted to clear that up as soon as possible."

Philip raised an eyebrow in surprise. "I thought my salary was the protection of life and limb."

Nicolas frowned. "Of course not! You'll be paid for the work you do just like everyone else. In the past, we've paid the blacksmith one hundred dollars plus room and board for the summer."

Philip's brow shot higher. That was more money than he had earned in his lifetime! "Is that what you're offering me?" he asked cautiously.

"You'll earn it," Nicolas assured him, knowing in intimate detail what remained to do on Cleftstone Manor before it could be completed and released to its future owner.

"What kind of smith work remains to be done?" Philip wanted to know.

"All the railings in the house and for the balconies," Nicolas explained. "The man we hired last year could make a lot of the hinges and hardware we needed, but he wasn't an artist. The sheriff says you have the talent to do the fine work as well as the everyday things."

"I've some talent," Philip allowed. "But I'll need better tools than these."

Nicolas bristled. Emerson would not appreciate extra expenses, not when they already had tools on site. The architect would not hesitate to spend necessary money, but he hated waste. "What's that going to cost?"

"Nothing if I can go home for a few hours. I have everything I need in my forge, but Shawn didn't have a wagon to transport my tools last night."

Nicolas nodded. "We'll hitch up a wagon and take a trip into town this afternoon," he decided. "I need to get the word out that I'm here and hiring and we need to replace some supplies that didn't make it through the winter. West made a list. We can go by your forge at the same time and pick up your tools."

"I owe you a fagot as well," Philip said. "I borrowed one this morning to finish an outstanding commission while I checked the state of the forge. The bellows, anvil and fire pit here are in good shape, but the hammers are not very good quality. I'd rather have my own."

"It's settled then.   We'll go this afternoon," Nicolas declared. He started to leave, then turned back. "West's making breakfast. You're welcome to join us if you're hungry."

Philip smiled genuinely, the expression lightening his features and giving him a youthful air that had been missing during their earlier conversation. Nicolas's breath caught in his throat as the desire he had suppressed while talking business came back to the fore. He could see why Parnell still referred to the blacksmith as a boy, but Nicolas knew only the man and so saw the beauty of the smile rather than being reminded of the boy the man had once been.

"Does the crew usually eat together?" Philip asked, banking the fire so it would still be hot later and so no stray sparks would escape. He ordered the forge quickly so that all was in readiness for his return.

Nicolas watched in silent appreciation, both aesthetic and practical. The harnessed power evident in every move the other man made appealed to the artist and lover that resided under the manager's practical exterior, making him long to reach for his sketchbook and pencils. The overseer in him appreciated the obvious care the blacksmith put into keeping his workplace and tools in good shape. He had found the blacksmith from the year before disappointingly lax and was glad of the opportunity to replace him with someone more conscientious. And if Hall could do the artistic work required, that would save them from having to order the expensive custom-made decorations and have them shipped to the island. Emerson did not believe in cutting corners, but he also appreciated opportunities for saving money.

Philip could feel Mr. Wells's eyes on him, but surreptitious glances in his direction did not reveal any of the other man's thoughts to the blacksmith. The overseer's face was a pensive mask even as his eyes followed Philip's every move. The expression could have hidden anything from indifference to disgust to a lust to rival Philip's own. Unfortunately, he did not know his employer well enough to know which emotions would show and which would be hidden. He would watch and he would learn, but for the moment, he could do nothing but meet Wells's eyes. "You said something about breakfast?" he prompted after a moment of tense stillness.

"So I did," Nicolas agreed, the words jerking him out of his thoughts and back to the present. "Let's go." He led Philip away from the forge and toward the campfire where they had assembled the night before.

As promised, Johnny had made breakfast – a large pot of black coffee, a batch of thick, rich oatmeal, and a rasher of bacon to share. Philip joined the other four men in eating, though he held his silence as they talked, listening and learning. It was clear that West and the other two men had worked with Mr. Wells before. Though they spoke to him respectfully, the ease of their conversation projected volumes about their relationship. Perhaps they were not quite friends, understandable given their respective positions, but the overseer listened to the suggestions West, Sullivan, and Malone made with an open mind and serious consideration. He saw as well that the manager had every intention of being involved in all aspects of the construction. That was all well and good as long as Wells did not try to tell him how to do his job. What needed to be done and when, absolutely, but not how.

"The timbers we used for scaffolding last summer are rotting," Carl informed his employer. "We'll have to get new ones if we have any hope of raising the marble and granite to the upper levels. The ones we have now might hold regular bricks, but the first time we tried to raise one of those blocks, the whole structure would come tumbling down."

"We'll find what you need in town," Nicolas assured the mason. "I don't want injuries on the site. That's not the way I work."

"That's why I told you about the wood," Carl replied with complete confidence. More than once, he had seen his boss stop construction to fix a problem that endangered the men. It was one of the reasons he left his lover every summer to come to this island to work. The pay was good and the conditions far better than on any other site he had ever worked. He would have preferred the comfort of home most of all, but he had to earn a living somehow.

Philip was surprised by the overseer's vehemence. He had never worked on a building site before, always working in the island forge with Vernon, but he had heard tales of workers killed or maimed by accidents because of cavalier attitudes and cutting corners. It was one of the reasons Vernon had always refused to work on the summer cottages that were springing up around the island. Even working from his own forge where he would be in no danger himself, he said, he wouldn't be party to endangering others. The shared outrage at the conditions they saw at some of the worksites had been one of the reasons Philip had been so hesitant to accept Shawn's plan for protection. It appeared, though, that this site, this overseer, were different.

"It might be a good idea to get an oilcloth for the forge, too," Philip spoke up, wanting to see what reaction he got. "I keep the fire banked pretty well, but sparks do escape occasionally, and if it gets dry like it did last summer, they could cause a wildfire."

"Do we have any in the storage shed?" Nicolas asked, turning to West. He had put the widower in charge of supplies several years ago when he noticed the man's knack for organization and numbers. It was one less thing for Nicolas to worry about and added to the rapport he had with his returning crew.

"We had one left last summer," Johnny replied. "I'll check before we go into town today and make sure."

Satisfied, Philip let the conversation swirl on without him, content in the knowledge that his concerns would be taken as seriously as those of the established crew. The discussion of stonework and painting, gardens and gazebos passed him by. He knew little or nothing of those matters, having spent all his time learning to work iron. Instead, he sipped his coffee and observed the men before him. Sullivan and Malone seemed of an age, a little older than Philip himself, but younger than either Johnny or Mr. Wells. Both were darkly handsome men, strong and overtly muscular. Johnny was slimmer, though Philip suspected his build hid a wiry strength that opponents would easily underestimate. While all three of them were attractive, they did not hold Philip's gaze or his thoughts. Those meandered consistently back to the overseer. Fairer than the others, he was nonetheless handsome, his blue eyes twinkling in response to a joke Johnny made. Like Johnny, the overseer was wiry rather than bulky, but he had more than proved his strength the night before when he wrestled with Philip. Certainly, part of that was the element of surprise, but even caught off guard, Philip was strong, made so by the work he did for a living. Mr. Wells had not only taken him down, he had kept the blacksmith down, a rarer feat, and proof of the overseer's hidden strength.

A part of him felt guilty for having such thoughts so soon after James's death, as if he were betraying his former lover the same way James had betrayed him, but James's faithlessness had already killed Philip's softer feelings for the bank clerk. He had thought himself in love, but he had sworn to himself long ago that he would never stay with a cheating lover. It had been too hard, as a boy, to watch his mother suffer through that before both his parents were killed in an accident. Finding out that James had been seeing Jason Leonard from Seal Cove, on the other side of the island, was all it took to extinguish any interest Philip had in a longer term relationship with James. All that had remained was the desire, which was not so easily snuffed out. Now it seemed that had been supplanted, too. Glancing back at the overseer, Philip found he did not mind. He knew he was probably setting himself up for disappointment, for the overseer surely had no interest in men beyond their role as his employees, but at least this time, the object of his attraction would be a man worthy of his respect as well.

Chapter 5

RAGE fills me, an unproductive emotion, I know, but one I am helpless at the moment to reject. The whelp has escaped me somehow, disappearing to parts unknown. I vented my frustration on the solid wood door of the pervert's house, taking great pleasure in watching the wood splinter, but the metal that ran through and behind it held, only adding to my anger. So the sheriff thinks he can hide the sodomite away somewhere. Let him try. Parnell is not as smart as he thinks he is. I will find the sodomite and when I do, I will eliminate another link in the chain of depravity that is taking over the island. Hall and Leonard will be next, then I will find out who else those two have been associating with. I will allow no trace to remain.

THE heavy wagon made its way slowly toward town, pulled by two irascible mules. Nicolas was perfectly content to let Sullivan handle the animals. West managed the supplies, Sullivan managed the animals, and all three of them helped him manage the men. Casting a sidelong glance at the blacksmith sitting beside him on the wagon bed, Nicolas wondered how much more difficult their job would be this summer because of Hall's presence. Some of the men he usually hired had very strong opinions about homosexuality, one of the reasons Nicolas had been so careful to keep his own preferences a secret. The blacksmith had no secrets any longer, at least not in that area, and it could well complicate matters. The overseer suppressed a sigh. They would just have to deal with problems as they arose. At least his three crew bosses seemed willing to accept Hall regardless of his past. They would help set the tone and silence whispers that Nicolas might not hear until it was too late.

They had barely entered the town when the blacksmith was hailed by a stout blond man. Sullivan looked back at Nicolas questioningly. The overseer nodded, indicating that he should stop the wagon.

"Philip," the man said again, slightly out of breath as he reached the wagon. "I heard the news. Are you all right?"

Philip shrugged. "I'm fine, Paul," he replied diffidently. "It was a shock, for sure, but I'd already said everything I had to say to him that night in the tavern." He flushed at the memory of the very public confrontation he and James had engaged in a week before James's murder. "I decided to take a job out at Cleftstone for the summer, so that'll keep me too busy to think about anything else."

"Paul!" A woman's shrill voice interrupted them. Paul turned around with a guilty look on his face. "I have to go," he told Philip. "Christine doesn't want me associating with you anymore. I'm sorry, Philip. I hope everything turns out for the best."

Before Philip could reply, his friend – his former friend – was hurrying back across the village green to his disapproving wife's side.

"Good riddance to him if he doesn't have more spine than that," Carl murmured in Philip's ear as he watched the scene unfold.

"He's a kind-hearted man," Philip replied, defending his friend automatically. "He befriended me when I first arrived on the island and no one wanted anything to do with the penniless orphan boy. His wife never liked me, even before she found out about James. This is the latest in a long series of attempts to keep him away from me. He won't stand up to her openly, but he'll sneak away whenever he can to help me out."

Johnny shook his head at the exchange. He understood the islander's reaction – he would have done anything Virginia asked and then some – but he also knew how much it must hurt Philip to be shunned by a friend that way. He only hoped the other villagers would be more tolerant. If not, they were in for a very long summer.

Seeing that the conversation was over, Eric urged the mules forward again, driving to the mercantile in town that supplied everything from lumber to ladies' undergarments. Jumping down from the buckboard, he tied the reins to the hitching post and waited for the others to join them. As they stepped onto the boardwalk, they were accosted by two of the local ladies.

"Mr. Wells!" one of the women called out. Eric turned his head in their direction, recognizing them but not sure which one had spoken. He avoided them, and all the local ladies, as much as possible. They were far too mercenary for his gentle soul. Besides, his heart was already set on a girl back home. He just had to wait for her to turn eighteen so they could wed.

Nicolas turned at the sound of his name, repressing a sigh when he saw the Misses White and Underwood bearing down on them. He touched his fingers to the brim of his hat respectfully. "Ladies."

"We heard you were back in town for the summer," Miss White began, hooking her arm through Nicolas's proprietarily. "We wanted to welcome you back and to make sure you heard the news."

"News?" Nicolas asked, not even feigning interest. The cousins were inveterate gossips and he was sure he knew what they wanted to tell them. He also knew what else they wanted, but he had even less interest in their persons than he did in their gossip.

"Why, yes," Miss Underwood replied, taking Nicolas's other arm. "We had a murder last week, and we wanted to make sure you knew about it."

"A murder?" Nicolas affected surprise, knowing he could not afford to act too uninterested in the ladies. They were lovely girls, if one liked the type, blond with long curls, elegantly attired and coiffed, slender, with curves in all the appropriate places. Unfortunately for them, those curves held no appeal for the overseer, their slender limbs no enticement. Revealing that, to them or to anyone, though, would be the end of Nicolas's career on the island, and he had a few houses to build still.

"It was quite the shock," Miss White related confidentially. "Why, just the week before, the dead man was involved in a scandalous scene at the tavern. It seems…" she lowered her voice "… that he and the blacksmith were lovers." She paused for effect.

"Stop carrying tales, Catherine," Philip scolded harshly, stepping from behind Eric into the women's view. "I know you don't have anything better to do with your time, but tell your stories to someone who cares."

Catherine and Rebekah both turned to face Philip, glaring daggers at him. "Philip," Rebekah gasped, "we didn't see you there."

"Like hell they didn't," Carl muttered, but Philip ignored him.

"What else were you going to tell Mr. Wells?" Philip demanded of the two women. "That I killed James in a fit of pique? That instead of being heartbroken over his death, I'd moved on to some other man? Or some other made-up tale?"

"We're drawing a crowd," Nicolas murmured, extricating himself from the women's grasp. "Ladies, if you'll excuse us, we're here to buy supplies for the summer. We really should go inside and make our selections." He tipped his hat again, gesturing with his head for the other men to precede him into the store.

Catherine and Rebekah continued to glower at Philip's retreating back. When the door to the store swung shut behind the men, the two women's eyes met. They did not speak – they did not have to – their thoughts were clear. They would not drag Mr. Wells into their gossip since they still had hopes for catching his eye, but the other man who had spoken was misogynistic enough to suit their purposes perfectly. A few well-placed words and everyone in town would know that Philip had a new lover.

Inside the store, Philip tried not to scowl. He had not held any real hope that his employer would be interested in men. That would have been too good to be true. To find, though, that the overseer's taste in women ran toward the cousins they had just met was almost more than Philip could stand. Surely Mr. Wells had better taste than that! With a sigh, he resigned himself to a summer of long, lonely nights, dreaming of something that could never be while resisting the image of his fantasy-made-flesh cavorting with the bitch queens of the island.

"Mr. Wells, welcome back!" the shopkeeper's voice broke into Philip's thoughts as he watched Mr. Waring cross the store to shake the overseer's hand. "And I see you brought your usual crew with you again." His eyes strayed over the group. "And a new addition this year."

"The sheriff recommended Hall's work to me," Nicolas replied firmly.

"And so he should," Hugh agreed. "Quite the artist he is. We'd miss him if he left the island. Now, what can I do for you today?"

Nicolas pulled the list of supplies they had made over breakfast from his coat pocket and handed it to the store owner. "It's quite a list this time."

Hugh scanned down the list. "I'll have to order some of the things, but I have most of it here already." He started around the store, gathering items and setting them on the counter. "I imagine you'll be hiring a crew again for the summer."

"Yes," Nicolas agreed. "The plan is to finish up Cleftstone Manor this summer, so I'll need plenty of willing hands."

"I'll put the word out for you," Mr. Waring promised. "Will you be needing a cook again? Katrina just asked me the other day if you were back on the island yet."

"We will need a cook. If Mrs. Waring would be willing, we'd gladly have her and your daughter cook for us again," Nicolas replied with a smile.

"They're willing. When shall I have them start?" Hugh asked.

"Tonight!" Johnny replied with a laugh. "Otherwise, they'll have to suffer through my cooking again."

"Don't let him fool you, Mr. Waring," Philip interjected, the shopkeeper's kind words emboldening him. "Johnny's a good cook. Mr. Wells just needs him for other duties."

Hugh chuckled. "It's just the five of you for now?" he asked Nicolas. When the overseer nodded, he continued, "I'll let her know. I'm sure she can whip something up for this evening."

"Thanks," Nicolas replied. "The pay's the same as last summer."

"That's more than generous," Waring accepted. "My son may come out to the site with her tonight. He's sixteen now and eager to work. He hoped you might let him swing a hammer."

"Harry's sixteen?" Nicolas asked with a shake of his head, remembering the little boy he had met his first summer on the island. "Time does fly, doesn't it? Have him come out. We'll see what he can do."

Mr. Waring gathered the last of the supplies and added everything up. Nicolas paid and the five men started carrying everything out to the wagon. The others had started back inside to get the rest as Philip bent to set down the load he was carrying. Just as he did, a shot rang out, the bullet embedding itself in the side of the wagon an inch from his ear. He dropped flat against the wagon bed, covering his head with his hands. He was not carrying a gun and knew he would be no match for a gunman unarmed. All around, people started screaming, seeking cover and searching for the assailant.

When no more shots were fired, Philip raised his head, peeking above the edge of the wagon. To his relief, he could see Shawn elbowing his way through the crowd. "Are you hurt, lad?" the big blond asked when he reached the blacksmith's side.

"No, just scared," Philip admitted. "Nobody's ever shot at me before."

"They shouldn't have gotten the chance today," Shawn retorted. "What's Wells thinking, letting you come to town alone?"

"He's not alone," Nicolas replied from behind them. "He came to town with the rest of us because we needed supplies and it seemed safer to bring him with us than to leave him at the site alone. I didn't expect somebody to shoot at him in broad daylight in the middle of town."

Shawn had to acknowledge the truth of that statement. Turning around, he faced the gathering crowd. "Did anybody see anything?" he asked in stentorian tones.

Back near the edge of the crowd, Rebekah looked at Catherine again. "Somebody tried to kill Philip," she whispered, her voice revealing her shock.

"Do you suppose it's because…" her gesture, a nod of her head toward the tavern where the argument between Philip and James had played out, filled in the missing words.

"I don't know," Rebekah answered, "but maybe we shouldn't spread any gossip about Philip and the other construction worker. Even if it isn't, I wouldn't want the sheriff thinking we had anything to do with it."

Catherine nodded her agreement. Gossip was one thing; being responsible for someone's death was something completely different.

GLEE fills me as I watch them from across the square. No, the shot did not succeed, but it did let everyone know the blacksmith is next in line. The sheriff will do his best to protect the deviant, but I know where the bugger is hiding now. It will take time to lay my plans, but I have time. Let the whelp think he's safe among the construction crew. He will learn better soon enough. For now, though, I should be seen to be a concerned citizen along with the rest. It would not do for the sheriff to note my absence.

Chapter 6

PHILIP chafed under the attention from every quarter. He really was a private man by nature, despite his public falling out with James. Being the center of attention, as he had been far too often since that day, was repugnant to him. He wanted only to be left alone to work and love as he pleased. He wondered, honestly, if that would ever happen now on the island. Given enough time, he could probably work again in peace, but he feared his every action would be viewed through the lens of his homosexuality, so that even something as innocent as his friendship with the sheriff or Paul would be viewed askance. This was his home and had been for fifteen years. He did not want to leave it, but he questioned if he would be able to stay and still live his life.

When Shawn was finally done investigating – fussing, Philip thought privately – he broke up the crowd, leaving the five men standing beside the wagon once again. He had learned nothing concrete from his attempts at investigation. More men than not carried a gun at their waists and Shawn could hardly go around seeing if any of them was hot from a recent shot. Even if one was, it did not necessarily mean anything, and if the killer was as smart as Shawn feared, he would not be carrying his weapon now. What bothered him most, though, was the surety that the killer had joined the gathering around them after firing the shot, hidden amidst the crowd of well-wishers and curious onlookers.

"Life sure is interesting with you around," Carl commented blandly when all but the sheriff had returned to whatever business occupied them before the shooting.

"I warned you someone was trying to kill him," Shawn interjected from his place by the wagon. "You should really get back to the job site where there aren't so many people around."

"We'll head that way just as soon as we go by Hall's forge to get his tools," Nicolas replied coolly. He understood the sheriff's concern, but he did not appreciate the meddling in his affairs.

"I can't work with inferior tools," Philip agreed in support of the overseer's statement. He knew how Shawn could be and did not want Mr. Wells to change his mind. "And no, you don't need to come with us. We'll be on our guard."

"Fine," Shawn snapped. "Watch yourself, though. I didn't go to all that trouble just to see you get yourself killed."

Philip's attitude softened at Shawn's obvious concern. The sheriff had been an older brother to the young orphan and that relationship still held sway at odd moments like this. "I'll be careful," he promised. "I'm not ready to die."

Shawn nodded and waved them on, stepping back as the wagon rolled forward and whispering a quick prayer for his friend's safety.

Eric drove the wagon slowly out of town in the opposite direction from where they came in, following the curve of the harbor toward Eden. They were nearing the outskirts of town when another group of men hailed them. "Hey, Hall!" one of them called.

"Keep driving," Philip told Eric. "I don't have anything to say to them."

Eric was surprised at Philip's comment, but he clucked to the mules to urge them forward.

"Hall!" the man called again, louder this time.

"What's going on, Mr. Hall?" Nicolas asked.

"They're the town bullies," Philip explained. "They've never liked me and they never will. They've limited it to words since I got old enough and strong enough to beat the shit out of them if they tried anything physical. It doesn't stop them from being inconsiderate pigs, though."

Nicolas knew the type. He had dealt with such bullies more than once on his crew. His solution was to fire them, but that would not help Philip deal with the townspeople.

"One not enough for you any more?" one of the four men sneered.

"Shut the fuck up, Parks," Philip retorted. "At least I can get a lover when I want one."

"Sodomite!" Parks shot back. "Unnatural freak." He started closer to the wagon, as if to reach for the mules' heads.

Carl's gun was in his hand and pointed. "Take a step closer and it'll be your last," he warned, as incensed by the ignorant words as Philip was, though they were not directed at him.

"Stay out of this, outlander," another of the men replied, beginning to circle the wagon.

"There are five of us and only four of you," Nicolas pointed out, not wanting this to degenerate. "Those odds aren't in your favor."

"Leave off, Bradley," Philip added. "You know I'm not going to lose my temper from your barbs. I'm not fifteen anymore."

"No, you're not," the third man, John Ferguson, agreed. "At fifteen, you were just a wimp. Now you're a sick pervert."

"That's enough," Carl declared, aiming his gun between the man's feet. He fired, the bullet raising dust at the tip of the man's boots. "Next time, I won't miss."

The four men backed off, knowing the shot would bring the sheriff, this close to town and so soon on the heels of the attempt on Philip's life. They continued to heap insults on Philip's head as they left.

"Let's go," Philip repeated. "Shawn knows where we're going if he decides to investigate the shot."

Eric glanced at Nicolas who nodded his approval. The entire confrontation left a bitter taste in his mouth, an all too vivid reminder of why he continued to hide what he was.

"Stupid shits," Philip muttered under his breath. "They wouldn't know an original insult if it bit them on the ass."

"Could one of them be the killer?" Johnny asked. "Shawn seemed to suggest the killer was targeting you because of your lover."

"Parks, Bradley and Ferguson?" Philip scoffed. "They wouldn't dare try anything with me. James, maybe. He wasn't the strongest of men, but they haven't gotten any closer to me than they were today, even in a group, since we were fifteen. They tried it then and I beat all of them. They still saw me as a skinny kid. They didn't know how hard I worked in the forge."

"What about the fourth one, the one who didn't say anything?" Johnny wanted to know.

"Martin Thomas," Philip replied. "He's the ringleader in a lot of respects, but I don't think he has it in him to kill someone. I'll tell Shawn about them the next time I see him. He can do what he wants with the information."

The wagon passed the end of the town's buildings when two more men called Philip's name. The difference in the blacksmith's reaction was marked. The smile that wreathed his face was as open as any the other men had seen on the younger man's face in the time they had known him. "Joseph! William!" Philip replied lightly. "How are you?" He turned to Eric. "Stop a moment, please."

The two men assured their friend they were well. "But what about you?"

"I'm doing all right," Philip promised. "I've got a job for the summer, though, so I don't know that I'll make it to play poker on Wednesdays for a while. I might be busy at the forge."

"We can come to your place to play if you want," Joseph offered. "We'll really miss you if you don't join us."

"I'm not staying at home," Philip told them quietly. "I've moved to the job site for the summer."

The two men's surprise was clear on their faces. "But why? After you worked so hard on your house, I was sure you'd never leave it. Lots of men ride in to work there."

"It was Shawn's idea," Philip explained.

"Why would the sheriff want you out of your house?"

"He thinks whoever killed James will come after me next."

Horrified, Joseph and William stared at their friend. "But... but... why would anyone want to hurt you?"

Nicolas listened to the exchange uncomfortably. They had avoided saying in town that Philip was actually living on the job site, though he knew some people would assume it. Philip obviously felt comfortable with these two, but he was not sure it was safe to trust anyone on the island, at least not until the sheriff had said they were not suspects.

"He thinks James was killed, well, because of me, because of him and me," Philip replied awkwardly. "I don't know if it's true or not, but it's not a chance I can afford to take."

Joseph's and William's faces fell. "Then I guess we won't be seeing you for a while."

"Maybe," Philip began, turning to Nicolas, "Mr. Wells, would it be all right if we had our weekly poker games on the site? It's just the three of us and two others, assuming Paul's wife will let him come now. After the scene in town, she might not, and then it would just be four."

Put on the spot, Nicolas did not know how to respond. His first inclination was to refuse because of the security issue, but he knew how important morale was and having Hall sullen and resentful would do nothing for the atmosphere on the job site. "Let me speak to the sheriff," he temporized. "If he thinks it's safe, I'll give my approval."

Philip frowned. These were his best friends. They would never do anything to hurt him! He reminded himself that Nicolas was not from the island and did not know them. Shawn would surely vouch for Joseph, William, and Matthew, and then it would be settled. "Fair enough," he agreed. Turning back to his friends, he added, "We've got to get stuff from my house that I didn't think to take with me yesterday. I'll send word to let you know about poker."

The two men nodded and stepped back, saying good-bye to Philip and the others.

"Poker?" Eric asked. "Now that sounds interesting. Would you be willing to have another player?"

"I don't see why not," Philip replied. "It's just a friendly game anyway, an excuse for old friends to relax for an evening away from our other responsibilities. I think I won a quarter once. That tells you what the stakes are like."

Eric chuckled. "Sounds like exactly what I can afford."

"I might join you, too," Johnny chimed in. "For the companionship, if nothing else."

"Johnny's good company if you don't let him drink," Eric joked.

Nicolas opened his mouth to speak, but before he could, Carl jumped in. "Now, boys, you know we don't drink at camp. That's only allowed in town. And don't come back until you're sober."

"You know why that's the rule," Nicolas insisted. "There's too much dangerous or expensive material on the site to have people at less than their best."

"I didn't say I disagreed," Carl protested. "We've helped you enforce that rule for as long as we've been crew bosses for you. I just wanted to make sure Hall knew."

Philip shook his head at the interplay. The interdiction on alcohol was not a problem. He and his friends rarely drank as they played. They did not need alcohol to liven up the mood. All it took was Matthew's and William's antics. Five minutes after they arrived, everyone was in stitches. "Thanks for telling me," he laughed. "I'll be sure to tell my friends if Mr. Wells decides to let us have the games on the site."

"You know," Johnny commented, "if Carl, Eric and I are there, Mr. Wells, there's no reason to fear for Philip's safety. After all, you know we weren't involved with the murder. Even if his friends were, which I find hard to believe, Philip would be safe because we wouldn't leave him alone with them anyway."

Nicolas considered the crew boss's comment for moment. They had a point and he really did not want to make Hall's life more difficult than it already would be given his forcible removal from his house. "As long as you're all there, I don't suppose it's a problem. Wednesdays, you say? Just let whoever's on guard know to expect them."

"Thank you," Philip said gratefully. He would have accepted whatever Wells decreed, but the thought of losing contact with his friends on top of everything else would have been disheartening. "Turn left here," he directed, seeing they had reached the lane to his house.

As they drew near the house, Philip caught a whiff of smoke. He knew he had not left a fire burning in either the house or the forge. Hackles rising, he tensed, praying wordlessly that he had a home to return to. The wagon pulled into the yard and Philip let out a pained shout. The house was standing, but two of the walls were singed. He jumped down even before the wagon rolled to a halt, running toward the building.

"Shit!" Nicolas cursed under his breath, vaulting out of the wagon and taking off after the blacksmith. He understood the impulse, but they had no idea if whoever had done this was still around.

Philip reached the door, relieved to see it mostly intact. The wooden planks would have to be replaced since they had been hacked at with an axe, but the iron plates and the metal bar that locked the door had held. The glass in the windows was knocked out, though. With trembling fingers, Philip fitted the key to the lock, afraid of what he would find inside.

"Wait, damn it," Nicolas ordered, grabbing Philip's hand before he could open the door. "You have no idea who might be inside."

"This is my home," Philip protested. "I built it myself. I have to see what damage was done."

"Let me go first," Nicolas suggested.

"If the killer did this and he's still inside, he'll be trapped and he won't care who comes in first. He'll hurt whoever's in his way."

"Fine, but I'm going in with you."

Philip relented with poor grace. "Fine." He opened the door and stepped over the threshold. To his relief, there was no indication the vandal had gotten inside.

"Is there anything from here you want to take with you?" Nicolas asked. "In case they come back."

Philip nodded and went to his bedroom, getting the necklace that had been his mother's. He had nothing else left from his life before he arrived on the island. He had enough problems smuggling himself aboard the ship. He could not afford to smuggle anything else. Slipping that into his pocket, he picked up the volume of poetry he kept by his bed, another indirect legacy from his mother. The volume itself had not come from her, but the love of the art had. Coming back out of the room, he mustered a smile. "Everything else I need is in the forge."

"Lead the way," Nicolas replied.

Philip left the house, securing the lock when they were both outside. It had kept the vandal out once. It would serve again if the bastard came back. He could do nothing about the broken windows, but they were small. Only a child would be able to squeeze through them. He walked toward the forge, letting out a shout of dismay when he saw the state of his workplace. His tools were scattered all over the ground, the handle of his best hammer shattered. The anvil was overturned, its base showing the same signs as the door. The bellows had been slashed and would have to be replaced completely. Only the brick forge itself seemed to have escaped damage. Philip grabbed his tools, checking the metal. While all the wood was broken, the metal itself was intact. "Stupid fucker," he swore under his breath.

Nicolas surveyed the destruction with a dispassionate air. He could only imagine what the blacksmith was feeling, seeing his space thus invaded. He tamped down the instinctive inclination to comfort the other man, unsure how his actions would be interpreted. He could still feel the echo of the other man's body against his from the night before and he feared that renewed contact between them, even of so innocent a nature, would cause his body to react in tell-tale fashion. While the result of such an action might be pleasant in the short term, he had to consider the rest of the summer and his career as well, and he doubted the blacksmith was looking for a new relationship so soon after the end of the last one. "What do you need from here?" he asked instead of offering the words of comfort that rose to his lips.

Philip handed the overseer the hammer in his hand. "I'll have to replace the handle." He grabbed the rest of what he needed and they rejoined the others there by the wagon.

Philip could read sympathy on the faces of the other three men, an emotion he did not know how to accept from these relative strangers. "If you want some help fixing things up around here, we could come out a few weekends and do some repairs," Carl offered. "It'll take less time with four sets of hands than with just one."

"Five sets," Nicolas corrected. He had not been able to take the first step on his own, but he likewise could not let this moment pass without saying something.

"Thanks," Philip said, his voice tight with emotion. These men who hardly knew him had accepted him in a way only his closest friends did, and not even all of them now that the truth was out about him.

Nicolas looked around the forest-encircled farmyard. "Let's get back to camp. I'll feel better when we're back on my territory."

The others agreed, loading Philip's tools into the wagon along with the supplies from town. When they were all settled again, on the buckboard or the seat, Eric slapped the reins on the mules' backs and headed back to the road.

As they drove back to camp, Nicolas's eyes continually scanned the roadside, alert for any threat. He told himself it was self-preservation and concern for his employees, but his reaction to the shot in town belied those thoughts. He had seen crew members injured before, even had one die on site when he was still a crew boss for a different architect, one who did not hesitate to cut corners. The fear he felt in town earlier had overshadowed even the grief he had known at the loss of his employee so many years ago. He could not pinpoint the moment when the blacksmith had gone from being another employee to someone special, but it had happened, time notwithstanding. Now he had to figure out how to live with that while still doing his job and maintaining his professionalism.

WIDOW Taylor watched silently as the sheriff made his way up her front walk, hand running irritably through his thick blond hair. Her eyes raked his muscular body, searching for any sign of injury, any hint that he had been involved in the shots she had heard from her seat on her front porch. Slipping away from the window, she returned to the kitchen and filled the tea pot from the kettle on the stove. Setting it and a few fresh cakes on a tray, she headed back toward the parlor just as the sheriff entered the house.

"Sheriff," she called in greeting, "I was just about to have some tea. Won't you join me?"

Shawn looked up from his perusal of the floorboards to see the lovely widow who haunted his thoughts far more than was wise. The white apron around her waist accented the indention as well as the swell of hips and breasts above and below. "I shouldn't..." he began.

"Why ever not?" she asked. "I have more than enough for both of us and I had something I wanted to ask you."

Shawn relented at the entreaty in her eyes, unable to refuse her anything when she looked at him that way. "I suppose it would be all right."

Hiding a smile at the bashfulness that so characterized their interactions – such a contrast to his demeanor with everyone else – she led them into the parlor and set the tray on a small table. She sat on one end of the loveseat, hoping he would join her. He never did, of course, but she always sat there anyway, in case today was the day he changed his mind. Pouring his tea and adding two lumps of sugar, just the way he liked it, she handed it to him. He took it and sipped slowly, his eyes flitting around the room to look at anything but her.

"I heard shots in town today," she observed as she poured her own tea. "Was anyone hurt?"

"No," Shawn hastened to assure her, "though I'm not happy that it happened at all."

"I have errands I need to run this afternoon, supplies I need to get from Mr. Waring's store. Will it be safe for me to venture out alone?"

Shawn's eyes flew to her face. "It should be," he replied, "though I'll escort you gladly if you'd like. Philip was the target, I'm afraid. As long as you're not with him, you should be safe."

"Philip?" she questioned. "Why would anyone want to shoot at him?"

Shawn hesitated only for a moment. The sweet woman had helped him take in the boy when he first arrived on the island. She could be trusted. "For the same reason Reed was killed."

Widow Taylor frowned. "That's not right," she protested automatically. "Mr. Reed was harmless and Philip is a good man."

"I agree," the sheriff answered immediately, "but it seems someone has taken an exception to his private life and thinks murder is the way to show it. And while he's the only one resorting to violence, I don't think he's the only one who feels that way."

The widow's face tightened. "Well, we'll see about that," she frowned. "I'm not without influence in this town and neither are you. I think it's time some people were reminded of all the good Philip does around here. We'd be lost without him now that Vernon's retired."

"You don't have to convince me," Shawn assured her, holding up his hands placatingly. "I may not understand his choices, but I'm not about to condemn him for them. The only person I'm interested in condemning is the man who murdered Reed and tried to kill Philip."

"You will," Widow Taylor stated with utmost confidence. "You'll find him and stop him in no time."

Shawn hoped she was right. Certainly, her faith in him and her determination to help turn the tide back in Philip's favor buoyed his own confidence, reminding him again exactly why he loved her. He stifled a regretful sigh. If only she felt the same....

Chapter 7

THE return to the camp was uneventful. They arrived just as Mrs. Waring and Holly did, Harry in tow. "Mr. Wells!" the young man called. "Da said you were hiring."

Nicolas smiled at the lad who had tagged along with his mother and sister for as long as they had been cooking for him. "That's right. How old are you now?"

"Sixteen, sir."

"I see. That's a good age to begin learning a trade. What part of building interests you most?" Nicolas asked, knowing how important it was for the young man to choose something he would enjoy learning.

"All of it!" Harry replied enthusiastically.

Nicolas chuckled. "With that attitude, you'll be an overseer one day for sure. In the meantime, I need to assign you somewhere as an apprentice so pick something for me, lad."

"I'd be glad to teach you to work stone," Carl offered.

"Or wood," Eric pitched in.

"Even the forge," Philip added, "if your father approves."

Harry looked back and forth between the three men. "I... I don't know." He looked back at Nicolas. "Where should I start?"

"With the stonework," Nicolas replied firmly. "That's the heart of what we do. While it's all important, the stone is the foundation for all the rest. If you find that it's not for you after a few weeks, we'll switch you to a different crew."

"Come on, then, lad," Carl said, cuffing the boy on the shoulder. "Let's get started."

"Now?" Harry squeaked.

Carl laughed. "Unless you're planning on helping your mother cook."

"No!" Harry exclaimed. "I'd rather work with you."

The men chuckled at Harry's answer as Carl led the boy toward the storehouse where the blocks of stone, marble, and granite waited. When they were out of sight, the others set about unloading the wagon, Johnny directing the storage of all the supplies. "Here's the oilcloth you wanted," he said, handing it to Philip when it came off the wagon.

"Thanks," Philip replied, setting it aside with his tools.

When everything was put away, Philip picked up the hammer with the damaged handle. "Eric, you work wood, don't you?"

The big man nodded. "Why?"

"Because I need new handles for some of my tools. I can do it, but it would take me awhile. I was wondering if you'd make one for me. I'll pay you when I get paid."

"That won't be necessary," Nicolas interjected. "It's part of the general repairs on the site. If there's a metal tool damaged, I'll expect you to repair it, too."

"Of course, but those are the crew's tools. These are mine."

"Most of us bring our own tools," Eric contradicted. "At least, those of us who are journeymen. We're just as particular as you are and this way we don't have to get used to new tools when we arrive at a site. You'll be sharpening adzes and chisels for me more than once before the summer's gone. Let me see what you have there."

Philip handed Eric the hammer.

"How long do you want the handle?"

Philip showed him and Eric nodded. "I'll work on it this evening. You'll be ready to go in the morning."

Nicolas smiled at the interaction between the two men. Creating the cohesive bonds that made a successful crew was always an iffy proposition. Some years it happened seemingly without effort and other years, it never quite happened. It appeared this year would be a good one, at least in that respect.

"We should get the rest of the camp set up. Sullivan, I'll let you get the tools fixed for Mr. Hall since he can't start work without them, but the rest of us need to get those tents pitched and the camp ready for the crew."

Philip and Johnny nodded. "Ever pitch a tent?" Johnny asked Philip.

"No, but I'm a quick learner."

"These are big tents. They'll sleep four, or six in a pinch. It'll take all three of us to get them up," Nicolas explained.

They spent the next two hours erecting the canvas tents and wooden cots that the construction crew would live in for the summer. Nicolas took advantage of the time to cast surreptitious glances at the blacksmith, admiring the strong, powerful body as they worked together to raise the poles and set the stakes that would hold the tents in place. He appreciated once again the younger man's strength as Hall maneuvered the heavy canvas, a job that often required a second set of hands. He eventually had to force himself to stop looking because he could feel his groin tightening at the sight of the powerful muscles flexing as they worked.

When they were done, they had a small village set up on the grounds of the manor. "Will you fill all of them?" Philip asked Nicolas as he marveled at the number of tents. They could sleep a hundred men in the canvas shelters they had set up, not counting the ones Eric, Johnny, and Carl were already using.

"And more," Nicolas replied. "The islanders don't usually stay on site, though they're welcome to if they choose. Most, though, would rather return to their own beds and their own families."

That, Philip understood. Given the choice, he knew he would choose his home over the sea of tents, if only for the privacy it provided. He was especially concerned about how the men who shared his tent would react to him once they learned he preferred the company of men, as he was sure they would if they spoke with anyone from town. Philip knew they need not be concerned – his attention was focused solely on the overseer – but the other men could not know that and he could not tell them, not when Mr. Wells had evinced such an interest in the ladies in town. Perhaps if the desire were mutual – just perhaps – he could assure them, but he would never put Mr. Wells, or anyone, in that position without being assured of the other man's interest and agreement.

"Mr. Wells!"

The three men turned at the sound of the female voice. Mrs. Waring stood at the head of the trail, ladle in hand. "Dinner's ready. The other men are already eating."

"We'll just wash up and be right there, ma'am," Nicolas replied, heading toward the pump. He worked the handle a few times to start the water flowing, then stripped off his jacket and shirt. He knew the water would be frigid, but he was hot and sweaty and wanted to clean up. He stuck his head under the fall of water, running his fingers through his shoulder-length hair, sluicing away the dust and sweat from the day. Later, perhaps, he would have time to take a proper bath, to wash away the salt air from his sea voyage, but this would have to do for now.

Philip's eyes bulged and his mouth went dry when the overseer removed his upper garments. He had pictured the man's body in his feverish dreams the night before, but the reality was even more fascinating. Mr. Wells's body was lean and hard, clearly a product of a lifetime of physical labor. His skin was pale from the long winter, but Philip suspected it would darken to a honeyed gold over the summer if the color of the man's hands was any indication. Philip hoped it would anyway, because watching him over the summer, watching the color deepen, would give him plenty of opportunity to store up images to fuel his fantasies. He knew his imaginings would come to naught given the attention his boss had paid to the women in town, but that would not stop him from dreaming of feeling that whipcord body against his own once again, moving over him, into him. His hands itched to touch, to learn the texture of the pale flesh. Trying to resist the temptation, he stuck his hands in his pockets. Then the overseer stood up, shaking his head like a wet dog. Philip coughed to cover a gasp. Knowing what he was feeling had to show on his face, he averted his gaze.

"Who's next?" Nicolas asked, using the kerchief he habitually wore around his neck to wipe away the water that ran down his neck and onto his chest.

Johnny glanced at Philip, but when the blacksmith did not immediately move to the pump, he performed his own ablutions, choosing simply to wet his bandanna and use it to wipe his face and hands.

"Your turn, Philip," he said, stepping back.

Nicolas envied the easy way Johnny addressed the blacksmith by name. He wanted that liberty for himself, but he had never taken it with any of the crew, even the three bosses. If he started now, someone would remark on it immediately. He hoped, although he wished he could deny it, that Philip would follow his lead and remove his shirt to clean up for dinner, giving the overseer a chance to see clearly what he had glimpsed that morning at the forge. It seemed the blacksmith was more modest, or at least more self-conscious, than that, though, because he simply splashed water on his face and rubbed his hands together under the stream of water.

When they were all presentable, they walked down to the small pavilion that sheltered the tables and chairs, giving the workers a place to eat out of the sun and rain. Mrs. Waring had prepared a veritable feast for the five men, a venison stew, cornbread, the early greens from the island farms and a strawberry shortcake for dessert.

Nicolas greeted her with a smile and effusive praise, the meal a luxury after weeks at sea. She replied with her usual indulgence, treating all the men, even the overseer, like she did her son.

Sitting together at one table, the men enjoyed a moment of tranquility in the quiet evening. Nicolas waited until they had poured themselves cups of coffee before bringing up business. "We need to decide how we're going to handle the extra security this summer, not just in terms of watches, but in terms of explaining the change to anyone who has worked for me in the past and knows how I've done things before. I think what happened in town drove home to all of us how serious this is. And while Mr. Hall is clearly the target, anyone could be struck accidentally."

"The first thing is that despite having tents up, Philip shouldn't be in a tent alone," Johnny declared. "At least that way, if the murderer gets past whoever's on watch, there's someone else right there to hear and stop the man. For the time being, you can stay with me, Philip. If you decide later you want to be in one of the other tents, that's fine."

"If I'm going to share a tent with someone, I'd just as soon share it with you," Philip replied. "At least I know you and know you aren't disgusted by me. Some of the others will probably react like Parks, Bradley, Ferguson and Thomas today."

"Not if they want to keep their jobs," Nicolas insisted. "Nobody harasses my crew, including other people on the crew. I hired you. If they have a problem with that, they can take it up with me." He saw the disbelieving look on Philip's face. "I'm serious, Mr. Hall. Even if there were no murder and this was just harassment, I would want to know about it, but given your circumstances, we can't afford to ignore any threat against you."

Philip shook his head, not in rejection, but in amazement. Only Shawn had ever defended Philip with the vehemence Mr. Wells was displaying. The difference was that he had known Shawn for years, but he had only met the overseer a day ago. He could not help but marvel at the situation. "I'll tell you if anyone says or does anything I can't handle."

That was not what Nicolas wanted, but it was, he realized, the best he was likely to get from a man so obviously used to relying only on himself. He fixed the crew bosses with a firm gaze, transmitting his seriousness to each of them. He would not tolerate anyone persecuting Philip on this job site. One by one, the three men nodded.

"Until we have a crew we can trust, I think you, Carl and I should share the night watches," Eric suggested. "Since Philip's staying in Johnny's tent, Johnny's effectively on watch all night, even if he's sleeping. Besides, if he takes a watch, that leaves Philip alone."

"The other option," Carl suggested, "is for all of us to use one of the big tents for the next few days. That way, we can split the watch four ways and still not leave Philip alone. We wouldn't even need to move our stuff, just our bedrolls."

"That's a good idea," Johnny agreed. "I'd feel guilty not standing a watch."

"As do I," Philip added with a dejected sigh, "though I don't know how I could since you're guarding me."

"As you say," Nicolas replied. "We knew what we were undertaking when we agreed to this last night. You certainly don't deserve to be shot at like you were today or be attacked verbally like you were in town. We'll do what's in our power to make sure it doesn't happen again. Who's taking first watch?"

"I will," Johnny said. "All I have to do tomorrow is finish up the supply inventory. Until we're ready to start actually setting stone, I'm not of much use."

"Not true," Carl, Eric, and Nicolas declared in one voice, all three of them knowing how much Johnny's organizational skills contributed to the smooth running of the camp.

Johnny chuckled. "It was a joke. I'll still take first watch, though. Who should I wake up?"

They quickly decided on the order of the watch. Eric and Carl rose to move their bedrolls into one of the big tents and get some sleep so they would be ready for their watches. Johnny went back to his tent for his rifle and started his circuit around the camp, leaving Nicolas and Philip sitting at the table facing each other over their steaming mugs.

"Shawn was right about you," Philip said after several long minutes of silence.

"Really? In what way?" Nicolas asked even as he told himself he should insist the blacksmith retire for the night.

"He said you were a fair man and that you'd make sure I was safe."

"I like to think of myself as being fair," Nicolas agreed, "and I'll certainly do my best to keep you safe."

"But why?" Philip asked. "I mean, if it were Johnny or Carl, I'd understand, but you don't know me, or didn't when

Shawn asked you to do this. Why do you care what happens to me?"

"Nobody deserves to be attacked like you were today," Nicolas repeated.

"Is it really that simple for you?"

It was not simple at all, Nicolas thought, but he could not tell Philip the rest of his reasons. He could not explain to the blacksmith that he, too, sought lovers among his own sex, that he, too, feared the kind of ostracism Philip had faced from some of the town's people, that he had taken one look at the younger man and fallen in lust and that everything he had learned since then only added to the attraction. No, it was not simple at all and sitting here with Philip only made it more complicated.

"Yes," he replied firmly, knowing it was a lie. He told himself he should send Philip to get his things and retire for the night, but he did not rise, did not say the words that would send the blacksmith from his side.

Philip had no answer to Nicolas's assertion and so he fell silent, waiting for the overseer to end the conversation. The other man made no move in that direction, though, so Philip stayed where he was, enjoying the opportunity to look his fill without trying to hide it. "How long have Eric, Johnny, and Carl worked for you?" he asked after a few more minutes of silence, wanting an excuse to hear the raspy voice again. He knew he would be hearing that voice in his head every time he touched himself for the rest of the summer and possibly beyond.

"Ten years," Nicolas replied, still surprised it had been that long.

"Why don't you use their first names?" Philip asked, surprised. "I mean, you hardly know me, but ten years? Surely you know them well enough to address them that way."

"It's not about how well I know them," Nicolas explained patiently. "It's about who I am and who they are. They're my employees."

"And you think they'd treat you with less respect if you used their first names? Or that I would? I owe you my life at this point. If I'd been home last night, I certainly would have gone out to investigate the vandalism to my homestead and he would have killed me, whether he simply shot me or whether he hurt me the way he did James. Nothing you could say or do could make me respect you less."

Even if I told you how much I want you right now? Nicolas wondered silently.

The flicker that crossed Nicolas's face was so subtle Philip was not sure he had seen it, but for a moment, he thought he saw a flash of desire in the overseer's deep blue gaze. "What does Mrs. Wells think of you spending your summers here on the island?" he asked impulsively, wanting to know if had indeed seen what he thought he saw.

"There is no Mrs. Wells," Nicolas replied flatly, afraid to ask what had brought on this line of questioning.

"Why not?" Philip inquired. "A well-set-up man such as yourself…. You must have plenty of choices."

"I would make a poor husband," Nicolas demurred honestly. "As much as I'm away with work, it would require a very patient wife indeed."

"You don't desire companionship?"

Lust shot through Nicolas as he thought of the companionship he craved but could not have. "You of all people know it's possible to find companionship without being married," he replied harshly. "I'm alone because I choose to be."

Every muscle in Philip's body went tense at the overseer's words. Yes, he knew it was possible to find companionship outside of marriage, but in his case, as the other man well knew, marriage was not an option. Did that mean…? He stared at Mr. Wells intently, trying to decipher the layers of meaning in the seemingly innocent words.

Seeing the look on Philip's face, Nicolas forced himself to stand. "You should get settled for the night," he declared, ending their conversation.

Philip watched him leave, retreating into the cabin where he would spend the summer. Slowly, he rose to his feet and headed for Johnny's tent to get his bedroll, the conversation playing over in his head again. *You of all people know…* Those words were the sticking point. Why say those words? Why not simply make the statement? Did it mean, could it mean, that

Nicolas shared his preferences, even returned his interest? He did not have the answer to his questions. He knew only that he had to figure out a way to learn what he wanted to know without losing his job. If he was right, perhaps his feelings were not so hopeless after all.

Chapter 8

SELF-DIRECTED anger raged through Nicolas as he stalked toward the cabin that was his home for the summer. He knew his last comment had gone too far, in more ways than one. He should not have attacked Hall the way he did, not when the blacksmith had so recently lost the lover to whom Nicolas had referred. He certainly should not have phrased the comment in so revealing a manner. He had all but screamed his desire at the other man, or so it seemed to him. He had walked away before Philip had a chance to reply. Philip... the blacksmith's question about names had been pointed, and it seemed to have served its purpose as well. He would not call Philip by his first name – he stood firm in that determination – but in his head, a line had been crossed, one he could never cross in reality.

Except that he had crossed it. Not in saying Philip's name aloud, but in everything he had done that afternoon to try to catch the blacksmith's attention. He knew, if he was being honest with himself, that he would never have stripped to the waist the way he had at the pump if Philip had not been there. Yes, he had worked up a sweat setting up the camp, but he had been sweaty before.

Yes, he wanted a bath, but a quick rinse under the icy pump hardly counted. The heat welling in him had little to do with the work they had been doing anyway, and removing his shirt and jacket had not been about relieving that heat, but hopefully adding to it. Unfortunately, as far as he could tell, the younger man had been unfazed.

He was beyond annoyed with himself. He had no reason to think he might catch Philip's eye, even knowing the blacksmith was interested in men. Hell, the man had lost his lover only a week before. It was completely unreasonable to expect Philip to move on that quickly. That did nothing to mitigate Nicolas's desire, though. His entire conversation with Philip after the crew bosses left for the watch and to move their things was motivated by an ever-increasing desire to capture Philip's interest. Of course, then he had run like a coward rather than brazening out the blacksmith's reaction.

That had to stop. Right now. He could not irresponsibly endanger his authority with his men or his position in town over an infatuation with the blacksmith, no matter how attractive he was. Philip deserved better than that, too. His loss was surely too recent for him to have any desire for a new relationship, and Nicolas could barely offer him that, not when the end of the summer meant an end to his residence on the island. His path was simple, really. Avoid time alone with the other man. He would not say anything that might be misinterpreted in front of the crew bosses or the crew. Only if they were alone would he dare say the kinds of things he had said to Philip today. Therefore, such opportunities were to be avoided.

Stripping off his dirty clothes and pulling on his nightshirt, he lay down and tried to will himself to sleep. While he was awake, it was relatively simple to force his thoughts away from Philip, but as he began to drift, images of the blacksmith slipped past his conscious control, and his libido sat up and took notice. Before he realized what he was doing, his hand had slid down his chest to his groin, rucking up his nightshirt as it went. With a groan, his hand closed around his hard flesh as he saw again the shadow of muscle moving under cloth as Philip worked the forge. In his passion-inspired imaginings, the blacksmith removed his

shirt, leaving his chest bare to Nicolas's gaze before turning back
to his work, letting the overseer watch as his muscles flexed with
the rhythmic pounding of the hammer. His fist on his cock kept
perfect time. Letting himself sink deeper into the fantasy world his
subconscious was providing, Nicolas took a step toward Philip,
then another, until he could touch the smooth flesh. The
blacksmith turned to him with a welcoming smile, setting aside his
hammer without hesitation, opening his mouth to the claiming kiss.

Nicolas's hand tightened around his aching cock as he
imagined what it would be like to kiss Philip, what it would feel
like to have the blacksmith's strong, calloused hand encircle his
erection. The movement of his fist sped up at the thought, leaving
him gasping for breath as his orgasm tore through him, Philip's
name on his lips as he came.

The feeling of release was soured by the realization that
once again, he had allowed his passions to rule him. This was the
second time he had brought himself off to thoughts of Philip with
absolutely no encouragement from the other man. Disgusted with
himself, he rose and washed away the evidence of his climax, then
pulled his clothes back on. He obviously would not be able to trust
himself in the cabin. He would relieve West on watch and
sublimate his energy into patrolling the camp. At least that way,
he would be doing something to protect Philip instead of making
the situation worse.

ACROSS the camp, in one of the large tents, Eric, Carl,
and Philip sat in the light of a small oil lamp, talking. "So how
long have you worked for Mr. Wells?"

"Ten years," Eric replied. "I think we started with him the
same summer, right, Carl?"

"Yeah," Carl agreed. "Ten years ago. I've worked with
other overseers in my career, but none of them compare to Mr.
Wells. I'll keep coming back to him as long as he has work to be
done."

"He seems to inspire incredible loyalty," Philip observed
casually, trying not to give away his interest to the other men.
That he would want to know about his employer was reasonable,

but he did not want to telegraph the depth of his fascination with the tall blond.

"He does," Eric concurred. "You'll find, probably, that more than half the crew he hires this year will be people who have worked for him before. He treats his men well, makes sure they're paid on time and in full, gives us all a place to stay and provides the board for the summer. He doesn't have to hire a cook. He could leave us all on our own to make do with our feeble cooking skills. He doesn't, though."

"It's not completely unselfish on his part," Carl interjected. "After all, if we don't have to spend time cooking, that's more time we can spend working."

"I'd rather work an extra hour or two than have to cook for myself!" Eric insisted.

"Me, too," Philip agreed. "I can do it if I have to, but just as often, I end up eating at the tavern or at Widow Taylor's boarding house."

"Not this summer," Carl declared. "Mrs. Waring is a fine cook. You won't need to head into town to get a decent meal."

"He can't head into town anyway," Johnny added from the entrance of the tent.

"Aren't you supposed to be on watch?" Eric asked.

Johnny shrugged. "Mr. Wells came and relieved me early. He said he couldn't sleep anyway."

Philip perked up at that. He would wait a while so as not to be obvious, and then he would see if he could join the overseer on his watch. He definitely wanted to continue their earlier conversation. "Is he always so solitary?" he wondered aloud.

"Yes," Johnny replied. "He shares some of the load he bears from the construction responsibilities with us, but he has always been a loner on a personal level."

"But he'll listen to anything you want to tell him," Carl commented. "Knowing I could talk to him is all that kept me sane my first summer here."

"He's the camp's confessor in a lot of ways," Eric agreed. "I think we've all spilled our worries to him at least once a summer."

"Who listens to his worries?" Philip inquired.

All three men shook their heads. "Nobody here, anyway," Johnny answered. "Maybe he has someone back in Boston."

"His wife, maybe?" Philip suggested guilelessly.

"He's not married," Carl informed him. "In fact, I've never even heard of him speak of anyone special, but surely he must have friends there."

Philip hoped so. The thought of Nicolas living such a solitary life saddened him. Nicolas deserved better than that. The thought brought an almost smile to his lips, despite the troubled thoughts. The overseer had made a similar comment to him earlier, about how he deserved better than to live in fear and persecution. For a moment, he wondered if they could give each other what they truly deserved. He had to remind himself not to jump to conclusions just yet.

Shifting restlessly on his cot, he found the perfect excuse to leave the tent and join Nicolas. "I need the privy," he announced. "I'll be back in a few minutes."

Eric rose immediately. "I'll come with you. You shouldn't wander alone, and I need to go anyway."

Philip smothered a curse. He could not very well change his mind now or refuse Eric's offer without an explanation he was not willing to give.

"Thanks," he said instead, knowing that saying the right things now would increase the likelihood of being able to slip away later. "It's probably safe with Mr. Wells on patrol, but that's no reason to take chances."

He and Eric left the tent for the little outhouse on the outskirts of the camp. The wind whistled eerily through the trees as they walked, the wispy clouds dancing across the face of the moon, casting odd shadows on the clearing where the camp stood. Suddenly glad he was not out there alone, Philip turned to look at Eric, seeking the reassurance of the other man's presence. He refused to let the killer keep him from functioning, but he could feel an edge of fear that had not bothered him until that day with the attempted shooting in town and the vandalism at his house.

They used the privy and returned to the tent. Eric doused the lamp as soon as they were settled, plunging them into the darkness and silence of the night and leaving them alone with their individual thoughts.

Eric's thoughts drifted to his sweetheart back home. Despite her youth – she was still six months shy of eighteen – she had captured his heart. He sighed wistfully as he thought of her... little Rachel Gibbons. Except that she was not so little anymore. To his delight, the little terror had grown into a tall, slender woman. The silken exterior hid a spine of steel, and Eric knew she was exactly what he needed, that having her at his side would push him to be his very best rather than drifting through life as he was so often tempted to do. He sighed again, missing the feeling of her hand in his, her lips beneath his own. Though they would wait until her birthday to wed, at her father's insistence, they had long since mastered the art of slipping away for a few stolen hours. He had not made love to her yet the way he desired, not wanting her to get pregnant out of wedlock, but that had not stopped them from learning each other's bodies in every other way he could think of. He rolled over on the cot, wishing he were alone with his thoughts. It would not be the last time he made that wish, he knew all too well. This was the last summer, though. He would marry Rachel this winter and if he returned to work for Mr. Wells next summer, they would take a room at the boarding house so he could return to her every night. Holding tight to that thought, he slipped into dreams.

Across the tent, Philip hid a muffled sigh of frustration. He was glad Eric had gone with him to the privy, but it had ruined the chance to slip away. Another time, he promised himself. He had all summer. The opportunity to speak with Nicolas again would certainly arise if he was patient. His thoughts led to a familiar swelling in his lower regions. He sighed again, knowing he could do nothing about it but dream. Trying to avoid thinking about the nagging ache, his thoughts drifted instead to James. That certainly doused any lingering arousal.

A part of him had wondered, still wondered since he first learned of James's faithlessness, why his former lover had cheated on him. He could not ever remember discussing the issue with James, yet surely it must have been clear to the banker that he wanted an exclusive relationship. Had he done something to drive

James away? He knew he was not the most polished of men. His apparel was of necessity coarse, the heavy fabrics protecting him from the cold in the winter and from the dangers of his job. James had known what Philip was before they ever became lovers. Surely that could not be the cause, yet Philip could think of nothing else.

He tried to pinpoint in his mind the moment when James first strayed. He flattered himself to think that they had shared some period of faithfulness before James's roving eye kicked in. Thinking back, he could identify a change in his lover's behavior about six weeks before their fight in the tavern. At the time, he had thought it was stress at work, with a new bank manager coming in and changing things, and that was surely part of it, but their relationship had not recovered after that, leaving Philip often alone and emotionally neglected even when James did come by and assuage his physical needs.

Hating the doubt that filled him when he thought of those times, Philip pushed the memories away, trying to dwell instead on the possibilities the future held, specifically one sexy overseer. Nicolas had none of James's softness, none of his perfumed clinginess, but Philip did not think he would miss it, not if he had the overseer's strength in its place. Certainly, his boss would not be disturbed by his blacksmith's clothes or the sweat and soot that were part of his job. James had never wanted to see Philip until after he bathed and was always harping for him to buy nicer clothes. Philip had stubbornly resisted, claiming he had no reason to spend money on more than his suit for Sunday when he was only going to sit around the house. Was that refusal part of the problem? Had his stubbornness driven James away?

He knew he was independent, some would even say cocky, but he had gotten where he was in his life by forging ahead, regardless of the odds against him. Had that caused his problems with James? Had the banker wanted someone more malleable? Could that be what Nicolas wanted as well? His heart quailed at the thought. Could he change so completely to suit the whims of a lover?

He was getting ahead of himself again. He had no idea if Nicolas was even interested in men, much less in him. Resigning himself to another restless night, he tried to still his thoughts enough that he could sleep. His fears followed him into his dreams, though, images of himself wearing a muslin dress and plain apron, playing the perfect wife, groveling at the overseer's feet, begging for scraps of the man's time and attention yet completely at his command lest he drive his lover away. With a muffled shout of anguish, he startled awake, sitting up in bed as he fought the humiliation of the nightmare.

No.

He would not subjugate himself that way. He would not give up who he was. He wanted Nicolas, yes, but if the perfect wife was what Nicolas wanted, he would be better off with one of the ladies in town. Despite his desire for the older man, the overseer was not worth losing himself in the process.

Chapter 9

THE sheriff thinks he's so smart, hiding the sodomite away where I can't get to him. Don't think I haven't tried, but the camp is too busy now during the day, with the construction starting and more men arriving daily. I tried at night as well, but they set a watch, and the pervert shares a tent with three other men. How they sleep at night is beyond me, but perhaps they share his sickness. I can't get at them right now any more than I can at him, but I will. They'll have to leave the Manor grounds eventually and when they do, I'll be ready.

It hasn't been a wasted week, though, not entirely. Reed had more than one associate on this island. Today there is one fewer. Parnell tried to warn the bugger, but he wasn't interested in what the sheriff had to say. Now he isn't interested in anything.

He repented before he died, begging for his life, promising to give up his homosexuality and live a good life. I might have spared him if he had repented before I began, but a confession, a promise made under torture has no value, especially when his first offer was not of repentance but of temptation. I took what he offered, to prove that I cannot be swayed. Only then did he repent. Worthless bastard.

With Leonard gone, the time has come to try for the blacksmith again. Then I will see who else has been infected by their perversions.

AS agreed, Philip met Joseph, William, and Matthew at the gate and let Mr. Cox, the man on guard, escort them to his tent. Johnny and Carl were already inside, lantern lit, cots arranged around a low box to provide a table. Eric had gone to refill the pitcher of water they kept at hand in lieu of the whiskey or ale they might have consumed at the local tavern if they had chosen to play there. The crew bosses had far too much respect for Mr. Wells's decrees to have alcohol on the construction site.

"Introduce us to your friends," Johnny prompted when the four men came in, a nod to Cox dismissing him back to his post.

Philip completed the introductions quickly, making known his oldest friends on the island, bar only the sheriff.

"Pleased to meet you," William said, holding out his hand.

Immediately, Matthew grabbed it and pulled it back. "I wouldn't do that if I were you," he warned Johnny. "He's been known to offer more than just a handshake."

"Matthew, I'm insulted," William replied with a mock scowl. "To think that I would insult Philip's new friends by slipping them a toad or some such... Really, what an idea!"

"It didn't stop you from doing it to me," Philip reminded him with a grin as he settled on his cot. He leaned over to Johnny and Carl and whispered conspiratorially. "They're really harmless, I swear, but they still think they're fourteen."

"Sixteen," Matthew insisted. "He was sixteen when he pulled that stunt on Miss Underwood."

"And she hasn't let him forget it yet," Joseph chimed in. "I'm the harmless one in the bunch."

"From the sound of it, none of you are harmless," Carl declared. "Let's see if you're as good at poker as you are at pranks."

William pulled out a deck of cards and set it on the makeshift table as Eric walked back in with the water. He set it down and immediately picked up the deck, inspecting it carefully.

"It's just a friendly game," Philip protested.

"I know," Eric replied, setting the cards back on the table, satisfied, "but I never play cards without checking them first. No chance of getting cheated that way."

"He lost his shirt once," Johnny confided in a loud whisper. "Right off his back. He hasn't been the same since."

Philip could not stop the shout of laughter that escaped him at the vision of Eric, shirtless and frustrated, after a game of cards. "And I suppose the card shark cheated?"

"Damn right he did!" Eric insisted. "Marked cards and an ace up his sleeve!"

"And none of our coats would fit him to get him back to camp," Carl added, dealing the first hand. "He had to ride all the way back out here without a shirt, with a cold breeze blowing. I didn't think he'd ever stop shivering. Ante up, gentlemen."

Joseph, William, and Matthew looked at each other, at the crew bosses, and then at Philip, deciding they liked the new additions to their game. Relaxing, they examined their cards, settling in to play.

Joseph looked at his hand in disgust. "I'm in," he declared, tossing out two junk cards before looking at Philip. "So how do you like working out here? Mr. Gibson wouldn't ever work on the cottages."

Philip glanced down at his own cards, squirming a little at the reminder, however oblique, of why he was here. He knew Matthew, Joseph, and William would never judge him for his orientation, but he was not sure the crew bosses would be as accepting. They had done as much as Wells to make him feel welcome, but that did not mean they would appreciate having his homosexuality rubbed in their faces. "Three for me. Mr. Wells is a fair man and he's certainly done everything he can to make me feel welcome here." He picked up the new cards and examined them. No help, really, but he would see how the game went. He had won with a weak hand before simply by bluffing his sometimes gullible friends. "I'm certainly safer than I would be at home."

"How do you figure that?" Matthew asked, folding.

"You saw the guards at the gate," Philip reminded them, keeping a close eye on the game. He knew how his old friends played, but he knew nothing about his new friends in that respect.

"The murderer would have a hell of a time getting onto the site. And I'm not stupid enough to go off site alone."

"Nor are we likely to let him," Carl added, studying his hand and the open faces of the three townspeople. Philip was more guarded, but then Carl understood exactly why he had reason to be. "Especially not after we found his house vandalized."

"What?" all three of Philip's friends exclaimed at once, rounding on their friend, game forgotten in their distress on his behalf. "You didn't tell us!"

"I haven't seen you," Philip protested. "I'm not keeping secrets, but it's not like I've been in town since we found out. It's only been a couple of days anyway."

"We've talked about going out to the house and helping him fix it up," Johnny interjected.

"Just tell us when," Matthew insisted. "We'll be there."

Philip sighed in resignation. He had planned to work on the house quietly, maybe with the help of the crew bosses, but primarily on his own when he had a chance. It was *his* house, after all. He had built it the first time and wanted to repair it himself, too. With his friends involved, he would be lucky not to have half the town showing up to help. He thought ruefully that perhaps his pariah status might finally be worth something. He doubted many people would really want to help the sodomite. "Saturday?"

SHAWN stared down at the body. The young man had lived in Eden, not in Bar Harbor, but his body had been found in Shawn's jurisdiction so it was his case. He had warned Jason Leonard earlier in the week that Reed's killer was almost certainly targeting Reed's associates. He had not used the word lover, knowing how defensive the suggestion would probably make the man. Maybe he should have said it. Maybe Leonard would have taken him more seriously if he had. He would never know.

With a sigh, he began the grisly process of making the corpse presentable enough to take to the mortician. The body was naked, bruised and bloodied, the gaping maw across the man's neck clearly the cause of death. He could only guess that Leonard had put up more of a fight than Reed. Either that or the killer took his anger at not being able to get to Philip out on this victim. Reed had not been beaten the way Leonard clearly had been. The thought chilled him. He knew the signs of acceleration in a murderer, and he saw them here. Knowing his friend, his little brother, was also a target strengthened his resolve to find this bastard and stop him.

This clearing was not very different than the one where he had found Reed. The biggest difference was the state of the two bodies. The only marks on Reed's body had been the blood on his throat and from his anus. Leonard, though, was covered in bruises, his face, chest, and back showing signs of abuse. Shawn wondered if the killer used the broomstick to hammer him before using it to rape him.

His eyes closed in fear and desperation, his imagination all too easily supplying images of Philip in place of the dead man. Pushing aside those thoughts – he had a job to do, one that if he did right would keep those visions from materializing – he started quartering the clearing, searching for anything that might help him trace the killer.

He decided almost immediately that the culprit had not caught Leonard there in the clearing. For one thing, the victim's clothing was not in evidence, despite his naked state. Reed's had been still at his house, along with evidence of a struggle. Shawn imagined Leonard's would be the same way. Still, he would search the surrounding woods just to make sure.

He studied the few footprints he could find in the leaf-covered ground, trying to determine if he was dealing with one killer or a band. He wanted to believe it was only one man, but the degree of violence made him fear that his murderer had an accomplice. Reed had been a slender man, not terribly muscular. It was relatively easy to imagine him succumbing to the strength of a single larger man. Leonard, though, was a farmer and had led a more active life. Unless he was unconscious, he should have put up a struggle, especially against just one man. He found no sign of a struggle in the clearing, though. If Leonard had been conscious during the abuse inflicted on him, he had been bound or it had happened elsewhere.

Returning to the body, he flipped it over, studying the ground beneath it. There was no puddle of blood there. Wherever the murder had taken place, this was not it. The placement of the body was deliberate then, a ploy to catch his attention. The killer was baiting him, reminding him of his relative helplessness.

Deciding he had learned all he could from the scene, he gently pulled the broomstick from Leonard's body – the town did not need those details – and lifted him into the wagon. Examining the broomstick, he mentally matched it up to the one he had found in Reed's body. It was the same pale spruce that the first one had been made of. He would go by Leonard's house later and see if he could learn anything else, either from the state of his home or from his neighbors, but he was not hopeful. No one had seen anything when Reed was killed. This, he feared, would be no different. Either way, he would keep this quiet as long as he could. If the murderer thought he had gotten away with it, he might be careless and let something slip Shawn could use. He would have to warn Philip, though.

TIRED after another long day but pleased with all he had accomplished, Philip returned to the tent he continued to share with the crew bosses for a clean shirt and pants. Johnny had rigged several outdoor showers, one the workmen could use to clean up and one that the three crew bosses and the overseer used. They had offered to let him use it as well so that he would not have to share with the general crew whose tolerance for his homosexuality was only minimal. The water was no warmer than the pump since it came from the same well, but the enclosure guaranteed some privacy and the spray of water offered a better bath than the pump. Of course, he regretted his wooden bathtub on the hearth at home, where he could heat the water and soak away the tension that built in his shoulders from the hard work at the forge, but he would have to wait for Shawn to catch James's killer before he could enjoy that luxury again.

Stripping down, he turned on the water and stepped beneath it long enough to wet himself thoroughly. Later, when the temperature rose, he would enjoy standing under the spray of cold water. For now, though, he moved away from it as quickly as he could. Grabbing the bar of soap, he worked up a lather and began running the washrag over his sweaty skin. As he cleaned up, his thoughts drifted back over the last week. He had honestly not believed Nicolas when the overseer said he would fire anyone who harassed Philip. That disbelief had lasted all of a day.

Two days after his arrival on the island, Nicolas had started assembling a crew, many of them men he clearly knew from years past. Philip recognized some of them as other islanders from the nearby towns. Others, he did not know. He overheard snatches of conversation over the course of the day and knew that James's murder was on everyone's minds. Most of the men were suitably horrified that someone on the small island had been killed, a sentiment Philip echoed silently every time he heard it expressed. One man, though – Philip did not know his name – had been quite voluble in his disgust for the entire situation and had adamantly condemned James and anyone involved with him. The man had made the mistake of appealing to others around him for support in his argument, becoming so effusive that he drew the overseer's attention. Nicolas had asked what was going on and been told. Calmly, he had asked the other man if he could contain his animosity enough to work with one of the deceased's associates. At the vitriolic refusal, Nicolas's face had hardened slightly, but enough that Philip had picked up on it. The overseer had opened the employment rolls he kept and crossed out the man's name.

"You're entitled to your opinion," he had told the other man, "but you need to find another job for the summer. I won't have you, or anyone, bringing conflict onto my site."

The man had spluttered defensively, but Nicolas was implacable. Eventually, the fired man had no choice but to leave. Philip only hoped he would bow out with good grace and not make matters worse. Even so, the memory warmed him as he fought the rise of gooseflesh from a cool breeze. Nicolas had not been obliged to fire the other man, one he had hired in previous summers. The overseer could have left Philip to fight his own battles when they came and suffer the scorn of the crew in silence. Instead, he had defended the blacksmith and guaranteed his ability to work in peace. Even more interesting had been the conversation his three new friends had in their tent that evening.

"I'm glad Mr. Wells sent Farr packing," Carl commented. "He always had something to say. He never crossed the line before today, but he wasn't an easy man to work with."

"You, too?" Eric asked, surprised. "I thought it was just me he irritated."

Both Carl and Johnny laughed. "Why didn't we figure this out years ago and ask Mr. Wells to get rid of him?" Johnny wanted to know.

"He'd do that?" Philip inquired curiously.

Johnny nodded. "He takes our advice seriously. The final decision is his, but if all three of us had gone to him with problems from the same man, he would have reconsidered the man's employment. It doesn't happen often, but we've gotten a few people dismissed in the past. Usually, it's for drunkenness or dangerous conduct, and it's usually a pattern before we take it to him, but he trusts us. That's why we're crew bosses."

Philip had looked for an opportunity to speak with Nicolas, to thank him, but the overseer remained determinedly elusive, so much so that Philip wondered if the man was deliberately avoiding him. If so, it was subtly done, Nicolas making a point of eating with a different group of men each noon and night so he could stay abreast of all the work on the site and all the undercurrents that ran between the different groups. Philip respected that and had not tried to impose, biding his time and hoping an occasion would arise. So far, the only time it had was when the overseer came to the forge with a request for something. Those moments, though, were brief and all business, something ineffable setting a tone that did not engender any kind of personal conversation.

Despite Nicolas's aloofness, Philip caught the overseer watching him. Not obviously, but definitely keeping an eye on him. He knew those lingering glances could have a hundred different explanations, none of them related to anything other than work, but they gave Philip hope nonetheless, because every once in a while, he would surprise a look of more than professional interest on Nicolas's face.

That hope had fueled his hypnagogic adventures, his imagination throwing up again and again the image of Nicolas's bare torso as he bathed the first day Philip spent on the site. In his dreams, though, he did not stop at looking.   Johnny was unsurprisingly absent in those nocturnal fantasies, and nothing kept Philip from indulging himself, his hands exploring the solid planes of the overseer's body, mapping every valley and plane.   In his dreams, Nicolas welcomed those touches and reciprocated enthusiastically.

Philip groaned as those images, as vivid in his waking mind as they had been asleep, sent fresh desire sizzling through his body. He was grateful for the time alone to shower. Carl, Eric, and Johnny had long ago worked out a schedule that gave each man some private time in the shower they shared. It had been easy to work Philip in as well, giving him the privacy he did not have in the tent at night to attend to the nagging ache that was his constant companion these days. His soapy hand slid down his torso to lather the curls around the base of his erection. Another low groan escaped as he closed his eyes and gave his imagination free rein.

His previous lovers had mostly been men like James, attractive in a boyishly pretty sort of way, slender and willowy rather than solid and strong, their bodies giving in to his so beautifully. He did not delude himself that Nicolas would give the same way.   No, the overseer was easily a match for Philip's strength as he had proven the night they met. Having felt the weight of the other man's body atop his, Philip found himself eager to repeat the experience, eager to know again the other side of the equation. He closed his eyes and conjured the sensations that had stayed with him for the past week, Nicolas's strength pitted against his and winning, Nicolas pinning him to the ground, moving over him, atop him.

Into him.

It only took a few strokes of his hand to relieve the tension that built predictably over the course of the day, the glimpses he caught of Nicolas as he worked stoking the ever-burning fire in his belly. With a muffled groan, he spilled his seed onto the soft, wet loam, watching it mingle with the soap that had slid from his skin. Sighing at the lack of true satisfaction from the self-induced orgasm, Philip turned on the shower again, washing away the soap and the evidence of his passion.

When he was clean, he shut off the water and began to towel himself dry, wishing again that he were at home in front of his fireplace where he could relax and not feel constrained to dress again immediately if he were so inclined.

Relieved that another long day had ended, Nicolas crossed the camp, towel in hand. He knew Eric and Carl would both shower after dinner and Johnny when he finished his watch. That had been their schedule for as long as they had worked for him, which meant the shower would be empty now, giving him time to clean up and relax a little before Mrs. Waring rang the supper bell. Rubbing absently at the back of his neck to dispel the tension from the day, he pulled open the door to the shower enclosure and froze.

There, in front of him, was the embodiment of every fantasy he had allowed himself this past week. Philip's shoulders were as broad as he had imagined, skin dark enough, even after the long winter, to tell Nicolas that the blacksmith preferred to go without a shirt in the summer. The solid torso tapered to a narrow waist and hips and the most beautiful heart-shaped bottom he had ever seen. His fingers itched to reach out and touch, to cup the firm globes and see if the skin was as soft as it looked. Philip lifted a foot and bent to towel it dry, the movement parting the man's nether cheeks and giving the overseer a glimpse of the bounty within. He must have made a sound because Philip's head turned and their eyes met.

"Mr. Wells."

Chapter 10

THAT damnable mask Philip was coming to hate dropped over the overseer's face immediately, leaving Philip with only the faintest hope that he had seen desire in the blue gaze before it was cut off. Forcing himself to keep his movements relaxed, he wrapped the towel tightly around his waist, covering the lower half of his body from view before turning the rest of the way around so that he faced the object of his secret fantasies straight on.

The jacket and hat that never seemed to leave Nicolas's body were absent now, leaving the overseer clad only in his pants and shirt, the tails of which brushed the tops of his thighs, a towel hanging from his hand at his side. The top two buttons on the shirt and, oddly enough, the bottom two, were open, giving Philip a glimpse of the lightly furred chest that had haunted his dreams, waking and sleeping, for the past week. He also caught sight of a sliver of skin above the waistband of the overseer's pants. It seemed Mr. Wells had lost some weight over the winter, for with no belt to hold them in place, they rode low on his hips, revealing a darker line of hair that bisected his belly and dipped beneath the line of fabric, tempting Philip's eyes lower. Unfortunately, the heavy cloth hid any possible evidence of interest on the overseer's part. Stifling a sigh and adjusting the towel to hide his own growing arousal, Philip forced his eyes up to Nicolas's face as he reached for his clean shirt.

Mortified to have been caught staring, Nicolas forced his eyes to stay fixed on Philip's face rather than wandering over the blacksmith's front as they had already done to his back. To his surprise, he saw no sign of rejection or outrage on the other man's face. In fact, he thought he caught a hint of... interest? He mentally shook himself to rid himself of such delusions. Philip was a young man with his whole life ahead of him, a life he had made very clear he wanted to live out on the island, not following an itinerant overseer wherever his employer sent him.

When he could trust his voice not to betray him, he said, "I didn't realize you used this shower. I'll pay more attention next time before I come barging in."

No need, Philip wanted to say, but he held his tongue. If his attention was not returned, such a comment could destroy the working relationship he had succeeded in building with his employer, a relationship he needed if he was to stay here in the relative safety of the camp until Shawn captured James's killer.

Even so, the reflexive way Nicolas moved the towel in front of him, as if to hide something he did not want Philip to see, gave the blacksmith hope. Not enough hope to do anything so brash as approaching the overseer, but enough hope to keep watching for other little signs of possible interest. He had been the pursuer in every relationship he had attempted thus far. It would not bother him to do so now as long as he had some guarantee that his attentions would not ruin his current situation. He was not ready to take that step yet, but the time neared, he thought, when he might have the assurances he needed.

Knowing the length of his shirt would preserve his modesty, Philip pulled the towel from around his waist and reached for his pants, stepping into them without looking away from Nicolas. "Don't let me keep you from your shower. You needn't worry I'll bother you," he said. "I'll be done here in a minute anyway."

He did not pause in dressing to wait for Nicolas's reaction, but he did keep an eye on the sexy overseer out of the corner of his eye to see what effect his comment might have had on the older man.

A tremor of desire ran through the overseer at Philip's words. He would not, could not admit it, but he almost wished the blacksmith *would* take advantage, *would* approach him with undisguised intent. Perhaps if he did, Nicolas could let himself give in, could console himself later with the thought that the decision had been taken out of his hands. It was the coward's way out and he knew it, hated it, but it was a step he could not take on his own. Too much was at stake. His eyes, though, never left Philip as he dressed, hiding the tawny skin that already occupied pride of place in his fantasies. Now, having seen the perfect concinnity of his obsession's form, he suspected his fascination would only deepen.

Philip's words pricked his pride, as he was sure the blacksmith had intended, but knowing that did not lessen the impact. Tossing the towel over the edge of the enclosure, Nicolas unbuttoned the next button on his shirt. He kept telling himself that he had done this once before already, that removing his shirt now was no different than a week ago at the pump. He kept repeating it, but he found he did not believe his own words, not when the overwhelming sense of intimacy intensified with each button he prised from its hole with fingers made clumsy with lust.

Philip stifled a gasp when he realized Nicolas had accepted his dare, beginning to undress before him. He desperately wanted to stay and watch the show, or even reach for the buttons himself, but he knew they would quickly near a line he was not sure they could safely cross yet. Besides, he had told Nicolas he was almost ready to leave. He delayed as long as he could, but far sooner than he would have liked, he had no reason to tarry. At least he had gotten another glimpse of the strong chest and pale skin that haunted his dreams. Picking up his towel, he walked to the door of the enclosure. "Enjoy your shower," he said as he left.

Nicolas's breath rushed out of him when he was finally alone, the tension of the moment draining away with his solitude. As he let his guard down, the rush of adrenaline he felt at finding Philip there and naked, augmented by his own frustrated desire, set his hands to trembling. He scrubbed at his face, struggling for control again. He could not do this! Philip was his employee, but that was the least of his reasons. The blacksmith was young, not even thirty, while Nicolas was nearing forty. Even if the younger man felt some attraction now, what would he feel when he was still in his prime and Nicolas well into his dotage? Then there was the issue of residence. Philip was clearly settled here on the island while Nicolas's work required a certain degree of transience. No building occurred on the island in the winter and while he had been here for several summers in a row now, he had no idea how long that would last. If the current boom ended in Bar Harbor, Nicolas would have to go elsewhere to find work. His pride would not allow him to be dependent on Philip. Even if it did, they would never be able to build a life together on the island given the climate of intolerance that had led to one murder and the vandalism to Philip's home and forge. No, he could not do this, for both of their sakes.

Having renewed his resolve, he finished stripping, throwing his pants over the top of the wall of the shower and turning on the water to begin cleaning up.

A few feet away, hidden by the thick foliage of the island forest, Philip listened and imagined what was taking place just beyond his sight. He saw Nicolas's pants land on the top of the shower wall and closed his eyes, his mind's eye conjuring up a vision designed to drive him mad with desire. He had spent the past week thoroughly, if discreetly, studying the overseer. He knew every line of the man's body as completely as he knew his own. He could see the long legs, devoid in his vision of clothing, muscular but lean, covered in the same dusting of hair that was sprinkled over the man's chest. The water was cold, he knew well, but that did not keep him from picturing the overseer's erection in all its glory, for surely such a fine specimen of masculinity would be equally well-endowed.

Wet from the spray, Nicolas's hand slid down to encircle the hard flesh that even the douse of cold water had not softened. As tempted as he was by what he had seen earlier, nothing short of orgasm would ease his tension now. He moaned softly as he tugged on his engorged cock. He wanted to indulge his fantasies and whisper Philip's name, but he dared not, remembering all too well how little privacy he truly had here. After all, had he not just walked in on Philip? And while there was no shame in self-pleasure, he did not want anyone to know of the secret lust he harbored for the blacksmith. Such knowledge could ruin him in the eyes of his employees.

The moan that drifted to his ears fueled Philip's fantasies. He knew the sounds of pleasure a man made, whether they were self-induced or wrung from him by an attentive lover, and Nicolas was definitely making those sounds now. It was a simple matter to arrange his mental image to fit the noise coming from the shower, Nicolas's fist closed around his cock, pumping slowly, a little twist to his wrist at the top, teasing the frenulum, then pulling back the foreskin on the downward slide, letting the purpled tip peek out. Despite his recent climax, the vivid image in Philip's mind sent desire rushing through him again, leaving him trembling with need. He wanted to slip his hand inside his trousers and caress himself as he knew Nicolas was doing, but if he were caught, if someone found him there, his obsession would be revealed and his situation made more complicated than it already was. He could not afford that. He would just have to deal with the unassuaged desire until he could find time alone again. Instead, though he knew it would only make his problem worse, he imagined himself in the shower with Nicolas, his hand replacing the overseer's, their bodies brushing together teasingly, intimately. He shuddered when another groan reached his ears.

Holding the vision of Philip naked and bent over in his mind, Nicolas tightened his fist and imagined thrusting into the blacksmith's tight channel, imagined the velvet depths closing around him, squeezing him firmly, massaging his aching cock until he came hard, as hard as he had ever come. He managed to silence the shout that wanted to leave his lips, Philip's name a supplication for fulfillment, but he could not stifle the long, low moan that accompanied his release.

Philip knew that sound, too, the one that accompanied a climax. He stayed where he was, fighting the urge to barge back into the shower enclosure and find his pleasure in Nicolas's body. If he had been sure the overseer would welcome him, he would have done it, his passion roused enough that his inhibitions were burned away. Only the thought that Nicolas might not be willing held him back.

When he looked toward the enclosure and realized Nicolas's towel was gone, he slipped away toward the camp, not wanting the overseer to find him spying.

Chapter 11

FINISHED with his shower, Nicolas dressed and returned to his cabin for his jacket and hat before walking down to where Mrs. Waring served dinner every night. He found his crew bosses there already, but he saw no sign of Philip. Frowning slightly, he opened his mouth to ask them where the blacksmith was when a flurry of noise near the corral drew his attention. He tensed when he saw the sheriff striding toward them with a scowl on his face. Whatever the man had come to say, it was not good news.

"Where's Philip?"

FACE down on his cot, Philip humped his fist desperately, trying to bring himself relief as quickly as possible. His tent mates were at dinner, so he had a few minutes of privacy, but he had no idea how long it would be before they missed him and came looking for him. He had no desire for them to find him thus engaged, though he was sure they would understand the need to release the tension that held him.

As much as he had enjoyed listening to Nicolas in the shower, hearing the other man's pleasure had predictable consequences, consequences that had to be addressed before Philip could show his face at dinner. His hips moved faster, pushing down into his fist and then pulling back up. He could not have said, if pressed, whether he was driving his dream lover into the mattress or being driven there himself. Either would have been preferable to another empty, self-induced climax, but for the moment, this was his only option. He could hardly walk around with a raging erection, any more than he could walk up and ask Nicolas to take care of it for him.

He wanted to roll to his back and slide his fingers into his clenching passage, but he resisted. The hand job he was giving himself could be brushed aside as no different than any man's self-pleasure, not at all related to his "condition" as he had heard one person call his homosexuality. He did not expect to be interrupted, but if he was, the other man might be embarrassed but not horrified. Coming in and finding Philip with his fingers up his ass would garner an entirely different reaction. He *needed* to stay here in the relative safety of the camp, which meant not doing anything to give Nicolas, or anyone else, a reason to ask him to leave. Oh, how he ached, though, to be filled, even if only with his own fingers! It had been so long since he had a lover he trusted to take him that way, but he would trust Nicolas if the overseer was interested. The thought of feeling Nicolas's weight on top of him, Nicolas's strength surrounding him, Nicolas's cock impaling him was enough to trigger Philip's release, his body shuddering hard with the surcease of passion. He rolled onto his side, his hand covered in a sticky mess.

"**WHAT** do you mean you don't know?" Shawn demanded angrily. "You were supposed to keep him safe!"

"He was safe the last time I saw him," Nicolas retorted. "He took a shower about half an hour ago. I saw him leaving as I arrived to take mine."

"This bastard doesn't need that much time," Shawn insisted.

Nicolas frowned. "Malone, would you escort the sheriff to my cabin? I'll go check Mr. Hall's tent and then join you there."

Shawn's frown matched the overseer's, but he did not persist, following the crew boss toward the overseer's cabin.

"He hasn't been alone for more than five minutes except for just now," Carl said defensively, feeling the weight of the sheriff's disapprobation.

"PHILIP?" Nicolas called , approaching the tent his crew bosses shared with the blacksmith. "Are you in there?" After the incident at the shower, he did not want to embarrass them both again by walking in on anything private.

Half-naked, hand covered in his own seed, Philip groaned where he lay on his cot, even as a thrill went through him at hearing the other man use his first name. It seemed his luck today for Nicolas to catch him with his pants down, literally as well as figuratively. He was tempted to tell the overseer to come in, to give the man another eyeful, but if Nicolas had come looking for him, something was surely going on. "Just a minute," he called back. "Let me finish getting dressed."

Nicolas arched an eyebrow in surprise, given that Philip had left the shower half an hour ago and had been dressed at the time. He waited patiently, though, for permission to enter or for Philip to come out.

Inside the tent, Philip wiped his hand and fastened his trousers, wondering what he should say to Nicolas if the overseer questioned his absence from dinner. He could not exactly give his real reason. He could just imagine how well that would go over. *Well, you see, Mr. Wells, I spied on you while you were taking a shower and hearing you get yourself off got me so hot and bothered that I had to come back here and jerk off. Of course, I did it while imagining your hands on me instead.* No, he would not be saying that to his employer. "You can come in," he offered as he sat down to pull on his boots.

Nicolas stuck his head inside the tent, the smell of sex wafting up to his nose immediately. His gut tightened as he imagined Philip lying there on his cot, stroking himself to completion. "The sheriff is here," he said without preamble, not wanting to address the rest of what he was thinking. "He's waiting for us in my cabin."

"Shawn?" Philip questioned, surprised. "What is he doing here?"

"I don't know," Nicolas replied, "but he was quite upset when you weren't at dinner and he realized you were alone."

"Mother hen," the blacksmith muttered, brushing his hands over the thighs of his trousers as if to straighten them as he rose. "Let's go see what he wants then," he suggested, not quite meeting Nicolas's eyes. It must have been incredibly obvious to the overseer what he had been doing, but the other man had let it pass without comment. Philip appreciated the gesture and so did not call attention to the fact that Nicolas had called him by his first name moments before. One good turn deserved another, after all.

They walked through the camp silently, neither willing to bring up any of the things that haunted their thoughts. The silence had just started to get tense when they arrived at the door to the overseer's cabin. Nicolas pushed it open and gestured for Philip to precede him inside.

Looking up from the seat he had taken at the table, the sheriff's glower eased as he saw his friend come in. "Are you trying to get yourself killed?" the big man asked, rising to his feet and embracing the blacksmith.

"What are you talking about, Shawn?" Philip demanded, his voice muffled against the sheriff's chest as he struggled gently against the tight hug. He did not care so much about getting away, but he did care about being able to breathe.

Nicolas tensed as he watched the two men embrace. He had interpreted the sheriff's protectiveness as a product of his job and his concern for the island's residents. Now, seeing how comfortable they were with each other, he wondered jealously if there was more to the situation than he had realized.

Philip squirmed a little harder when Shawn still did not release him. "Let me go, you big oaf," he demanded affectionately. "You'll give me ideas."

Shawn pulled away immediately. "Not my type, lad. Not my type."

Philip chuckled. "Why do you think I didn't want to waste my time?" Growing more serious, he took in the concern on his friend's face. "So what brings you out to see me?"

Looking at the overseer, Shawn gestured to the table. "Do you mind if we sit? This may take awhile."

Nicolas nodded and sat, motioning for the others to do the same, feeling unworthy at the sense of relief that went through him at the teasing exchange. The sheriff really did see the blacksmith as a younger brother.

Impatiently, Philip took his seat. When Shawn sat as well, he asked again, "What's going on, Shawn?"

"There's been another murder," the sheriff explained. "In Eden."

"Who?" Philip asked softly, afraid he knew the answer.

"Jason Leonard," Shawn replied slowly, not sure what Philip's reaction would be.

"Who?" Nicolas asked, not recognizing the name.

"A local farmer," Shawn began diplomatically.

"James's other lover," Philip interjected dully. He had no reason to keep the truth from Nicolas, and the overseer needed to understand the threat, since Shawn clearly considered this one.

"And you think this is related to the first murder?" Nicolas clarified, sure that was what the sheriff's presence signified but not wanting to jump to unfounded conclusions.

"I know it's related," Shawn replied, his face tightening at the memory of finding the two bodies.

Philip's eyes shut briefly as he tried not to think of the details Shawn had revealed to him, the one fact that made these murderers incontrovertibly a threat to his life as well. The image would not leave him, though, and while he was angry at James for cheating on him, angry at Leonard for being the other man, neither of them deserved what Shawn had described.

"Not that I don't trust you to do your job, but a little more detail would be helpful," Nicolas cut in, not seeing Philip's reaction.

"Tell him, Shawn," Philip said quietly, though he did not really want to hear it all again. "He needs to know everything since he agreed to help protect me."

Shawn nodded and turned to Nicolas. "I told you the murderer was targeting Philip because of his history with Reed. I left out the details that made me believe that. When I found Reed's body, he hadn't just been murdered. He'd been raped with the handle of a broom. Not wanting there to be any more backlash against Philip than there already was from their fight, I didn't tell anyone but Philip, so the only other person who knows is the murderer. Leonard was abused the same way." Shawn saw no reason to mention his conversation with Widow Taylor. There was no chance she was involved and it was simpler to leave her name out of the conversation entirely.

"God," Nicolas muttered, "that's sick!" Every fiber of his being shuddered in protest at the thought of anyone being forced to endure that kind of abuse. It was one thing to have sex with a willing lover, working his fingers and his cock inside an eager body. Having such an act forced upon him… his eyes sought Philip, saw the tension in the set of the blacksmith's shoulders. Over his dead body would anyone have a chance to hurt Philip that way!

His hands clenched with the effort of keeping them at his sides, of not reaching for the blacksmith and making aloud the vow he had already sworn in silence. Inwardly, he scoffed at himself, at the thought that Philip would even consider accepting such a promise from someone so much older. The younger man deserved someone his own age, his own generation, not some graying old man with nothing better to do than lust over someone almost young enough to be his son. "What else do you know?" he asked, trying to keep the conversation going. Philip might not want promises of protection, but Nicolas would do anything he could, use any knowledge the sheriff had, to keep the blacksmith safe.

"Reed lived in Bar Harbor," Shawn continued. "It makes sense that his body would be found here, although I found him outside of the actual town, thank God. Leonard, though, is from Eden, yet I found his body near where I found Reed's, another fact I didn't share with anyone. The murderer, sick bastard that he is, wants my attention and he wants Philip. I don't see any other explanation for the facts."

"Do you have any idea who it is?" Nicolas asked.

"I know who it isn't," Shawn replied, "which is some help, but not a lot. It isn't an outlander. Whoever this man is, he's either native to the island or has been here for some time."

"How do you figure that?" Philip asked with a frown.

"He knows the island well enough to slip around," Shawn explained, "to convince both Reed and Leonard to go with him peacefully. I went to both their homes after their murders, and there was no sign of forced entry, nothing to indicate that they put up any kind of a struggle while they were at home. If they weren't taken from home, then they were taken by someone who knows the island and their routines well enough to grab them without being noticed. I talked to their neighbors and no one remembers seeing or hearing anything unusual the nights they were killed."

"That's saying something then," Philip agreed. "James had really nosy neighbors. He wouldn't let me come to his house because he said they'd find out about us for sure. He was always complaining about them and their meddling."

Privately, Shawn wondered how much of that was the neighbors and how much of it was Reed's way of making sure Philip did not find out about his cheating ways. Either way, it was irrelevant now. The neighbors had not heard or seen anything useful, which told him he was dealing with someone who knew the island and its inhabitants well enough to avoid arousing suspicion.

"He's a big man," Shawn continued, "big enough to carry a dead body to the spot where I found them. There wasn't enough blood at either murder site for them to have been killed where I found them, and there wasn't any sign of a wagon or hoof prints, so after he was done with them, he carried them where he wanted them found and left them there. Another reason to think he's a long-time resident."

"Are you sure it's just one man?" Nicolas inquired.

"God, I hope so," Shawn swore. "I'm having enough trouble imagining someone I know doing this. To think that it's more than one person makes it even harder. Honestly, though, I don't know. I couldn't distinguish clear footprints in either clearing to be able to tell how many were there. Leonard fought. Reed's body didn't show any real signs of struggle, but Leonard had bruises all over. Either the killer is getting angrier because he can't get to Philip, or Leonard fought. Given his size and what I know of his personality, it certainly seems consistent with his character, which again means the killer is a strong enough man to take Leonard down, or there were two of them."

"So what do we do now?" Nicolas asked.

"I keep looking, trying to find someone who saw something, trying to find something to give me a place to start," Shawn answered. "You two stay out here and do everything you can to keep Philip safe. We have no idea who he'll attack next, but Philip is still a target."

Philip slumped in the chair. Shawn said he wanted Philip to be safe, but the blacksmith wondered if he would ever truly feel safe again. The murderer was out there, stalking him. It was just a matter of time.

"I don't know what else to do," he told the other two men honestly. "Already, I've left my home to come here. I'm sharing living space with three other men. I'm surrounded by people all the time. I know it's necessary, but I feel like I'm going to burst with the strain."

"You could move in here," Nicolas suggested, the words out of his mouth before he realized he had said them. He flushed, knowing they were motivated by more than just a concern for Philip's safety, but he did not rescind them.

"Here?" Philip repeated, looking around the small cabin. "Why?"

"Because it's four walls and a door that locks instead of just a tent," Nicolas explained. "And it also gives you a little privacy at least. You still won't be alone during the day, but you won't have to sleep next to three other men at night."

Philip frowned as he considered his options. Yes, it was four walls and a door. Yes, it was a little more privacy. It was also a lot more temptation. Glancing up at the handsome overseer, he pondered that. For days, he had been catching glimpses of possible interest from Wells, feeling the overseer's eyes on him when he was working, though the older man looked away every time Philip tried to make eye contact. Even now, Nicolas would not meet his eyes, making the blacksmith wonder what he would see in those lapis eyes if they did meet his. Interest? Desire? Lust? Maybe it was time to stop resisting temptation and find out for sure.

"All right," he agreed, looking over at Shawn. "Satisfied now?"

The sheriff looked back and forth between the two men, catching undercurrents he could not quite identify. He suspected there was more to this suggestion than met the eye, but he could see no reason to speak against it. "It'll help keep you safe."

Nicolas sat there in shock, the conversation swirling about him as the sheriff and the blacksmith continued to talk. He could not even have said what they were discussing, his mind too caught by the fact that Philip had agreed. The object of his secret desires would be moving into his cabin that evening, or in the morning at the very latest. He could not quite believe this was not some dream, thrown up by his subconscious mind to torture him with all he could not have. He reminded himself firmly that Philip sought safety, not a lover, in his agreement to move in. He would treat the blacksmith now the same way he had been treating him – like any other member of the crew.

Except he was not just any other employee. He was admittedly homosexual, devilishly attractive, and seemed at times to be attracted to Nicolas. The combination was almost more than the overseer could stand. Philip would not revile him for his preferences, would not call him an unnatural freak and send him away. The blacksmith might still reject his advances, for any number of reasons, but disgust would not immediately follow any admission of interest on his part. And maybe, just maybe, the speculative glances he intercepted from time to time meant something more, something… real.

Chapter 12

SAFE.

He was supposed to be safe at the work site.

That was the despairing thought that went through all three men's minds as they stared down at the heap of torn fabric that had been Philip's bedroll and spare clothing.

Nicolas had held back in his cabin, keeping himself from reaching out to offer comfort of any kind, not sure how the blacksmith would react. Seeing his shaken face now, he could not stop a reassuring hand from lifting to the younger man's shoulder.

Philip shivered at the touch, unable to deny the desire it sparked in him even as he fought with the reality of what he was seeing and the implications it raised in his mind. The murderer had been here.

On the site.

In his tent.

And if he had come even a few minutes earlier, he would have found Philip there alone, hand on his cock, guard completely down. He shuddered at the thought, glad now for the safety Nicolas's cabin represented. Four walls and a door that locks. That was what Nicolas had said. At the time, Philip had been more interested in the proximity it would provide him to the overseer, but now he truly understood the value of the offer.

"I guess moving me just got easier," he quipped in a shaky voice, nudging the pile of rags with the tip of his boot. "I'll need to go into town tomorrow, or I'm going to be seriously underdressed."

"Don't make jokes," Shawn scolded, mind racing as he tried to assimilate this new information in light of his earlier conclusions. He told himself it could be a coincidence, but that did not ring true. He had a murderer targeting homosexuals and Philip's belongings destroyed. He could see only one logical conclusion: the murderer had made it onto the job site. "Who's guarding the camp right now?"

"No one," Nicolas admitted. "Everyone's at dinner, or should be, except us. The men should be finished soon and they'll be wandering back to their tents, to sleep or to take showers in the facilities West rigged for them. The watch will start at sundown. It hardly seemed necessary before that."

Shawn frowned. "It might be necessary after all," he pointed out. "Either the murderer sneaked onto the site while your crew was at dinner, or else he's already here."

"One of the crew?" Philip asked, his eyes darting back and forth between the two men. "But how is that possible?"

Shawn shrugged. "Everyone knows Mr. Wells hires locally when he can," the sheriff pointed out. "You've heard them talking at the tavern. They like to work for him because he's fair, pays well, and looks out for his employees' well-being."

"Most of the locals don't stay on site," Nicolas observed. "They return home to their families for the night."

"How long ago did you let them go?" Shawn inquired.

Nicolas pulled out his pocket watch, glanced at it, and replied, "About an hour and a half."

"But someone was here in the tent until I came to Mr. Wells's cabin to see you," Philip interjected. "Johnny, Carl, and Eric all came back before dinner. They were here when I went to take my shower. And my stuff was fine when I left. So whoever did this, he was here in the last half an hour."

Shawn nodded. "Then the question is who lingered after his shift. That ought to be easy enough to determine. If you don't mind, Mr. Wells, I'll ask a few questions before I head home. I'll leave you to help Philip get settled in his new lodging."

"You know," Nicolas said slowly, "it might not be the murderer. I mean, I've seen this kind of petty vandalism before from men who would stoop to this but not go so far as murder. All it takes is enough intolerance. Coloreds, Irishmen, Jews... I've seen them all victimized, and I'm sure you have, too."

Even as he spoke, his thoughts slipped back to another camp in another state, almost twenty-five years before. He had just signed on as an apprentice to the resident mason. Over the course of that summer, two of the crew had been discovered in *flagrante delicto.* The reaction had been immediate and harsh, their belongings trashed, their work sabotaged. The overseer had not fired them immediately, but the other men had made the working and living conditions so miserable that the two men had finally quit in despair and frustration. Nicolas had resolved that day never to let anyone he worked with discover his own leanings. A few moments of pleasure were not worth the risk.

"There are hateful people everywhere, and it's not limited to Philip," Nicolas finished, glancing at the blacksmith. "Have you noticed anyone here on site giving you unpleasant looks? You haven't reported anything to me, but then again, would you?"

Philip considered the question, thinking back to the previous days. "I really haven't noticed anything," he replied honestly. "There was the one man you fired early on, but I haven't felt uncomfortable with anyone since then."

"Would you tell him if anyone had said anything?" Shawn challenged. "I know how you are, Philip, but we're not talking about just a little bullying. Whether the murderer did this or just a petty vandal, he's out to hurt you if he can. I'm glad you'll be safe behind a locked door again, and not alone where you could be lured out."

"I'm not that stupid," Philip protested. "I really haven't noticed anything, and yes, I promise I'll say something if I do. After the damage to my house, I won't take reckless chances."

Glancing out at the darkening woods, Nicolas held up a hand to stave off Shawn's reply. "Before you two get into that, I think we ought to go back to my cabin. The murderer shot at Philip in broad daylight in town. Now that it's getting dark, and with the cover of the woods, we're sitting ducks out here like this."

Both men agreed and Philip gathered the pile of torn clothes, hoping something would be usable enough to get him through the night and into town the next day.

Returning to Nicolas's cabin, Shawn rounded on the blacksmith, preparing to light into him for not notifying him of the vandalism to his house. "Before you start," Nicolas chuckled, easily reading the sheriff's intentions on his face, "Hall hasn't eaten and my dinner was interrupted. I'm going to get us something while you two are talking."

Both men nodded, neither taking their eyes from the other as they prepared for the argument to come. As soon as the door shut behind Nicolas, the shouting began. "Why didn't you tell me?"

Nicolas shook his head and walked back toward the mess area to gather two plates of food. Mrs. Waring always made more than enough, so he was not worried about there being food left for him and Philip. His thoughts were centered instead around the predicament he had landed himself in.

His cabin only had two rooms, not counting the mudroom where he left his boots, coat, and hat each night, and while his bed was large enough to share with a lover, Philip was *not* his lover, could not be his lover. There was simply no way for that to work between them, not as anything more than a summer fling. Nicolas had grown beyond that years ago. His relationships, when they occurred now, happened with the hope of something permanent. That he had not found what he sought said more about his own high standards than about his intentions when he began each of his affairs.

With Philip, neither of his requirements were even possibilities. Philip was as fixed in Bar Harbor as Nicolas was in Boston, his professional reputation, his friends, his history giving him a place in society that he would lose completely if he moved elsewhere, which meant that their relationship had no hope of permanence, his primary requirement. The other one, discretion, was equally impossible to fulfill given the current situation that had Philip and his preferences on the minds and lips of the entire island. Even those, like the sheriff or Philip's friends, who were not criticizing the blacksmith, were still talking, and for a private man like Nicolas, that sort of public scrutiny made him incredibly uncomfortable. No, he would simply have to treat Philip like any other employee and arrange a cot in the main room of the cabin for the blacksmith to sleep on, no matter how much he wanted the younger man in his bed.

Gathering two plates and filling them with the thick stew Mrs. Waring had made for dinner that night along with fresh biscuits, Nicolas returned to his cabin, hoping the worst of the shouting would be over by the time he got back. He understood why the sheriff would want to know, not only because of the threat to Philip's life, but also, quite simply, because Philip was his friend. He also understood Philip's motivation in keeping his own counsel. He had seen already how incredibly protective of the young blacksmith Parnell was. With the addition of the vandalism to his house... well, Nicolas did not know what more the sheriff could do, but he could easily see Philip preferring not to find out.

Silence greeted his ears when he stopped outside the door to juggle the plates so he could go inside. The scene that met his gaze did not surprise him at all. The two men sat on either side of the table, their steely gazes locked stubbornly, neither one speaking. When his entrance drew their attention, the sheriff rose immediately. "I'll be getting back to town then since this one doesn't need or want my help."

Philip snorted but held his tongue. He saw no reason to inflict their argument on the overseer when he had no part in its making.

Nicolas nodded. "Thank you for coming out and letting us know what's going on with the investigation," he said civilly, knowing they could not afford to alienate the sheriff completely. "You're always welcome on the site."

Shawn ducked his chin curtly and started toward the door. "I'll remember that." He glanced back at his friend, still sitting motionless at the table. "Take care of him."

"I will," Nicolas promised as Parnell disappeared into the night. He thought ruefully that the sheriff would probably not have chosen those particular words if he had known the vein along which Nicolas's desires ran, but he reminded himself firmly that his attraction for Philip had no chance of a happy ending and so was better left unexplored. Going back into the cabin, he took out silverware and offered a set to the blacksmith.

"You should eat."

Philip nodded and accepted the utensils, eating his meal in awkward silence with no idea what to say to the overseer now that they were alone. He kept hoping Nicolas would say something to start the conversation, but the overseer seemed no more at ease than Philip himself.

Their meal finished, the two men stared at each other awkwardly. Nicolas had made the offer on impulse, and Philip had accepted for the same reason, necessity adding to it after finding his belongings vandalized. The impulse that had landed them there could not make the situation less uncomfortable, though, not with the unspoken attraction simmering between them. Philip summoned a hesitant smile.

"Thank you again for letting me stay here," he offered before glancing at the door. "If you'd like, I can reinforce the cabin door when I have time, make it like mine at home."

Nicolas looked over at the simple door. It had a lock on it, true, but it would not stand up to the kind of determined assault the killer had inflicted on Philip's house. "If it's not too much trouble," he agreed.

"Not when it's my safety at risk," Philip pointed out wryly. "I'd spend a lot more time than the few hours it will take to make some struts to reinforce the door in exchange for knowing he won't get in here."

"He'd be a fool to try," Nicolas insisted, opening a cupboard door and showing Philip the Colt revolver inside. "I don't carry it with me on the site because we've got explosives – not to mention that I don't want to set that tone – but it's here if you ever need it."

Philip nodded. "It's not the kind of thing we're supposed to need in a civilized town," he agreed. "This isn't Wyoming or

Kansas. We're an old and established community, a lawful place. I can't remember the last time Shawn had to deal with anything more than just a few men getting drunk on a Friday night."

Nicolas smiled. "That's one of the reasons I love coming here in the summer. It's so peaceful compared to the bustle of Boston."

"I've never been to Boston," Philip admitted, his heart beating a little faster at the honest smile on the overseer's face. He had seen the other man smile before, but not like this. Not just for him. "But I was born in New York, and I remember how noisy it was all the time. But here... just listen."

Silence fell between them, comfortably this time, as they listened to the soft night sounds: the crickets, the birds, the gentle lap of the ocean against the shore. "You don't hear any of that in Boston or New York," Nicolas agreed.

They shared a quiet smile, caught in the shared enjoyment for a moment, before the awkwardness reasserted itself. "So... um... where do you want me to sleep?" Philip asked.

Chapter 13

THE next morning saw Nicolas, Philip and Johnny on their way to town, guns strapped openly to their belts as they rode. While they all hoped such a display was unnecessary, they refused to take chances with Philip's safety. Fortunately, the ride to town passed uneventfully.

"Mr. Wells, Philip," Mr. Waring called as they walked into the mercantile, "I wasn't expecting to see you for another few weeks after all you bought the last time you were here."

"We had a little trouble last night and Mr. Hall needs some new gear," Nicolas explained.

"There was also some trouble out at my house and I'll need to get some materials to fix it up," Philip added.

"What's happening to this town?" Mr. Waring muttered as he came out from behind his counter. "Tell me what you need and we'll get you set up. If it's much, I'll give it to you on credit and you can pay me over the course of the summer."

"That isn't necessary," Philip protested. "I can pay…"

"I'm sure you can, and I'll let you, but don't skimp on what you need for your cabin or yourself just because money's tight. That's all I'm saying."

Philip nodded, overwhelmed by the generosity the shopkeeper was showing. He knew he had enemies in town, but he forgot, sometimes, that he also had friends, outside those he spent most of this time with. He had spent so long seeing himself as an outsider, an outlander, that he did not always see how much the town had come to accept and depend on him.

Walking around the store, he gathered a few shirts and trousers to replace the ones that had been shredded, having decided his garments were too damaged to repair. He would give them to Widow Taylor for her quilting guild to use. Maybe they would make him another quilt for the winter, to give him a spare to use when he had to wash the one on his bed at home. He was suddenly glad he had not brought it with him to Cleftstone. If he had, there would be nothing more left of it than of his clothes.

"Do you have a spare bedroll or blankets?" he asked, looking for Mr. Waring.

"What did they do?" the shopkeeper asked, taking note of what the blacksmith had already selected. "Destroy everything you own?"

"Everything I had in my tent at the site anyway," Philip replied acidly. "They left the cot intact, but then, that belongs to Mr. Wells, not to me."

"Does the sheriff know?" Mr. Waring inquired insistently. "Whoever did this should be punished."

"He was with me when I found the damage," Hall explained. "He's looking for whoever did it, but he isn't hopeful he'll find out who it was. Nobody saw anything and everybody who was supposed to be on the site was at dinner when it happened. The same thing with my house... I wasn't home so all I have is the damage and no idea who's responsible."

"What do you need for your house?"

"New glass in all the windows, though I imagine that will have to be ordered from the mainland. I can just keep the shutters closed for now since I'm not living there at the moment," Philip replied. "I'll... we'll," he corrected, glancing back at the two men who had come to town with him, "go out to the house on Saturday when we're not working and see what repairs we can do. The wood on the door will have to be replaced completely. The man hacked at it with an axe, although he couldn't get past the lock. There's some charred wood elsewhere, too, as if he tried to smoke me out." Philip shuddered. "I'm almost glad I wasn't there, because it would have worked if I had been."

Mr. Waring's scowl grew darker. "This kind of thing shouldn't happen in a civilized town."

A muffled curse drew their attention and they looked up to see John Ferguson walking into the store. Philip's eyes flew to Johnny, then to Nicolas, both of whom were moving in his direction, flanking him in a show of silent support.

"Excuse me for a minute," Mr. Waring said to Philip. "What can I help you with, John?"

"Just looking," Ferguson drawled arrogantly, weaving his way through the counters toward where Philip stood with the other two men. "Well, what's this?" he asked nastily, looking up as if in surprise. "Haven't seen you around, Hall. What rock did you crawl under? Or have you holed up with some other pervert?"

Before Philip could reply, Mr. Waring appeared at Ferguson's elbow. "If you have business in my store, I'll be happy to help you," he interrupted coldly, "but if you've just come in to make trouble, you need to find somewhere else to start it. I don't have the time or the patience to tolerate it in my store."

Ferguson looked around the room instinctively seeking support, but the other couple in the mercantile had the same disapproving looks on their faces that Waring wore on his. Spitting tobacco juice from his mouth, he glared at Philip. "This isn't over, Hall."

Mr. Waring grabbed Ferguson's arm and propelled him from the store. "It is for now," he spat. "And don't come back either. I don't have any use for your kind in my establishment. You can ride to Eden for your supplies from now on."

When Mr. Waring came back inside, Philip offered an immediate apology. "I'm sorry. I was hoping it was early enough that I'd avoid that kind of trouble. I certainly didn't mean to bring it into your store."

"You didn't bring anything into my store except your business," Mr. Waring replied smoothly. "Ferguson's the one that came in here starting trouble." He looked at the dark tobacco stain on his floor. "He and his cronies have hated you since you arrived here, though I have no idea why, but no matter what they said or did, never once have I seen you start anything. Now, finish gathering what you need. I have a mess to clean up."

Philip's guilt redoubled as he watched the shopkeeper fetch a bucket and mop, but he knew better than to argue with Mr. Waring. He gathered the rest of what he needed, saying he would pick up the materials for his house on Saturday morning. Mr. Waring looked up from his mopping to acknowledge the comment and take note of what Philip had purchased.

As the three men left the store, Johnny murmured, "You're a better man than I am, Philip Hall. I would have punched the ignorant bastard in the mouth a long time ago and been done with it."

Philip laughed bitterly. "I did that once. They haven't bothered me physically since, but nothing seems to stop their comments."

Nothing ever does, Nicolas mused silently, yet another reason why he took such care to keep his own inclinations private.

THE following few days were excruciating in their tension, as the two men measured each other and learned to deal with one another in private as well as public. Public was relatively easy still, each falling into his role on the site with simple competence. Philip continued to work the forge, repairing tools damaged by the winter damp and cold, and learning the shapes of the fittings needed for the various parts of the manor. He would wait until he could see more of the shape of things before beginning work on the decorative metalwork to adorn the railings and banisters of the interior galleries and exterior balconies. Nicolas had not given him strict instructions on what would be needed, and he hoped he would have the freedom to be creative with the designs. He also took the time to fashion bars to reinforce the door of Nicolas's cabin. They were easy enough to make, and knowing he was doing something to account for his own safety made him feel better about imposing on the overseer's privacy the way his presence surely did.

Nicolas had not said anything, even obliquely, to make Philip feel like he was unwelcome. On the contrary, the overseer's expression was almost always warm and open, at least when they were alone, but Philip noticed that Nicolas never lingered in the kitchen area in the evenings, always retreating to his bedroom and shutting the door firmly behind him. One night, the blacksmith had snuck to the door and pressed his ear against it, trying to figure out what the overseer did each night. He could hear shuffling sounds, but nothing to give him any sure idea. He had hoped to hear more sounds of Nicolas's pleasure, perhaps inspired by his presence in the next room, but if Nicolas indulged himself, he either did so in near silence or outside the cabin, for no such sounds reached Philip's ears at night.

Nicolas, meanwhile, kept a close eye on those he considered the most likely suspects, based on Shawn's deductions and his own knowledge of his crew. A quiet word with the crew bosses ensured they would do the same. It irked him to think he was so poor a judge of character as to have worked with many of these men for years without ever sensing the hatred that motivated the kind of violence perpetrated against the murdered men or against Philip's house and belongings. A few of them were hotheads, and he and his crew bosses had broken up more than one fight over the years, but while the vandalism might be explained that way, the murders could not. The destruction of Philip's gear, however, seemed to suggest that the murderer was one of his employees.

He managed to stay in control of himself well enough during the day, the various aspects of his job keeping him too busy for thoughts of Philip, but each night seemed longer than the last, knowing that only a thin wall separated him from the object of his desires. That Philip took advantage of the relative privacy of the cabin to relieve his tensions at the end of the day made resisting temptation even harder. Knowing what was happening just beyond his bedroom wall, he closed his eyes and imagined Philip with his hand on his cock, stroking slowly, firmly, repetitively until he came with a muffled groan. Every night, Nicolas strained his ears listening for that sound, hoping despite himself that he would hear his name on the blacksmith's lips. He would lie in bed, his own erection throbbing, until he was sure Philip slept before giving himself relief, the heel of one hand firmly between his teeth to smother any noises that might escape.

Nicolas awoke in the middle of the night four days after Philip moved in with him with the undeniable need for the privy. He had forced himself, the previous nights, to stay in his room until after he heard Philip fold up his cot in the morning, not wanting to add to the temptation already assailing him, but he knew he would never be able to wait until morning. Pulling a pair of trousers on under his nightshirt, he slipped as silently as he could through the darkened kitchen and out the door, being careful to close it quietly behind him. Finished with his business, he returned inside, slipping off his boots and locking the door carefully. He was almost to his bedroom door when a sound drew his attention to the sight he was trying to pretend did not exist. Unable to help himself, he moved on silent feet to the end of the cot where Philip slept, his eyes raking the blanket-swathed form in the pale moonlight that streamed through the window.

In repose, Philip's face looked younger than his years, the lines of care and sorrow erased from his brow. The almost boyish features in no way detracted from the attraction Nicolas felt. On the contrary, they showed him a side of the blacksmith he imagined few people now saw. Of its own accord, his hand reached out, as if to touch, catching himself as his hand hovered inches above Philip's face. For a moment, he warred with himself before pulling back and turning away. Yes, he suspected Philip would not send him away, but he needed more than that before he could commit himself. With a sigh, he walked back into his bedroom and shut the door firmly behind him.

In the main room of the cabin, Philip's sigh echoed Nicolas's own. He had no idea what was holding the overseer back, but he knew one thing now for sure. The older man was attracted to him. If Nicolas had tarried but a moment longer, Philip would have reached for him, issued the invitation that thrummed in his heart and loins. Nicolas had turned away, though, just as Philip started to reach for the hand that floated above his head. He did not know what had changed Nicolas's mind, what had caused him to leave when he did, but waiting for the overseer to act was clearly not an option. He would have to take matters into his own hands if he intended to have Nicolas as his lover.

He had tried being subtle, sending the same kind of signals he had noticed from James before they started seeing one another: looks to express his interest, listening attentively to everything Nicolas had to say (not that it was difficult since the overseer was a well-traveled, well-read man). That had clearly not succeeded with Nicolas the way James had with him a little over a year ago, which meant he would have to try something else. His mind raced as he considered the possibilities.

Telling Nicolas flat out how he felt.

He could do that, but he suspected it would only result in excuses, reasons why they could not be together, and while he was sure he could refute any argument Nicolas made, he was equally sure the overseer would not be won by logical argument alone.

Showing Nicolas how attractive he found him.

The close proximity of the cabin would make it easy to touch the other man under the guise of casual interaction, slowly acclimating Nicolas not only to his presence but also to his touch until he came to expect, even desire it. It would be easy enough to do, but would it be enough? Would Nicolas see it for the expression of desire that it was or would he dismiss it as part of the normal interactions of sharing their living space?

That left him with just one option: seduce the older man in earnest.

SATURDAY morning dawned cool but clear, with the promise of a warm day once the sun reached its zenith. Philip stood outside the caretaker's cabin enjoying the ocean breeze on his face. Like many of the cottages, Cleftstone Manor was being built on the coast. The manor itself blocked the view of the ocean from the cabin where he now lived, but it could not block the wind that gusted wildly around the solid stone and tugged at his hair and clothes. Closing his eyes, he tipped his head back and let the sense of renewal that came with dawn wash over him and through him.

He had grown so used to thinking of himself as being alone, even when he was with James, that finding himself now with friends offering to help rebuild his house and the possibility of a lover on the horizon would take some time to assimilate. He still had no idea if he would be able to rebuild the life he had before his preferences came to light, to love freely without enduring the constant scorn of the townspeople, but he did know, at least, that he could live here still. He had fully expected to be ostracized completely, but it had not happened. Now that the shock was wearing off, the majority of the town had returned to treating him as they always had.

A noise behind him drew his attention and he turned to look back at the little cabin nestled among the trees, still cast in their shadows and the shadow of the manor. It would not take long, though, for the sun's rays to illuminate the rough-hewn wood. In that moment of quiet dawn, he and Nicolas, framed by the doorway, could have been the only two people on the island, in the world.

"You're up early," Nicolas commented quietly, drinking in the sight of the blacksmith backlit by the early dawn light. His breath caught in his throat despite himself as he marveled again at how the man could be so beautiful without sacrificing any of his masculinity. Nicolas had known pretty boys before, boys who stole his breath with their appearance but were too slender, too willowy to truly be called men. Philip had no such problem. The breadth of his shoulders proclaimed him every inch a man in his prime, the epitome of masculine perfection. The dark hair was limned with gold as the sun rose above the roof of the manor, bathing them both in its light. Finally, Nicolas forced himself to tear his eyes away. However beautiful, Philip was not for him.

"I wanted to watch the sunrise," Philip explained with a shrug, not sure what to make of the odd look on Nicolas's face. "It seemed like the day for it. I didn't mean to disturb you."

"You didn't," the overseer assured him. "I was already awake when I heard the door open. I thought I'd better check and make sure everything was all right."

Philip nodded and turned back toward the shore. "Everything's fine," he replied, realizing that for the first time in a long time, he believed those words.

"Mr. Wells, Philip?" Johnny's voice interrupted, shattering the illusion of their isolation. "I've got some breakfast ready if you want to eat before we head out."

The two men turned away from their contemplation of the dawn and each other and followed the crew boss to the dining tent. Carl and Eric were already there, helping themselves to eggs and bacon. "No bread," Johnny apologized. "I'm not much of a baker and there wasn't any left from what Mrs. Waring brought yesterday."

Philip shrugged. "Tell me there's coffee and I'll forgive you anything else." He could not tell Johnny that he was having trouble sleeping because his dreams left him wracked with desire.

They ate quickly, discussing what they hoped to accomplish that day as they hitched the wagon and started into town to pick up the building materials they would need to repair Philip's homestead. The glass would not be ready for some weeks, but Mr. Waring had assured them he had plenty of lumber and nails to replace the damaged door and charred timbers on the house and in the forge.

Arriving at the mercantile, they loaded the supplies. "I'm sorry I can't come out and help," Mr. Waring told them as they put the last of the wood into the wagon. "I just can't leave the store on a Saturday. Harry's got some chores to do for his mother, but I'll send him out as soon as he's done. If nothing else, he can hold the boards in place for you while you work."

"You don't have to do that," Philip protested, amazed at the offer. Even after the conversation in the shop the other day, he still expected ambivalence more than acceptance.

"'Have to' doesn't figure in," Mr. Waring insisted. "You need help; Harry can help you. That's just being neighborly. You'd do the same if something had happened to my store."

Philip had to admit Mr. Waring was right on that count. Shawn and Widow Taylor had made sure his sense of civic duty was strong, even before the community had accepted him as one of them. Recent events notwithstanding, this was his home and he would do what he could to contribute. "Thank you," he offered finally. "We'll look for him later this morning, then."

Mr. Waring acknowledged the blacksmith's thanks with a bow of his head, sending the wagon on its way with a wave before turning back into the store, shaking his head still at the thought that anyone of his acquaintance would treat Philip this way.

Philip's house was in the same state they had left it in after discovering the vandalism. He breathed a sigh of relief that the vandal, whoever he was, had not come back attempting to finish his destruction. It had been hard enough to lose his clothes and bedroll. To lose everything he owned would have been devastating.

"Why don't you work on the forge since we don't know exactly how you want things and we'll work on replacing the damaged boards on the house itself?" Eric suggested, surveying the scene with a critical eye when the wagon rolled to a stop.

"Hall shouldn't be alone at the forge even if he's within shouting distance of the house," Nicolas intervened immediately, wanting to offer to accompany the blacksmith but not daring to make the offer.

"You're probably right," Carl agreed immediately. "I'll work with him in the forge."

Philip hid his disappointment carefully. He had hoped Nicolas's comment would be followed by an offer of his own assistance, but he could hardly insist. Fortunately, he enjoyed Carl's company and would find it no hardship to work with him for the day.

They had almost finished unloading the wagon when Matthew, Joseph, and William rode into the yard. "Starting without us?" Matthew quipped.

"Trying to avoid the real work?" Philip retorted automatically, though a smile danced around the corner of his lips.

"You know Matthew," Joseph chimed in immediately, "never do yourself what you can get others to do for you."

Matthew feigned injury but he could not keep the expression in place for long in the face of the laughter from all sides. "So what do you want us to do?"

"The door's going to have to be completely rebuilt," Philip declared, examining it again. "I'll need to take it off its hinges and see if any of the metal's damaged. Hopefully, it's just a question of replacing the wood. I guess you can help switch out the burned boards elsewhere on the house."

They set to work, the sound of hammering interrupted only occasionally by a call for assistance or a curse as a hammer slipped and caught a tender thumb. The day warmed quickly away from the coastal breeze and long before lunch, they were all down to their shirtsleeves, the islanders soon removing even their shirts in an attempt to escape the heat.

Nicolas found himself looking for excuses to go to the forge with this question or that so he would have another opportunity to ogle Philip's bare chest, the way the muscles moved beneath the smooth skin, darkening slowly as the weather warmed. It was the first time he had found the younger man working shirtless, but obviously not the first time the blacksmith had eschewed the garment while outside. His fingers itched to touch, but they were never alone, Carl or one of the others always within sight. It was probably a good thing, he admitted to himself, not sure he would be able to stop if he let himself start.

The sun had just reached its zenith when the sound of a wagon drew their attention. Mrs. Waring and Harry sat on the buckboard as the wagon came into the yard, sending Philip, Matthew, Joseph and William scrambling for their shirts.

"Sorry, ma'am," Eric apologized, putting his own shirt back on. "We didn't expect you today and so weren't watching our manners."

Mrs. Waring smiled tolerantly. "Please don't worry," she assured them. "It's nothing I haven't seen before." Gesturing back to the wagon, she added, "I've brought lunch."

Philip flushed. He had used all the money he had on hand to pay for the supplies they were now using on his house. "Can I pay you for it…?"

"Not a cent," Mrs. Waring insisted. "I won't hear a word about it. You boys eat and enjoy. I can't help you fix the house, but I can make sure you don't go hungry."

"Say 'thank you, Mrs. Waring'," William prompted from Philip's elbow.

"Thank you, Mrs. Waring," Philip repeated obediently, head reeling at the generosity as the others went to the back of the wagon to fix themselves a plate.

RETURNING to his cabin at the end of the day's work, steeling himself for another night of resisting temptation, Nicolas was pleased to find the door locked even though he knew Philip had returned from the showers an hour earlier. That meant the blacksmith was taking the threat to his life seriously. They had not talked about it much since the night Philip moved in with him, preferring to discuss the progress on the manor rather than rehashing the same territory. There had been no new vandalism, either to Philip's property or elsewhere on the site, since that night, lulling them into a sense of security. Nicolas reminded himself occasionally not to be fooled into laxity simply because the murderer was biding his time, but he was happy to let Philip enjoy as normal a life as possible under the circumstances.

Pulling out his key, he let himself in, calling out to let Philip know it was him, though it was probably unnecessary since he was the only other one with access to the cabin.

Philip's breath caught in his throat when he heard Nicolas come inside, stopping in the mudroom to remove his boots, coat and hat. His name on the overseer's lips only added to the tension investing his body. In public, Nicolas remained stultifyingly formal, calling him Mr. Hall whenever they met, even today as they had worked on his house, but in the evenings, in the privacy of the cabin, he had relented and started calling Philip by his given name. To hear it now, with all that he hoped would soon transpire, added an extra jolt to the desire already sizzling along his nerves. Closing his eyes and letting everything else leave his mind, he relaxed back into his chair and sighed Nicolas's name.

The whisper of sound was almost too soft, leaving Nicolas wondering if he had heard it. Stepping into the room, he froze, the sight that met his eyes more than his mind could process all at once. There, in the middle of the kitchen, sprawled across one of the chairs, sat the embodiment of his desires, fully dressed still except for the open placket of his trousers. His hand disappeared inside them, stroking languidly, smoothly. The dark brown eyes opened and met his. "Nicolas."

There was no mistaking the invitation in the sinful voice. Even as his feet carried him forward toward the vision that had haunted his dreams, sleeping and waking, he was shaking his head. "Philip, we can't," he protested helplessly.

"Yes," Philip insisted emphatically. "We can. Don't deny that you want to," he continued, his voice husky and low. "I've seen the way you watch me. I can read your desire on your face. I won't stop you. I want this as much as you do. Come, Nicolas, touch me the way you want to. Make me moan your name again, because of what you're doing instead of because of a fantasy in my head."

He held his breath as he waited for Nicolas's reaction. The events of the previous night had convinced him of the overseer's interest, but that did not make this less of a gamble.

The raspy voice, the beckoning words shattered what little remained of Nicolas's control. He was on his knees at Philip's side in a heartbeat, his lips closing over the blacksmith's mouth, silencing him, tongue surging inside and claiming him. This was the forbidden fruit in every way, and yet it tasted, it felt *so* right. With a moan, he gave in completely, his hand sliding down Philip's chest and inside his open trousers to find bare skin and fulfill one of the many fantasies that had driven him to distraction since his arrival on the island.

Philip sighed in relief when Nicolas fell to his knees at the blacksmith's side, his lips parting eagerly as the overseer's mouth captured his. He had known Nicolas was a masterful man. To have that carry over to the lover fired Philip's blood with all the heat of his hottest forge, and his mouth melded with Nicolas's the way hot iron melded beneath his hammer. Finally, he had met his match, a man strong enough to claim him rather than wait to be claimed. Philip responded passionately, his body leaning into the heat of the other man's, his head falling back beneath the lustful onslaught, heart softening like metal in the coals even as his muscles hardened in preparation for what would surely be a rapturous explosion as he accepted Nicolas's claiming.

When the strong, callused fingers closed around his cock, Philip moaned into the kiss, his hips arching forward, driving his shaft through the tight fist, reveling in having a hand other than his own on his aching flesh. His hands lifted slowly to settle on the wiry body that pressed against his own as Nicolas leaned over him. He kept his touch light, letting his desire come through their kiss rather than through his touch. When he was sure Nicolas would not pull away, when he had joined his lover in the big bed in the next room, then he would give free rein to his desire and learn the firm contours of his lover's form.

The heat of Philip's skin burned away what little remained of Nicolas's inhibitions. He worked the blacksmith's erection with easy confidence, his hand moving with the effortless assurance of an experienced lover, bringing all his expertise to bear, wanting to feel the younger man's release.

Perhaps if Nicolas had been hesitant or fumbling, Philip might have held back, might have drawn out the encounter, but Nicolas's fist touched him exactly the right way, stroking firmly, smoothly, with a little twist of his wrist at the head, designed to rub his foreskin against the sensitive frenulum. Throwing his head back, he came hard, his seed coating Nicolas's hand and soaking into the trousers and shirt he had not dared to remove earlier.

Gasping Nicolas's name as the aftershocks continued to rock him, Philip reached for the buttons on the overseer's shirt, knowing instinctively that if he let Nicolas get away, his seduction would be even more difficult. "Let me return the pleasure you gave me," he murmured.

Philip's words startled Nicolas into pulling away, his head shaking in automatic denial. "No," he said again, "I can't."

Before Philip could protest, Nicolas had retreated into his bedroom again, the door shutting firmly behind him.

"Fuck!" Philip muttered, his body replete, his mind completely unsatisfied. Yes, Nicolas had gotten him off, but that was not what he had wanted, or rather, not all he had wanted. Still, he knew now that he could break down the overseer's defenses, could get past his hesitations. The trick would be to do so in such a way that he stayed in control so that Nicolas could not run from him. Pondering that, he pulled off his soiled clothes, changing into his nightshirt and setting up his cot for the night. He would sleep on it and see what he came up with in the morning.

In the other room, Nicolas leaned against the door, his body clamoring for him to return to Philip's side, to let the blacksmith make good on his offer. He ached with unspent passion, his pulse throbbing unbearably in his cock, in his heart. He had broken, had given in to temptation, but he could not let it continue. Philip was not looking for a relationship. If he were, he would never have approached Nicolas the way he had. And Nicolas had no place in his life for a summer fling.

Lifting his hand to his face, inhaling the blacksmith's musky scent, he groaned, the smell only adding to his arousal. Resistance faltering, his tongue flicked out and tasted the cooling cream. For a mere moment, he allowed his imagination to supply a different scenario, one in which he lapped at the salty fluid from its source, sucking on and swallowing the thick shaft he had just now fondled. Unable to stop himself, he tore open his trousers, thrusting his clean hand inside and jerking himself quickly. It only took two strokes before his own essence covered his hand, leaving him trembling with Philip's name on his lips.

Groaning again, in frustration this time, he pushed away from the wall and forced himself to get ready for bed. He could hardly ask Philip to leave, but he had no idea how he would face the other man the next morning over breakfast, or the following night when it was time for bed again. He would simply have to keep himself under control, no matter what provocation Philip threw at him.

Chapter 14

"**So** why the change in venue?" Matthew asked as Johnny led him, William, and Joseph to the caretaker's cabin.

"It's safer," Johnny replied simply.

"Safer?" William repeated. "Did something happen?"

Johnny nodded. "You'll have to ask Philip for the details, though."

"He didn't mention anything on Saturday," Joseph said.

"He wouldn't," Matthew reminded them. "We've always had to pry his troubles out of him, no matter how willing he is to help us with ours."

Johnny thought that sounded a lot like someone else he knew, but he did not make the comparison aloud. The other three men did not know Mr. Wells and to talk about him seemed disrespectful. Rapping lightly at the door, he opened it and gestured for the others to go inside.

Carl, Eric, and Philip called greetings immediately before Philip introduced his friends to the overseer.

They settled around the table, Joseph handing the deck of cards to Eric to inspect before they started. With a nod, Eric examined them and then started to deal. "Ante up."

They all looked down at their hands, evaluating, making decisions.

Philip tossed in his penny and waited for the bets to make their way around the table. With eight of them playing rather than four, the pot grew faster than usual, even the minimum bet bringing it to almost a dime already. He looked at his hand. A pair, but a low one, and a Jack high. Not much of a hand, but better than some he had played – and won with – in the past. Studying the faces of his friends, new and old, he debated how to play the hand. "Give me two," he decided after a moment, tossing in another penny.

At Philip's left, William tossed in his second penny, taking two cards, and turned to his friend. "So what happened that we're playing here instead of in your tent?" He scowled down at the cards and looked to Philip for an explanation instead.

"Somebody vandalized my gear in the tent," Philip explained uncomfortably. "We decided it'd be safer for me here, with a door that locks."

"First your house, then your gear!" Joseph exclaimed, folding his cards and setting them aside. He had nothing but junk anyway. "And there's been another murder, too!"

"I know," Philip replied, watching as one by one, the three crew bosses added their pennies and took more cards.

"The sheriff came and told us Thursday night," Nicolas added, waiting to see what the others still playing would do. His flush would hold against enough hands to make it worth betting again.

"Thursday?" Matthew repeated, looking at the bets on the table and at his own hand. He had a pair of nines with an ace high, enough to make it worth another round anyway. Tossing his penny in and taking two more cards, he looked expectantly at Philip to see what the blacksmith would do.

Philip looked down at his cards again, biting back a smile. His two sixes and a Jack had been augmented by another six and another Jack. "Check," he commented before answering William's question. "He came to see us Thursday night, the same night we found my things vandalized. The same night I moved in here."

He waited, half expecting some expression of shock or disgust from his friends. Instead, all three of them nodded. "Makes perfect sense," William declared. "Walls, a locked door... much safer, although probably a little crowded."

Philip shrugged. "It won't hurt me to sleep on a cot until Shawn catches this bastard." A thought struck him suddenly. "Wait, when did you find out about the murder?"

"Sunday afternoon," William replied, tossing his cards aside. "I fold. A man from Eden rode over after church to see if anybody had seen or heard from Leonard. Seems Leonard never missed church on Sunday and so when he didn't show up, people got worried. Shawn said he'd been killed and that he'd been waiting to investigate before he told people about it. He didn't say when he found out, though."

Nicolas raised another penny, letting the conversation flow around him. The friends obviously used this time to catch up on all the happenings in town and each other's lives. He saw no reason not to glean what information he could about the generally private blacksmith from the unguarded interactions.

Matthew considered his cards again. He could stay in the game, hope Philip was bluffing, and take his chances with the overseer, but with only one pair, even with the ace, he really had little chance of winning. Cutting his losses, he folded.

"Call," Philip said, matching Nicolas's bet.

Nicolas considered pushing, but it was a friendly game after all. "Let's see what you've got," he declared, laying out his flush.

Philip's face broke into a grin as he laid out his full house. "Sorry, old man," he teased. "This pot's mine."

The crew bosses' eyes widened at the quip, but the overseer did not seem to be offended, just laughing and holding up his hands in defeat. "Next time," he joked back.

"I know you're not supposed to speak ill of the dead," William commented to Philip as Eric shuffled the cards and offered them to Joseph to cut, "but I still don't understand how Reed could possibly prefer Jason Leonard's company over yours."

The observation left everyone frozen for a moment. "What?" William asked defensively. "Leonard was a barely educated nobody who was scarcely making ends meet enough not to lose his farm. I don't have to like men that way to see the difference between Philip and Leonard."

"I'm not that big a prize," Philip insisted diffidently.

"Oh, no, you don't," William declared as Eric called for the ante. "I'm not going to sit here and listen to you put yourself down. You're a smart man with a steady job and a fabulous sense of humor. You're kind and generous to a fault. You don't get angry over nothing and you'd do anything for a friend. Isn't that right?" He looked to Joseph and Matthew for validation. They both nodded slowly, not completely comfortable with the context of the comment but definitely in agreement with the content.

Nicolas listened in silence to the ode to Philip's stellar qualities. He had already observed most of them himself, but he would add a few traits he doubted the blacksmith's friend would feel comfortable including: the breadth of Philip's chest, the silkiness of his dark hair, the way his pencil-thin moustache and light beard accented the fullness of his lips, the way his brown eyes darkened even further when he found his release. Shifting slightly as his body reacted to the direction of his thoughts, he forced himself to focus on the cards in his hand and the play around the table. Such thoughts, if he allowed them at all, were best reserved for moments of complete privacy.

"ARE you sure this is a good idea?" Nicolas asked for the fifth time as he watched Philip saddle their horses.

"Yes," Philip insisted. "You have your Colt, I have my rifle, and nobody knows where we're going. Let me show you the island, Nicolas, the parts of it that only a full-time resident would have had the time to discover."

"Oh, all right," Nicolas acceded, admitting to himself that he would enjoy a day away from work. The men had the day off, but they were still around, still asking questions or wanting his opinion. Only by leaving the site completely would he have any peace. The day was unseasonably warm, the sun shining with enough strength to make him reconsider whether he should wear his jacket. He fingered the collar until Philip reached up and caught his hand.

"Wear it," the blacksmith urged. "It's sometimes windy on the coast, and I wouldn't want you to get cold."

Nicolas arched an eyebrow at Philip's shirtsleeves and vest, but the younger man was a permanent resident, more accustomed to the extremes in temperature than he was. Mounting, he waited for Philip to lead the way out of the camp to whatever destination he had chosen for the day.

They rode in companionable silence, one of many changes the previous few days had wrought. Philip had not tried again to seduce Nicolas actively, choosing instead to bestow small, simple touches on the overseer every chance he got. The first time he had done so, Nicolas had pulled away reflexively, as if afraid that any encouragement would lead to more than he was ready to handle. Philip had not pushed, biding his time instead and waiting for another opportunity, brushing his hand lightly over the back of Nicolas's neck and then moving on as if his heart were not pounding wildly in his chest, as if the touch were as simple as it appeared.

Nicolas had stared at him piercingly, but when Philip had made no other move, the overseer had gone back to what he was doing.

In the intervening days, the surprised looks that followed those initial caresses had stopped, until Philip could touch Nicolas with that same deceptive casualness any time they were alone in the cabin. If all went as planned, any illusion of casualness would disappear before the day was over. If all went as planned, by the time the afternoon was over, they would be lovers in fact, not just in Philip's fantasies.

The wind was indeed brisk as they started out down the coast, but Philip set a vigorous pace, the exertion enough to make the cool breeze welcome, and as they cut inland, following a trail Nicolas could not see but assumed must exist given Philip's confidence, it settled somewhat, leaving the overseer wishing they would return to the coast for a respite from the heat of the sun.

The meandering path Philip had chosen did eventually lead back to the coast, on the leeward side of the island, far enough off the beaten path that he hoped to avoid both the summer residents who had begun to filter back onto the island over the past week and the locals seeking a quiet place to enjoy a sunny Sunday afternoon. The rocky promontory he had in mind was remote enough to serve his purposes and sheltered enough from the wind, he hoped, to allow them to disrobe, at least a little.

Dismounting, Philip tied his horse in a stand of trees and waited while the overseer did the same. When the older man stood beside him, ready to descend toward the coastline, Philip held out one hand, the other carrying his rifle. "Watch your footing," he warned. "The rocks can be slippery if the waves have been high."

Nicolas hesitated as he stared at the outstretched hand. It was another of those temptations he had been trying to resist. While he had grown accustomed to Philip touching him, he had not reciprocated, unwilling to allow himself that freedom for fear of losing control once again. His dreams had been haunted, though, memories of the one kiss they had shared, of the feeling of Philip coming beneath his hand, of the taste of the blacksmith's release rushing unchecked through his sleeping thoughts and sometimes, despite his best efforts, his waking ones as well. He almost refused now, almost insisted he could navigate the rocks fine by himself, but pride goeth before a fall, and he could not afford to be injured. If Philip felt it necessary to warn him about the footing, the least he could do was accept the younger man's wisdom and experience. Taking a deep breath, reminding himself of all the reasons to stay in control, he closed his fingers around the strong hand, letting Philip help him over the rocks almost to the tip.

Philip had not been sure Nicolas would accept his help, but he was glad he had made the offer. The feeling of the overseer's warm, hard hand in his, by Nicolas's choice, was electrifying. He took a deep breath, absorbing the jolt of lust, as he led the way over the scraggy outcropping to a large, flat rock well out from the tree line but far enough from the water that the spray at low tide would not reach them. Sitting down and leaning back on his elbows, he waited for Nicolas to join him.

Keeping a respectable distance between them, Nicolas sat beside Philip on the marbled granite, stretching his long legs out in front of him to enjoy the warmth of the sun, unfastening the gun belt that he wore uncomfortably, not accustomed to its slapping against his thigh. He set it aside, but within easy reach, the sheriff's harping about constant vigilance fresh in his mind. Despite the heat from above, he was glad of his jacket, for the breeze, though gentler than when they started out, was indeed cool.

For a time, they rested there in comfortable silence, wispy clouds passing overhead, occasionally muting but never quite blocking the sun's rays, the gentle susurrus of the waves lulling them into deep relaxation. Eventually, Philip sat up a little, his hand going to Nicolas's arm as he drew the overseer's attention. "Sit up very slowly," he murmured. "A seal decided to join us."

Carefully, Nicolas lifted himself enough to see the very end of the promontory and the dark seal that had pulled itself onto the rocks. A smile lit his face as he watched the plump creature stretch itself in the sun.

"It had the same idea we did," Philip whispered, "an afternoon relaxing in the sun."

"Smart beast," Nicolas chuckled just as softly, so caught with watching the animal that he did not even think to pull away from Philip's hand. "How long will he stay there?"

Philip shrugged, scooting a little closer to Nicolas to get a better view of the seal. "Five minutes or several hours or somewhere in between," he replied. "It depends on whether something startles him and what kind of mood he's in."

Nicolas nodded as Philip lay back down beside him, his own gaze still fixed on the fascinating creature. He had seen seals before, but never this close.

Keeping his gaze fixed on Nicolas's face – the overseer was far more interesting to him than animals he had seen hundreds of times – Philip smiled at the rapt look on the older man's face. Taking advantage of his distraction, Philip moved his hand from Nicolas's arm to his thigh, hoping by the time the blond realized, he would be used to the touch. It seemed to be working, for Nicolas did not pull away as he continued to watch the seal. Biding his time, Philip settled in to wait.

The seal lingered for a time, holding Nicolas's attention despite the distraction of Philip's hand on his leg, not quite high enough to do more than tempt him, but definitely there, impinging on his awareness enough to have his body tingling lightly. When the seal had enough of the sun and flipped itself into the water,

Nicolas lay back again, the silent lecture running in his head as he admonished himself to pull away, to rebuff Philip's advances. The helping hand earlier, the hand on his arm to get his attention – those could be explained away innocently, though Nicolas was beginning to think nothing Philip did could be called truly innocent, but the hand on his thigh could not be explained away so easily. Yet there was nothing threatening about the touch, and he could not bring himself to pull away, not when it felt so good to let someone touch him again after so long. Relaxing again, he shifted so his arm rested under his head, giving him some cushion from the hard surface beneath them, unaware of the picture he unwittingly presented to the younger man, his arm pulling his shirt up to reveal his lightly furred belly.

Having shifted onto his side when Nicolas lay down, Philip was fully appreciative of the inviting sight. He stayed as he was for a few moments, drinking in the long, lean lines of the blond's body. Eventually, the temptation became too much for him. Leaning over his soon-to-be lover, he explored the line of dark blond hair with his lips and tongue.

Nicolas's eyes shot open when he felt Philip's mouth on him, protests dying on his lips as lust jolted through him again, unstoppable in its intensity. His mind conjured one last, half-hearted protest, but it stood no chance against the swiftly mounting passion, not when he had desired this since almost the first time he saw the blacksmith. Their eyes met, blue and brown gazes catching, holding, as Philip nuzzled the edge of Nicolas's shirt, pushing it higher to reveal more creamy skin. "Philip," he murmured, starting to sit up.

Philip laid a restraining hand on the strong muscle, rolling the dice one more time. Boldness had worked before. Hopefully, it would work again. "Tell me, honestly, that you don't like the way it feels, and I'll stop."

"Feels good," Nicolas admitted after a moment's final hesitation, reaching down to tangle his fingers in the unfashionably long mahogany hair as he subsided to the rocks. He still feared he would regret this later, but at the moment, he could not bring himself to care.

"Then you'll really like this," Philip replied with a teasing grin, capturing the short hairs between his teeth and pulling up slightly, not enough to hurt, just enough to tantalize. He had not known, up until the moment Nicolas had spoken, whether his advances would be accepted, but now that he had Nicolas's cooperation, he intended to keep the overseer so lost in passion that he would not think of stopping, not until Philip had what he wanted: a lover.

Philip was right. Nicolas liked it quite a lot, his fingers tightening in the younger man's hair, urging him on.

Thrilled with the overseer's reaction, Philip followed the line of hair to where it disappeared into Nicolas's trousers. He ran his tongue along the waistband as his fingers fought with the buttons holding them closed. Nicolas's breath caught as he realized what Philip intended. Twice now, Philip had surprised him this way, overwhelming his senses with passion before his logic could convince him to walk away as he knew he should. He found that confidence incredibly arousing, irrationally so since it undermined his common sense, yet it was the one approach against which he had no defenses, a fact Philip seemed to know and exploit instinctively.

Finally freeing the fastenings on Nicolas's trousers, Philip slid his hand inside, his fingers following the line of downy hair lower, to the wiry nest at the root of Nicolas's cock. He carded his fingers through the thick curls, teasing momentarily before finding the length of hardening flesh and drawing it out into the cool air.

Nicolas's gasp brought a smile to Philip's face. Taking the sound as encouragement, he stroked the thick shaft firmly, his mouth moving lower along the arrow of hair, enjoying the rasp against his lips, the friction against his own short beard and thin mustache.

Nicolas squirmed beneath the mélange of sensations, the sting of cold air, the heat of Philip's callused palm, the tug of the blacksmith's lips on his treasure trail. He so rarely gave another control this way, even when he had taken long-term lovers in the past. To simply lie back and enjoy Philip's attentions this way felt... hedonistic... decadent... positively self-indulgent, yet the younger man had taken control so swiftly, so thoroughly, that

Nicolas had almost no choice, short of pulling away, and even that option had disappeared when he had given permission. He prided himself too much on his honesty to deny how good it felt to allow Philip's caress, to give Philip control. Then a wet tongue swiped over the tip of his cock and all thought flew out of his head, leaving him prey to his lover's ministrations.

Philip savored the burst of tangy flavor, his hand continuing its rhythmic stroking, simply enjoying the moment.

"Please."

The whisper from above him surprised Philip. Having wrung permission from Nicolas, he had not really expected further encouragement, at least not in words. To hear that husky voice pleading with him now was more than his control could handle. Lips parting, he worked his way down the thick shaft, taking as much of it as he could into his mouth, sucking strongly.

Nicolas's hips bucked wildly as he felt the moist cavern of Philip's mouth enclose him. "So good," he gasped, knowing it would take almost nothing for him to find his release.

Philip would have smiled if he could have, but the cock stretching his lips prevented that. Instead, he hummed softly in appreciation of Nicolas's encouragement, steadying his lover's hips to keep the other man from gagging him. The overseer was better endowed than Philip's past lovers had been. It would take him some time to get used to accommodating Nicolas's full length. His body shivered in delight at the thought of accommodating him elsewhere. First things first, though. Sucking harder, he let his fist cover what his mouth could not encompass, working the shaft with all the skill he possessed, determined to make this climax as powerful for Nicolas as the one he had experienced at Nicolas's hands.

A hoarse shout tore from Nicolas's throat as he gave in finally to the furor burning through him. He had not allowed himself to want this, except in the dark recesses of the night, and since touching Philip, he had denied himself even that release. To have those fantasies made flesh, here in the light of day, was more than he could contain. His body trembled with uncontrolled need as he gave in to a surge of sensation as powerful as the tides that had carved the rocks on which they lay. Just as relentlessly, his climax swelled through him, lifting him on the waves of desire and sending him flying as his orgasm hit, much like the spray from the surf when it reached the shore.

There was only one acceptable outcome, after such a powerful climax, as far as Nicolas was concerned. His pulse had not even begun to steady, his breaths still came in pants, but he reached for Philip, needing his lover in his arms, needing that contact to reassure himself that this was more than purely physical, that Philip cared about him at least that much. And then, he would see about giving the younger man some return on the surfeit of pleasure he had just received.

Nicolas's movement caught Philip's eye and he pushed up onto his elbows, body hard and aching for release. Seeing the offered embrace, he shifted, moving that way, ready to be enfolded and held the way he had not been the last time they came together. Before he could settle, before Nicolas's arms could envelop him, though, he heard the sound of horseshoes striking on rock.

"Shit," he muttered under his breath. "Someone's coming, and we dare not let them find us like this."

Swiftly, Nicolas pulled Philip into his arms, well aware of the approaching horses, but he could not let his lover go quite yet. Closing his lips swiftly, roughly over Philip's, he plundered the mouth that had so recently pleasured him, moaning softly when he tasted his release on the other man's tongue. Releasing him, knowing they did not have time to linger, he started to fasten his trousers. "Tonight," he murmured, promise deepening his voice.

Curses rolled around Philip's mind as he stepped away, body aching for release, heart aching for contact. He had succeeded – Nicolas had accepted him as his lover – but the victory was bittersweet in his mouth, their afternoon of discovery marred by the imminent arrival of others. It did not even matter who approached. It only mattered that the moment of bliss had been shattered.

Having fixed his trousers, Nicolas bent to pick up his gun belt as four men came out of the trees. The overseer recognized them instantly as the bullies who had hassled Philip in town the day someone had shot at him. Face hardening, he buckled the belt around his waist, hand resting on the butt of the gun.

Philip sighed in resignation as he saw Thomas, Parks, Bradley and Ferguson approach. Of all the people on the island who had to discover them, these were by far the worst. While he still considered them mostly harmless, they would have no qualms about spreading whatever rumors suited them. He was sure when they were done, they would be saying they had found him going down on Nicolas instead of simply standing near him on the rocks.

"Well, well," Bradley snarled when he saw the other two men standing on the rocks, "what have we here?"

"Looks like two freaks to me," Parks scorned. "Been corrupting the outlander, Hall?"

Nicolas saw the fury come into Philip's eyes. "Just ignore him, Philip," he murmured. "He can't do anything but blow smoke."

"I was just showing Mr. Wells around the island," Philip replied, struggling to heed Nicolas's advice and stay calm. He knew he could take any one of them still, had once taken all four of them in a fight, but he and Nicolas were not the only ones armed this time, unlike the last time they had met the other men, and he had no desire to see his lover shot.

"Showing him around your ass, more like," Ferguson sneered.

Before he could stop himself, Philip had the rifle on his shoulder and aimed at the men. "I suggest you leave," he spat. "And take your insults and nasty slurs with you."

The ruffians backed off, not wanting to provoke a gun fight. As they reached the tree line, Thomas turned back. "You should watch who you associate with, Mr. Wells," he called. "They're killing sodomites on the island."

Chapter 15

NEITHER man moved until the bullies disappeared through the trees and the sound of hoof beats faded.

"We have to tell Parnell," Nicolas said immediately when he was sure the others were gone. "They can't threaten you that way."

Philip's eyebrows shot up. "Nicolas, they've been threatening me since we were kids. They can't do anything to me."

Nicolas shook his head, too aware of the threat to his lover to let any suggestion of harm go unchallenged. "The one who called us freaks, the one who accused you of showing me around your ass – " Nicolas's mouth twisted against the vulgarity of the words "– they might be harmless. But the last one, that one was different, and we're going to town to report it to the sheriff."

"And explain to him what we were doing?" Philip asked softly. "Explain to him that you were fastening your gun belt when they found us?"

"You offered to show me the island," Nicolas retorted logically. "I took the gun off to sit more comfortably on the rocks and put it back on when we were ready to leave. The men found us at that point." He stroked Philip's cheek tenderly. "I'm not ashamed of what happened between us, but it *is* personal. Parnell doesn't need to know about it any more than those close-minded bastards do. Please, Philip. Report this to him. Help him do his job."

"All right," Philip agreed, sure Nicolas was overreacting and that Shawn would see it the same way, but if it would make the overseer happy, he would go along.

They walked quickly back to their horses and mounted, heading toward town. Though he did not mention it aloud, Philip was privately relieved the animals were still there. Stranding the two men on a remote section of the island was exactly the sort of prank his nemeses would play.

As they rode, Nicolas played the scene that had just transpired over in his mind, trying to separate boyhood rivalries from true adult threats. The three younger men, he could dismiss with relative ease. Everything about them – their words, their body language, the way they banded together – branded them simple bullies who had never outgrown adolescence. The other one, though, the one whose name Nicolas did not know, was different. He still rode with the other three, still participated silently in their childish taunts, but his stance told another tale. This was no overgrown adolescent, and his parting shot sent chills down Nicolas's spine.

He had known almost since his arrival on the island that Philip's life was in danger. The sheriff had made that clear from the first time they spoke. Then, it had simply been another human being who was threatened. Now, though... now it was his lover they were threatening and every possessive, protective instinct Nicolas possessed was rearing its head, demanding he keep Philip safe. He glanced sideways at the blacksmith, his powerful shoulders moving in easy time with the horse's gait, every line of his body projecting his confidence as he rode. Forcing his eyes back to the trail, he let the realization rock through him.

He had fallen in love.

Despite his attempts at keeping his distance, despite his silent lectures, his heart had flown, finding its new perch in Philip. He knew the blacksmith did not feel the same. He had just lost his lover, for Christ's sake! He could hardly expect the younger man to offer his heart so soon, did not even know if the blacksmith was interested in that sort of relationship. His body, it seemed, was a different matter. Somewhere deep inside him, Nicolas knew he should question that, but his tender heart ignored it. When it had been only physical attraction on his part, he had been able to resist temptation, but with his heart now engaged, he would take what he could get, storing memories away for the cold, winter nights in his garret in Boston.

The pattern of the horses' hoof beats changed as they neared the town, slowing over the cobblestones, not wanting to draw attention to themselves. Philip led the way through town to the boarding house where the sheriff had his lodgings. "He won't be in his office on a Sunday," he explained when he saw Nicolas's surprised look. "He has rooms in Widow Taylor's boarding house." He paused, then added mischievously, "Though not the rooms he wants."

"Oh?" Nicolas asked, not sure how else to respond to that comment.

"He's had designs on the widow since long before she was a widow," Philip explained, "but he's too damn honorable to do anything about it, even now that she's free."

THE sun beat down with surprising intensity for spring as Shawn turned the furrows of earth in Widow Taylor's vegetable garden. She had commented the day before that it needed to be done, and so he had gotten up early that morning and started on it before she could do it herself. Now, many hours later, he had worked up a sweat and a thirst. Leaning on the hoe, he wiped his arm across his brow, leaving a smear of dirt on his face. Movement at the kitchen door caught his eye and he turned, in time to see the lovely, dark-haired widow step out into the sunshine, a heavy tray balanced between her delicate hands. "Come have something to drink, Sheriff," she beckoned, setting the tray on the wrought iron table that graced the stone patio. "You have more than earned a break."

Nodding, Shawn set his tools safely against the garden wall and joined her at the table. Immediately, she removed the light scarf from around her neck, revealing the creamy skin of her neck and shoulders. Leaning forward, she wiped it across his forehead. "You left a trail of dirt behind," she explained quickly, setting the scarf aside and pouring tea into two cups. Without asking, she added two lumps of sugar to the sheriff's cup before offering it to him.

Shawn smiled his thanks, raising the cup to his lips and gulping quickly to hide his reaction to the sudden expanse of bare skin before his eyes. He was working up the courage to speak, searching for a way to finally reveal his interest, when he heard someone calling his name. Silently cursing the intrusion, he nonetheless rose from the table. "I should see what's going on."

"Of course," Widow Taylor replied with a gentle smile. "Duty calls."

Shawn would have given just about anything to have the right to lean over and kiss the softly upturned lips before he left the enclosure to attend to his obligations. Unfortunately, he had no such right, and so he left with only a smile in farewell. Seeing Philip outside, however, erased all thoughts of the lovely widow from his mind. "What's wrong?" he asked, sure his young friend would not have dragged the overseer into town without a good reason. "Has something happened?"

"Yes."

"No."

The two men glared at each other mildly. "Obviously, we have a difference of opinion," Philip added. "Can we go inside? I'd rather not explain in the middle of the street."

Shawn looked down at his muddy clothes. "I'm too much of a mess for Widow Taylor's parlor. We'll have to go to my office."

The three men walked quickly down the street to the sheriff's office, Shawn sitting at his desk, the other two across from him when they got inside. "So what's going on?"

"Nothing," Philip insisted. "Just Thomas and his cronies being stupid again."

"I'd hardly call the last comment 'being stupid'," Nicolas retorted.

"Stop!" Shawn ordered. "Philip, tell me what happened. No commentary, just facts. Mr. Wells, when he's done, you can tell me anything you think he left out, but don't interrupt him."

Quickly, Philip explained his suggestion of visiting the island, how he and Nicolas had ridden down the coast and stopped to enjoy the sun and breeze for a few minutes. "We were just getting ready to leave when Thomas, Parks, Bradley and Ferguson rode up. They made a few stupid comments, implied a lot of things, made a few threats, and left. The same stupid shit they've been doing since I got here."

Shawn sighed. "What did they imply?" he asked, though he was sure he knew. The four men had always enjoyed taunting Philip and as they had gotten older, it had invariably involved sex in one way or another. Once the truth of Philip's preferences had come to light, the men had taken every opportunity to denigrate the blacksmith for his choices. Finding Philip alone, however innocently, with another man was surely more temptation than they could resist.

"That we were lovers," Philip replied, unable to stop the flush that colored his cheeks as he thought of how close they had come, how much he wanted those implications to be true. Ferguson had intended to be vulgar and insulting when he accused Philip of showing Nicolas around his ass, but Philip would do so willingly, even eagerly when the opportunity arose. His groin tingled at the thought.

The sheriff nodded. He had expected as much. He was somewhat surprised the overseer had agreed to go off alone with Philip, not because of any fear that the blacksmith would press unwelcome advances, but to avoid precisely what had occurred that day. However innocent their outing had been, the bullies had undoubtedly now painted Nicolas with the same brush they used to tar Philip's name. "Mr. Wells," he said, turning to the blond, "is there anything you want to add?"

"Yes," Nicolas replied firmly, shooting a sidelong glance at Philip. "As they were leaving, one of them turned back and… I don't know if it was a threat or a warning, but he told me to be careful who I associated with since they were killing sodomites on the island."

"Fuck!" Shawn muttered, his hand slamming onto the desk. "Did either of you tell anyone that Reed and Leonard were violated before they were killed?"

Both men shook their heads.

"Which one said that, Philip?" the sheriff demanded, his mind racing as he calculated the implications of the man's statement. After Philip's fight with Reed, no one in Bar Harbor

had any doubt about their relationship, and Leonard's name had
been mentioned, but only in passing. He had deliberately kept the
information about the rapes from everyone except Philip and the
overseer, yet someone seemed to have figured out the common
thread. Either that or someone was the murderer.

"Martin Thomas."

"He just became my primary suspect."

"MR. WELLS," Johnny called, consternation in his
voice, "we've got a problem."

Nicolas frowned as he swung down from his horse. He had
enough problems already, with the additional threat to Philip, the
possibility that he, too, had now been targeted by the killer, and the
realization still rocking his soul that he had fallen in love despite
himself. "What's going on?"

Johnny held out a pile of slag. Nicolas took it and
examined it carefully. He could barely see the outline of the
chunk's former shapes. "The hinges?"

"All of them," Johnny agreed with a nod. "We were sitting
in our tent, enjoying a few moments' rest, when this came sailing
through the canvas, still warm from the forge. We searched, but
we couldn't find any trace of the culprit."

"When did this happen?" Nicolas demanded, wondering if
there was any way Martin could have done this before he found
them on the coast.

Johnny glanced at Eric and Carl. "An hour ago?"

"At the most," Carl agreed.

"Shit," Nicolas muttered, taking the slag and turning to
Philip. They had assumed, after the vandalism to Philip's gear,
that the murderer and the vandal were one and the same. If that
was true, then Martin could not be the murderer since it had been
little more than an hour since he had left them on the coast. If it
was not true, then they had two men with vendettas against Philip.
Neither thought was reassuring. "Can you melt this down and use
it again or is it a complete loss?"

Philip took the dross from Nicolas and examined it
carefully, his hands trembling as he digested the implications of

what had happened. "I'll have to melt it down again and see," he replied hoarsely. "I'll get started on it right away."

"Tomorrow will be soon enough," Nicolas assured him. "Sunday is a day of rest."

Philip's eyes darkened as he remembered Nicolas's promise from earlier. "You're the boss."

"Malone, if you'd take Mr. Hall back to the cabin, I'll see to the horses."

Handing his mount's reins to Nicolas to take to the corral where they kept the horses on site, Philip walked with Carl back to the cabin, letting himself in and locking the door behind him. Boots, hat and coat remained in the mudroom when he walked inside and slumped into one of the chairs, his heart pounding as the full gamut of emotions from the day overwhelmed him.

He had high hopes for what the evening would bring, yet a part of him held back. Shawn had not said anything explicitly, but he had not needed to. Philip had understood the hard look the sheriff had shot him as he and Nicolas had departed. *Be careful*, it had said clearly. Philip had not needed to ask why he was being warned. Even if Shawn was wrong, and Martin was not the murderer, he and the others were terrible gossips. News of his association, real or imagined, with Nicolas would be all over town before the sun set, and that would surely bring the overseer to the attention of the killer, whomever he was, not to mention bringing the censure of the town down upon them. His face hardened.

Nothing he could do now would change, stop, or even slow the rumors his nemeses would spread. Short of leaving the island, which he steadfastly refused to do, he would not be able to save Nicolas from speculation. Whether he kept the overseer at arm's length or embraced him fully as his lover, their names were linked in society's eyes, and that was enough to put the other man at risk. That being the case, nothing need hold him back.

The door to the cabin opened, the familiar grind of metal as the lock unlatched and then was thrown shut again bringing Philip out of his thoughts. *I ought to oil that*, he thought idly as he waited for Nicolas to appear in the door from the mudroom. Then he thought better of it. As morbid as it seemed, the sound of the lock turning would provide that much more warning if the murderer found a way into the cabin. Before he could remonstrate himself for his dismal attitude, Nicolas stepped into the room in his shirtsleeves and sock feet, a look of predatory intensity on his face.

Philip's eyes widened as he absorbed the intent stare, the prowling grace as Nicolas approached him. The overseer had told him before they were interrupted that they would finish what they had started when they returned home that night, but somehow, he had expected the older man to change his mind, to beg off because of the threat of exposure, not to mention the threat of murder. It seemed, though, that Nicolas had no such hesitations. Heart pounding, mouth suddenly dry, he rose to his feet, needing to meet his new lover on level ground.

Nicolas closed the space between them in two large strides, another step pinning Philip against the rough-hewn wall. "If you don't want this," he growled, "if you were just amusing yourself or passing the time today, tell me now."

Philip raised his chin. "This?" he questioned, challenge heavy in his voice. He knew what Nicolas was asking, but the overseer was the one who had repeatedly pulled away from their interactions, not him.

Nicolas's face tightened, desire warring hard with his control. "Us," he ground out between clenched teeth. "As lovers." He could not be any clearer than that, not without saying far more than he was ready to reveal.

Huffing sharply in disbelief, Philip lifted his hands to thread into Nicolas's blond hair. "*I* haven't been the one backing away," he pointed out archly. "*I've* wanted this since the moment I saw you. I think the real question is whether *you* want this."

No answer came in words, Nicolas's lips closing over the younger man's the only response he could muster. For a moment, they fought for control, neither willing to give an inch in this battle of wills their mutual seduction had become. Then Philip's grip eased slightly, his head tipping back, a subtle submission to his lover's dominance.

Immediately, the fire between them calmed, still there, still warming them, but no longer driving them. Nicolas lifted his head to stare down into the mahogany eyes, dipping his head swiftly to steal sips of breath from Philip's lips, the contact sweet now rather than commanding. A soft moan rewarded his efforts and he let his lips trail slowly up the strong cheekbones, caressing the slight stubble and then the smooth skin above it before settling at his lover's temple. "Come to bed with me."

Chapter 16

"YES," Philip whispered, already backing toward the door, his hands sliding from Nicolas's hair to his hips to draw his lover with him. He had dreamed of this moment, never truly believing it would come to pass, and now that it had arrived, he intended to seize it with both hands. Desire tightened his stomach, leaving him quivering with anticipation.

Philip's enthusiasm fired Nicolas's blood, leaving him chafing against the confines of his clothes. Guiding them through the narrow doorway and into his bedroom, he kicked the door shut and reached for the buttons on Philip's shirt, his lips never ceasing their peregrinations across the younger man's face, always returning to his lips but never lingering.

Philip's hands moved to his chest to help with his disrobing, but Nicolas caught his fingers and lifted them to his lips, kissing them tenderly before returning them to his hips. "Let me," he requested softly as he undid the next button, then the next.

Philip could feel himself becoming pliant in Nicolas's arms, the combination of forcefulness and romance stealing any impulse to resist, to assert his own dominance. He had dreamed of finding a lover strong enough in mind and body to command his respect and submission, not by force but by the sheer potency of his presence, but he had almost given up hope. Now, a most pleasant lethargy stealing his will to do more than accede to Nicolas's wishes, he felt those dreams renewed.

Sliding the shirt from Philip's shoulders, Nicolas's hands moved across the wide expanse of his lover's back, feeling the puissant muscles slacken beneath his touch. A sense of power swelled through him at having such an effect on a man of Philip's strength and dynamism. He did not speak of it, not wanting to shatter the magic of the moment, but his lips settled over his lover's, expressing his amazement and gratitude through his worship of the sweet orifice.

Philip's head fell back, offering his mouth completely as Nicolas explored tenderly. Their first kiss had been fiery, spurred on by Nicolas's surprise and Philip's rampant desire. This one, though no less passionate, had far less urgency, Nicolas taking his time, lingering over each exquisite curve, each welcoming cranny. Philip met him breath for breath, tongue twining around his own to welcome him in and beckon him back when he raised his head finally to gasp for air and control. That afternoon, he might have rushed the moment, but now, with the realization of the depth of his emotions in the forefront of his thoughts, he would linger lovingly, lavishing every ounce of tenderness, every drop of pleasure he could muster on his lover's beautiful body.

Philip's eyes, which had closed beneath the beauty of their kiss, opened as Nicolas lifted his head, meeting his lover's beryl gaze, breath catching in his throat as he absorbed the look of open admiration. Boldly, he took a step backwards, holding Nicolas's eyes as he did. His hands worked the buckle on his belt, pulling it off and tossing it aside before settling on the buttons of his heavy pants.

Nicolas took a step forward, but stopped when Philip shook his head sharply. "Just watch," he husked, undoing the buttons one by one until his pants hung open, low on his hips.

"Take them off," Nicolas requested hoarsely. "Let me see you."

Philip smiled seductively as he slowly pushed the thick cloth from his hips, revealing paler skin than on his upper body and an arrow of dark hair leading Nicolas's eyes downward to the thick shaft that rose from its nest of wiry curls.

Stepping from the pile of cloth at his feet, Philip backed the remaining distance to the bed, his hands sliding smoothly over his skin, never lingering, never stroking his most sensitive places, stoking his arousal without making any move to assuage it. That would be Nicolas's task.

The vision in his bed tempted Nicolas as little else ever had. Mesmerized, he matched Philip step for step until he stood, knees touching the edge of the mattress, eyes locked on his lover's profligate beauty. His hands itched to touch, yet he held back, not out of lack of desire or intention of stopping, but simply because he could not quite believe he had the right.

Pushing up on one elbow, Philip reached out, sliding his hand over Nicolas's hip before sitting up completely to begin divesting his lover. Nicolas stood quiescent under his ministrations, as the blacksmith slowly parted cloth and revealed pale skin stretched over hard muscle. Philip's fingers traced the heavy sinew alluringly. "You should lie down here next to me," he purred. "Your mattress is much more comfortable than mine. If I'd known, I might have let you lure me in here sooner."

"Lure you?" Nicolas asked with a throaty chuckle, shedding his pants and kneeling on the bed, straddling Philip's legs. "I seem to remember trying to keep you out."

Philip looked around, eyes twinkling, smug satisfaction playing across his lips. "That seems to have worked so well."

Nicolas laughed again and swatted playfully at Philip's thigh. "I can always get up again," he retorted, though he knew he would not. He had plotted his course and nothing short of Philip's refusal would change it now. Given that Philip had ensconced himself in Nicolas's bed, the overseer felt relatively secure in his lover's willingness.

Rather than allowing Philip to formulate a reply, Nicolas lowered his head and captured the blacksmith's lips again. Immediately, Philip returned to his reclining position, drawing Nicolas down with him so that the older man's body covered his own, skin to skin, heat to heat, twin moans tearing from both throats.

Dragging his lips away from Philip's, Nicolas slid them slowly down the line of corded tendon connecting jaw to shoulder, nipping lightly, little jolts of sensation that he could feel echoed in the twitch of Philip's cock, but nothing that would leave a mark and incriminate them later in the eyes of anyone who might be watching. "I've wanted to do this since the night you arrived at the site," he admitted, sucking strongly at the sturdy collarbone, knowing Philip's shirt would cover any mark he might leave there.

The avowal surprised Philip. He had suspected the attraction after a time, but he never would have believed it started that far back. "What changed, that you finally gave in?" he gasped as his lover's lips teased his skin, circling his nipple without actually touching it.

"You did," Nicolas answered simply. "Your forthrightness, your courage." He pushed Philip's arm over his head and followed the strong curve of muscle with his lips. "I would watch you, you know," he murmured against Philip's skin, "imagining what you would look like without a shirt. I kept hoping I'd find you bare-chested one day so I could see."

"You didn't get a good enough view when you walked in on me after my shower?" the blacksmith teased breathlessly, his other hand tangling in Nicolas's hair, encouraging him.

"That was later," Nicolas replied, his lips finding a strong wrist and worshipping there before moving back down. "I was dreaming of you long before that."

"Look all you want," Philip gasped, arching into the tender caresses.

"And touch?" Nicolas asked, though he knew the answer. "And taste?"

"Yes!"

Giving them what they both wanted, he sealed his lips over one dark nipple, his fingers plucking gently at the other one. His tongue laved the taut skin, learning its flavor, its texture, lavishing pleasure on his lover. Feeling Philip begin to move beneath him, he increased the suction, intending to drive them both wild with lust.

Philip's moans turned impassioned as the tormenting lips left one side and moved to the other, repeating the caress on his other nipple. He arched immediately into the touch, his hands clenching tightly on Nicolas's shoulders as he searched for an anchor in the storm of passion. Part of him knew they had barely begun and already he felt himself drowning in the morass of sensation. The thought of all that still remained left him trembling.

"I watched you," Nicolas whispered, lifting his head enough to meet Philip's eyes, "the day we set up the tents, the way you moved as you handled the heavy canvas, the way your muscles strained and stretched your shirt. I kept imagining what it would feel like to touch you." His hands slid lower, caressing Philip's abdomen, the lines of his muscles etched clearly as they tightened in response to the touch.

"You took your shirt off that day," Philip replied, wanting to turn the tables at least a little, "when we were cleaning up for dinner. It was all I could do not to touch you. I would have given anything that night for a little privacy, but with Johnny lying only a few feet away, I couldn't even find relief thinking about you." As he spoke, his hand crept lower, memories of that night combining with the passion driving him now. Before he could take himself in hand, though, Nicolas caught his wrist again.

"My turn," the overseer growled, closing his hand for the second time around his lover's hard shaft. This time, though, he did not hesitate, did not question. His hand stroked insistently.

Philip's hips bucked reflexively, driving his cock through Nicolas's fist. "This is going to end too soon if you keep that up," he gasped.

"Then I'll just have to get you worked up again," Nicolas teased, his hand moving faster.

Philip shook his head. "Not like this," he pleaded. "I want you inside me when I come this time."

Nicolas froze, fighting for control against the urge to bury himself immediately in his lover's body. "Soon," he promised. "Just as soon as I know you're ready."

"Hurry," Philip pleaded.

Nicolas leaned up and kissed Philip, hard and fast. "Don't move," he instructed. "I don't have anything here to make you ready for me."

Philip lay back on the bed, body throbbing as he watched Nicolas walk across the floor and into the main room. He was back in seconds, but even those moments of separation were too much for the blacksmith. He reached for Nicolas with one hand and the bottle he held with the other. Uncorking it, he poured some onto the overseer's fingers. "Hurry," he repeated, his thighs parting invitingly.

"You are too irresistible for your own good," Nicolas scolded even as he slid oil-slick digits into the dark crease, seeking the gates to paradise.

Philip lifted his knees, planting his feet firmly on the bed to give himself the leverage he needed to push up into Nicolas's touch. "Hurry," he said a third time. "I need you inside me."

Knowing he would never be able to stay in control with Philip's husky voice inciting him to riot, Nicolas captured the alluring lips again, silencing his lover's words as he started to prepare the puckered opening. He knew Philip had taken lovers in the past, but his ring of muscle was as tight as any virgin. "Have you done this before?" he asked suddenly, remembering the way his crew bosses had described Reed.

"Not in a long time," Philip admitted, trying to relax against the intrusion.

The honest answer gave Nicolas the control to slow his caress, despite Philip's moan of protest. Philip might claim eagerness – and the rampant erection pressing against Nicolas's stomach certainly supported that claim – but Nicolas refused to risk hurting his lover. He took possession of the blacksmith's mouth again and set about distracting him as he continued his tender preparations.

Philip floated on a sea of bliss, Nicolas's tongue teasing his, Nicolas's fingers stretching him, the force of his desire leaving him putty in his lover's hands. He wanted to encourage the overseer to hurry as he had done before, but the words did not come. He settled for moaning into his lover's mouth instead, lifting his hips against the probing fingers.

Slowly, Nicolas delved and stretched the tight sheath, preparing it for his generous girth. Philip's sensual undulations urged him on, the tenor of his lover's moans letting him know when he found the nub that would drive the younger man wild. Working it deliberately, he brought Philip to the verge of release, the tremors in the blacksmith's thighs a sure sign of his impending climax. Withdrawing his fingers, he gentled the dark-haired man with tender touches as he stretched out at his lover's side. "Do you want to turn on your side? It might be easier for you that way."

Philip shook his head vehemently. "I want to feel your weight, to see your eyes as we make love," he insisted, urging Nicolas to rise up over him.

The overseer obliged, kneeling between the widespread legs and pulling Philip's hips up onto his thighs. "Relax for me," he urged

Philip's eyes closed as he felt the tip of Nicolas's cock nudging his entrance. He pushed back against the pressure as much as he was able given his position, but he was not about to complain, especially not when the hard shaft finally slipped inside, the angle driving the head firmly against the sensitive bundle of nerves inside him. His head thrashed back and forth as he gasped. Above him, he felt Nicolas freeze.

Hearing what could well have been a sound of pain, unable yet to interpret the expression on Philip's face, Nicolas stopped his inward progress, unwilling to do anything to hurt his lover. As he did, the part of his mind not overcome with passion pointed out that he was able to stop, that his concern for Philip far outweighed his desire. He had never been a selfish lover, but never had it been this easy to put his partner first. Then the sienna eyes opened, passion-glazed and burning as brightly as his lover's forge. "Move."

The single, terse command broke what little restraint remained and Nicolas surged forward, seating himself completely within the throbbing passage. This time, he had no doubt what the moan that escaped Philip's lips portended. Pulling back slightly, he thrust again, watching his lover closely to find the perfect rhythm and angle to drive the other man wild.

It took almost no time at all, the accumulated desire from the afternoon combined with Nicolas's careful preparation leaving Philip with no control and even less patience. Without even a touch to his pulsing erection, he clenched tightly around the welcome invader, a hoarse cry tearing from his throat as his climax took him.

The rippling of strong muscles massaging his cock brought Nicolas to the edge as well. He struggled to hold back a little longer, but Philip pulled his head down for a kiss, shattering what was left of the overseer's control. Giving in, he came hard, filling the tight sheath. He tried to support himself on trembling arms, but Philip knocked his arms out from under him, pulling him down atop the blacksmith.

They lay like that, bodies still intertwined, for some time before Nicolas's cock finally softened enough to slip from its sheath. Rolling to his side, keeping his arms firmly around Philip's shoulders, he shifted until his lover's head rested in the crook of his shoulder.

For a time, Philip was content to rest there, enfolded in Nicolas's embrace, his thoughts drifting as he let himself imagine such comfort for months and years on end. Eventually, though, reality intruded again. Pressing a kiss to the line of muscle, he murmured, "So what happens now? Am I going to find myself banished to my cot again before the night is over?"

Nicolas tensed, knowing this conversation could not possibly end well, but he shook his head. "Not unless that's where you'd rather be."

"I'd rather be right where I am now," Philip averred.

"It can't change the way we interact outside the cabin," the older man warned, ever the overseer.

"I know that," Philip insisted, "and I'll act however you want out there, as long as in here, you let me love you again."

Nicolas's heart clenched at those words, his longing for them to pass beyond the realm of the physical so strong that it hurt. He nodded, unable to speak right away for fear of revealing his deepest desire.

It was enough of an answer for Philip, though, who snuggled deeper into the embrace, clearly settling in for the night. Nicolas breathed a sigh of relief and closed his eyes, reminding himself once again that he had known from the beginning that anything between them could only be temporary. It was cold comfort as he drifted into dreams of a lifetime with the man in his arms.

Chapter 17

SHAWN drew rein in front of the barn on Martin Thomas's property, shouting a greeting that he hoped would bring the other man out from wherever he was hiding. Reminding himself that he had nothing more than suspicions and not to jump to unwarranted conclusions, he swung down from his horse and looked around for a place to tie it up sheltered from the light drizzle that grayed the day. "Thomas," he called again when the man did not immediately appear, "are you here?" He almost hoped Thomas did not hear him. Looking for him would give Shawn all the excuse he needed to search the property.

"Coming, coming," Thomas's voice grumbled from behind the house. Shawn waited patiently until the man strode into view, getting the lay of the land in his head, just in case. The house – the glorified shack – sat with its back to the lake, only enough of the surrounding forest cut away to keep any large branches from landing on it during a storm. The barn, in slightly better shape, sat to one side of the clearing, nearest the road that led to the property. Those were the only two structures he could see, but Thomas could well have a shed or two hidden away in the woods. It would be just like the secretive man to do so.

"I'm going to put my horse in your barn," the sheriff called, starting toward the structure as if he had every right to go where he pleased, and in truth, very few people on the island would deny him that right.

"Be my guest," Thomas gestured magnanimously. Just because he did not like the sheriff was no reason for the man's fine horse to suffer unnecessarily. He followed the blond inside, keeping a sharp eye on him. He did not like anyone wandering around on his property unsupervised.

Shawn frowned when the big man followed him inside. He had hoped for the opportunity to look around a little, perhaps even to find something to give him some leverage in his questioning. He could not peek and poke at will now, but nothing could stop him from observing carefully as he walked the full length of the barn to the last stall, settling his horse inside. The place was a rat's nest, full of abandoned farm tools, old burlap sacks, scraps of wood, but nothing he could pinpoint as being overly suspicious.

He removed his horse's bridle, hanging it on a nearby nail, but left the saddle in place. He had no intention of staying longer than necessary. He took his time, ignoring Thomas's hovering presence. The man seemed tightly wound, on edge, even more than the typical reaction to having the sheriff around for no reason, but then, Thomas had always been brusque, extremely protective of his privacy. Shawn would have been more suspicious if the man had thrown the doors open wide in welcome. Other than his three cohorts, Shawn had never known him to choose willingly to be around people. That he had sold his parents' house in town and moved almost to Eagle Lake had surprised no one, least of all the sheriff, who had watched him become more and more anti-social as he grew older.

"What do you want, Sheriff?" Thomas asked testily when the older man took his time stabling his horse. "I know this isn't a social visit."

"I have a few questions for you," Shawn replied firmly, his voice brooking no argument. "Why don't we go inside where we can talk more comfortably?"

"Not interested in talking to you," Thomas retorted immediately.

"I know you're not," the sheriff agreed, taking a step closer to the other man, bringing his physical presence to bear. Thomas was not a small man or one easily intimidated, but Shawn had learned early the power of his own size and how to use it without ever laying a finger on his suspect. "But your two choices are to talk to me here or to ride into town with me and talk to me in my office. I figured you'd prefer to do it here."

"Damn lawmen," Thomas muttered, gesturing for the sheriff to precede him out of the barn, "think because they've got a badge they can make a body do whatever they want."

Shawn could not let the insult pass, not when his success or failure depended so completely on the way his constituents viewed him. Grabbing a handful of Thomas's shirt, he shoved the man against the wall. "You want to reconsider that statement?" he ground out, lifting just enough to let the other man know he was strong enough to enforce his edicts physically if it came to that.

Thomas glared at him but raised his hands placatingly, knowing he could never beat the sheriff in a fair fight, especially not when Parnell already had him pinned. "All right," he spat. "We'll go inside and talk."

He stomped across the yard and into the house, sitting down mutinously at the kitchen table and glaring at the sheriff. "Ask your questions and then get the hell off my land."

"Where were you night before last?" Shawn began bluntly.

"Asleep in my bed, of course," Thomas answered swiftly. "Where else would I have been?"

"Out," Shawn suggested. "Carousing with your friends. Killing Jason Leonard."

Thomas's face contorted with rage. "How dare you?" he roared.

Shawn was on his feet instantly, leaning threateningly over the other man. "I dare because it's my job," he reminded Thomas. "Two men have been killed in the past month and I want to know who did it."

"So why are you asking me?" Thomas demanded irritably.

"Why did you threaten Mr. Wells when you found him and Philip Hall out along the coast yesterday?" Shawn countered immediately.

"What are you talking about?" Thomas bluffed.

"Yesterday," Shawn repeated, "you and your buddies encountered Hall and Wells while they were out riding and as you were leaving, you warned Wells to be careful who he associated with because 'they're killing sodomites on the island.' Explain."

"It wasn't a threat," Thomas replied sullenly. "I was just trying to warn him."

"Why?"

"He's an outlander. He doesn't have anything to do with what's going on around here. No reason he should get caught up in something that isn't his affair," Thomas explained as if it were perfectly obvious. "Besides, isolated as the construction site is, I wasn't sure he was aware of what had happened and I wanted to make sure he knew what he was getting into."

"Your friends seemed to think the two men had been up to something… illicit," Shawn observed, watching closely for a reaction even as his own face hardened at the possible double entendre in the man's words. The look of distaste that crossed Thomas's face was clear.

"My friends don't always know when to keep their mouths shut," was the other man's only reply.

Shawn frowned. He had hoped Thomas's reply would explain the expression on his face, but it seemed the farmer was too savvy for that. "Their vitriol makes them obvious suspects in Reed's murder, you know," he pointed out. "Since you obviously don't share their opinion, though, you won't mind if I look around, will you?"

"You think because I live out here by myself, I'm stupid," Thomas declared defensively. "You might be the sheriff, but I don't have to let you go poking around on my property because of it. You can bluff and bluster all you want, but this is still my land and I've still got rights, so get your horse and get the hell off my property."

Knowing he truly did not have the leverage he needed to force the issue without something more than his suspicions, Shawn stood up straighter and glanced around the cabin one last time. "What happened to your broom?" he asked sharply, seeing the rough splice that had been done on the handle. Revulsion filled him as he remembered the broken handles protruding from the dead men's bodies. Keeping his feelings off his face as best he could, he studied Thomas, trying to decide if the man had the size and strength to subdue the two victims, to strangle them to death and rape them viciously enough that they bled. He reminded himself repeatedly that Philip had beaten this man and his three friends in a fight and was still more than his match physically. It was poor consolation.

Thomas looked up, his gaze suddenly hard. "It broke while I was doing some cleaning up," he answered coldly. "I fixed it as best I could until I can afford to buy a new one. That's not against the law, is it?"

Shawn stiffened angrily. "Listen here, you ignorant bastard," he growled. "You're right that I can't force you to let me search your property, but I'm watching you. If anything else happens, you better have a damn good alibi."

Not giving Thomas a chance to reply, he stormed out of the house, slamming the door behind him. Everything pointed to Thomas being the murderer or at least involved in the murders, yet none of it was proof, certainly not enough for him to arrest the man. He briefly considered sending a telegram to the circuit judge to see if he would be willing to come to Bar Harbor sooner than usual, but the circumstantial evidence was too flimsy to truly hold up. He needed proof before he could do more than bluff and bully. He would keep an eye on Thomas as best he could, hoping he would do something to give himself away, but he had other responsibilities as well that would keep him from shadowing the man day and night. He would just have to hope the layers of protection he had arranged for Philip would be enough.

AT the end of another long day, the two men walked back toward the cabin they shared, keeping a respectable difference between them, though Nicolas knew that would change as soon as the door to the cabin closed behind him. If the ruffians from town had spread rumors as Philip feared they would, the gossip had not yet made it to the work site, and no one there seemed to think anything of seeing the overseer and the blacksmith together, a turn of events that pleased Nicolas immensely since it allowed him to keep a close eye on his lover for safety's sake without raising any alarms. He could not spend all his time at the forge, regardless of how much he enjoyed watching the play of muscles beneath Philip's thin shirts, but he could drop by often, both to check on the progress of the work and on the blacksmith himself.

Wiping his arm across his forehead, Philip sighed. "What a day! I'm so hot that even a cold shower will feel good."

The vision of Philip in the shower flooded back into Nicolas's head, giving way to another, even more seductive image of sharing that experience with him. "Would you rather have a warm bath?" he asked softly, though he did not see anyone within earshot. "We can use the tub in the cabin, heat some water, and enjoy a leisurely bath in front of the fire."

"We?" Philip teased. "I don't recall inviting you to join me."

The urge to pull Philip to him and kiss him senseless, just to prove that he could, was nearly overwhelming, but Nicolas resisted. They were nearly to the cabin and there was no reason to take unnecessary chances with their haven just feet away. "Wait until we get inside," he growled.

Philip smiled. His lover was so easily provoked to possessiveness, a trait Philip found incredibly appealing. Picking up the pace slightly as anticipation made him hard, he unlocked the door and stepped inside, shedding his boots as always. When Nicolas had done the same, the blacksmith's smile widened. "You were saying?" he goaded.

Even as he recognized the prod to his instincts, Nicolas gave in to them, backing Philip against the wall of the mudroom and kissing him thoroughly, possessively, his hands flying over his lover's upper body, caressing as he had learned the younger man enjoyed. Immediately, his lover arched into his touch, leaving them both panting.

"Still want to take a cold shower without me rather than a warm bath here with me?" he demanded, one hand sliding lower to cup Philip's buttocks, his hips pressing forward to grind his cock against the blacksmith's answering hardness.

"No," Philip gasped, unable to carry on the teasing charade any longer. He had known passion before, known desire, but never like this, never so that it stole his breath and every rational thought in his head. Yet one touch of Nicolas's hand sufficed to have him achingly aroused, desperate for another caress, another kiss, another press of the overseer's hard body against his.

"Then get the buckets so we can start filling the tub," Nicolas instructed, pulling back though part of him wanted nothing more than to spin Philip around and take him right there against the wall. He had promised his lover a bath, though, and a bath he would deliver.

Philip almost protested, almost insisted that he no longer wanted a bath, but following Nicolas's instructions would ultimately lead to a far more fulfilling evening and so he released his grip on his lover's hips, pulling his boots back on and grabbing the buckets that stood by the door.

When he came back in from the pump, he saw Nicolas had built up the fire and pulled out a large wooden tub, big enough to hold two as long as they were willing to be close. The thought of squeezing into the tight space with his lover sent another shot of arousal through him. He suspected they would not be doing a lot of bathing.

"Make yourself comfortable," Nicolas suggested, taking the buckets from Philip and setting them to heat by the fire.

Philip's eyes sparkled as he considered the various ways to interpret that statement. Already, Nicolas had shed his vest, his shirt hanging open as he prepared their bath. Quickly, Philip stripped to the waist, not even bothering with the pretense of leaving the cloth around his shoulders. He wanted Nicolas to notice him, to touch him, wanted far more than just a bath from his lover, and he had no qualms about enticing the other man to get what he wanted.

Nicolas glanced up from the fireplace to see his lover's bare torso limned in gold, the flickering light of the flames casting shadows where normally there were none. He paused for a moment, simply looking at the image before him. "Sit down," he suggested quietly, turning his back to open a cabinet and pull out a small journal and pencil. "Let me draw you while we wait for the water to warm up."

Philip's eyes widened in surprise, that request not at all what he had expected. He saw no reason to refuse, though, and so nodded his permission, settling self-consciously in a chair. "I didn't know you drew," he commented into the silence broken only by the crackling of the fire. The lack of conversation and the sudden intense scrutiny left him feeling unaccountably uncomfortable.

Nicolas nodded his response, perching on a chair across from Philip so that he had a clear view of his subject. His pencil flew across the paper as he sketched in the lines of his lover's body, drawing almost as much from memory as from sight, the now-familiar planes of Philip's form coming to life on his paper. "Turn your head to the right a little," he instructed, glancing up to study the play of shadows on Philip's face. "I want the light from the fire on your skin more evenly."

Philip moved according to Nicolas's directions, his sense of unease growing progressively.

"Relax," Nicolas scolded, seeing the tension in the blacksmith's shoulders as he began filling in those details.

"I can't," Philip admitted. "I don't know how to sit here and let you draw me."

Comprehension dawned and Nicolas smiled, rising from his seat and setting his journal aside for the moment. He crossed to Philip's chair and knelt at his lover's side. "I don't do portraits, usually," he explained. "I draw landscapes, and I draw my lover. Sometimes, he's real, like you are. Sometimes, he's a figment of my imagination, an amalgam of men I have known and loved in the past. Either way, I draw him – you – because I'm fascinated with what I see. Every stroke of my pencil, every line I draw, is a caress, a moment of intimacy."

"But it's a one-way intimacy," Philip pointed out, struggling to explain what he himself only barely understood. "It doesn't matter that you admire me when we're making love because I'm admiring you in the same way. But this is different. I feel like an object instead of a person."

"You're not," Nicolas promised. "You're my lover, whom I'm worshipping a different way. That's all."

Philip nodded slowly, fingering the collar of Nicolas's shirt. "At least take this off so I can admire you, too, while you work."

"That's quite the twist on 'an eye for an eye,'" the overseer joked as he shed the concealing cloth.

Philip shrugged. "Do you mind?"

"No," Nicolas assured him, kissing him quickly. "So, can I finish my drawing now?"

"I suppose."

Nicolas returned to his sketchbook. The tension had not completely faded from Philip's shoulders, but it was better than before, enough that he could call up the relaxed lines of his lover's arms from memory.

Philip consciously reminded himself to relax, not wanting to interfere with Nicolas's drawing, but his mind kept going back to the overseer's comment about whom he chose to draw. As uncomfortable as it made him to think about Nicolas drawing him, it bothered him even more to imagine the overseer alone, conjuring up men from his past. Would he be one of those memories after the summer was over? Would Nicolas take pieces and parts of him later to add to some invisible ideal lover? The thought made him feel ill.

Suddenly determined to be the lover Nicolas remembered, he slid his hands down his chest, circling his nipples teasingly until the overseer looked up at him again, eyes suddenly darkening. "Want me to stop?" he husked.

"No," Nicolas choked out, his hand moving quickly to fill in the image of Philip touching himself. Despite the leanings of his own heart, he knew that once the summer ended, so would their affair. Back in Boston, he would have only his memories to keep him warm through the cold winter – his memories and his drawings.

Philip's eyes closed as his fingers continued to touch and tease. He could hear the scratch of Nicolas's pencil as it moved over the paper, recording his movements. Eventually, the urgency of the sound slowed. Opening his eyes again, Philip met Nicolas's heated gaze. "Finished already?" he asked, his voice rough with desire.

"Not even close," the artist groaned, knowing he would never be truly finished with Philip.

Finding his footing as he realized that Nicolas was as affected by their game as he was, Philip slid his hands lower to trace along the waistband of his pants. Nicolas's eyes flashed lapis lightning, making Philip smile.

"Open them," he suggested.

"Only if you do the same," Philip retorted even as his hands moved to the buttons.

Nicolas set the pencil on the table long enough to open the placket on his trousers, his eyes never leaving Philip as he reached blindly for the graphite again, hand flying across the page to fill in the details now revealed to his eyes. He wished momentarily for his pastels so he could fill in more than the outline of his lover's form, but they were in Boston in his lodgings there. He could always finish the image over the winter, for he had only to close his eyes to see the same image that met his eyes.

He had finished the bare outline of the drawing, looking up to check a detail, when Philip's movement caught his eye. His lover's hand had slipped beneath the fabric of his trousers, cupping his sac, rolling it suggestively in his palm. Gulping down a deep breath, Nicolas set the sketchbook aside and checked the temperature of the water. Finding it plenty warm for a bath, he stripped the heavy denim from his hips and poured the steaming water into the tub. "Bath time," he declared, submerging himself slowly, his open arms inviting Philip to join him.

Philip stripped with alacrity, joining Nicolas in the tub as quickly as he could. He sighed in delight as his lover's strong arms closed around him. Though only a couple of days had passed, he had grown used to being held instead of always being the one to hold. He leaned back against Nicolas's wiry chest and let the heat of the water ease the aches of the day's work. Smithing had been his profession for years, but he still felt the strain of his exertions at the end of the day.

Hearing the sound that escaped, Nicolas settled his hands over the strong muscles of Philip's chest, kneading firmly, not to arouse but to soothe. The groan of relief that followed made him smile even as he intensified his efforts. "Just relax and let me take care of you."

As he sank deeper into the water and Nicolas's caress, Philip murmured, "As long as someday soon, you let me take care of you, too."

"Deal," Nicolas agreed absently, his mind already focused on the moment at hand, at making *this* moment a perfect one for his lover. He kept his touch light, imbuing every caress with the panoply of emotions welling within him. Every kiss, every stroke spoke of his love, of his devotion to the man in his arms, though he knew Philip did not feel the same. That did not matter. He cared only for expressing what he felt in the silence of his heart in a way he knew and understood.

Philip quickly became lost in the sensation, overcome by the tenderness, the gentleness in Nicolas's caress. He had touched and been touched before, but never like this, never with this… sensitivity, this devotion to Philip's pleasure. He knew Nicolas had a home in Boston to return to and so had little hope of their affair lasting beyond the arrival of fall, but surely the overseer could not touch him, love him this way if all he felt was a passing attraction, a transitory lust that would end with the season. Heart beating faster, he turned in his lover's arms, intending to pour out his emotions with the same wordless fervor.

Their bodies moved together in the elemental dance of longtime lovers, flowing one into the other with no hesitation, no fumbling, every touch, every caress fraught with the emotions driving them. Their eyes met and held as Philip straddled Nicolas's hips, riding his lover with languid ease, their gazes never parting as they pushed each other closer and closer to paradise. When the moment came, when they could no longer hold back the passion their movements inspired, they collapsed against each other, never looking away, each warmed by the emotions they thought they read flickering in the other's eyes.

LOOK at him. He acts as if he has every right to be there, as if he were not some freak that violates every law of nature. He will learn the error of his ways soon, though it is too late for him to repent. He will pay for the errors of his ways on this earth and answer to his Maker in the next life. I cannot allow such pestilence to remain on the island. It is my duty as a God-fearing man to rid our fair shores of his filth. The sheriff thinks he can stop me, can find out who I am, but the Lord's will protects me. He can seek all he wants, but I will evade him as I have done thus far, and his plans to protect his precious friend will fail. They post guards, but they are only human, susceptible to bribes and persuasion like any other man. A few well-placed dollars gave me access to their "closed site," and a little patience has netted me the blacksmith within reach. He is a bigger man than Reed or Leonard, but not so big that I cannot subdue him. There is no need for a weapon now. That will come later, as I punish him. I will bring him to his knees with my hands alone. Just as soon as he turns his back.... Now!

He thinks to struggle, thinks he can escape me, but his physical strength is nothing compared to the power of the Lord that gives me strength. I have come to know the resistance of the human body, and his will give in just as the others did. He can fight me all he wants, but eventually, he will succumb. Already he weakens beneath my hands. Another few minutes and he will collapse as the others did, and then I will have him. I wonder if he will beg as the others did, if he will plead for his life, for an end to his torment, or if he will be stoic. It will not matter. He will die as the others did. Just a little....

"Philip!"

Shit! The overseer! He, too, will pay, for interfering even if he has done nothing else. I do not believe that, though. There is too much evidence to the contrary. He has fallen under the blacksmith's evil spell and when I have finished with my current cleansing, I will return for him. He thinks that because he is an outsider, he will be safe, but he is just another example of all that is wrong with our island, the corrupting influences from outside perverting our youth and weakening us. His time is not yet, but he will pay.

Nicolas briefly considered giving chase, trying to bring down the man who had attacked Philip, but his lover was lying unmoving on the ground, and checking on him seemed of far greater urgency.

Falling to his knees at the blacksmith's side, he laid a hand on Philip's chest, checking to see if he could feel any sign of life. To his relief, the dark eyes opened and met his, a hoarse cough signaling Philip's attempts to breathe.

"Just relax," Nicolas urged, raising Philip's torso as he slipped behind his lover to support his weight. "Relax and breathe. I've got you now and I won't let him hurt you."

"Did you see him?" Philip gasped weakly, his head spinning still from lack of oxygen.

"Only his back," Nicolas replied, "and only from a distance. I didn't recognize him, but I'm not sure I would have unless I knew him well. You didn't see him?"

Philip shook his head. "He…" a fit of coughing interrupted his words. When he could speak again, he finished, "He caught me from behind. The first thing I knew was his hands around my neck choking me. I tried to fight him." He coughed again, reliving the feeling of helplessness.

"Easy," Nicolas soothed. "You're safe now." He could feel the terror gripping his lover and fought to keep his own actions gentle and reassuring. That did nothing, though, to still his pounding heart or ease his own frazzled nerves. A minute later and Philip would surely have lost consciousness, leaving him completely at the mercy of the madman. It did not bear thinking about, yet he could do nothing else. "Do you think you can walk back to the cabin?" He wanted to sweep Philip into his arms and carry him back, but he doubted he could carry him that far.

"I think so."

Shifting to Philip's side and slipping his shoulder under his lover's arm, he started to rise. "Lean on me," he admonished when he felt Philip struggle to stand.

Relieved, Philip let Nicolas bear the bulk of his weight as they headed slowly back toward the cabin. They had nearly reached it when he heard Johnny call their names.

"What happened?" Johnny asked, approaching them. "Is Philip hurt?"

"Get the sheriff," Nicolas replied tersely. "The killer almost had another victim today."

Johnny's face blanched and he nodded. "I'll ride into town right away and be back as fast as I can."

"I'm going to take him in the cabin and lock the door," Nicolas explained. "I don't want to leave him alone. Tell Sullivan and Malone what happened and have them keep an eye on things while you're gone."

Johnny nodded again. "Stay safe." With that, he took off running toward the unfinished manor to speak to the other crew bosses before heading for town.

"Come inside," Nicolas urged, fishing in his pocket for his key. "You need to rest."

Philip limped alongside the overseer docilely until they were inside and the door was locked behind them. As soon as he heard the bolt slide home, he turned in Nicolas's arms, kissing him desperately. "I don't want to rest. I want to prove to myself that I'm still alive."

Chapter 18

NICOLAS gasped beneath the onslaught, not used to this level of aggression from his lover. Philip had never been passive, but neither had he ever taken charge to this degree. This was a side of the man he had suspected existed, but had never seen. Philip had admitted it had been a long time since he had taken a lover the way he had accepted Nicolas, yet the overseer knew he and Reed had been lovers, which meant the blacksmith had to have been the dominant one in the relationship. He had been cognizant of the gift of trust that first night, when they had talked about it, without having really considered the rest of the equation. The rest of the equation was now pushing him firmly against the wall of the mudroom, clearly intent on accosting him. Not that Nicolas required much persuasion. His head fell back against the mudroom wall, giving Philip complete control of their interaction.

Body trembling still with a mixture of fear, adrenaline, and lust, Philip recognized the surrender in Nicolas's actions and took full advantage of it, stepping closer and grinding forcefully against his lover. His hands scrabbled against fabric, kept from tearing it only because Nicolas helped him pull the cloth away, leaving the older man's body bare to his touch and his gaze. The urgency in his blood drove Philip's hands to move faster, harder, driving them both closer and closer to the point of no return.

Nicolas gasped as a hard, callused palm closed around his cock, stroking him rapidly, leaving him aching. He understood Philip's need to claim, to control, and he gave in to it without hesitation. His lover had been nothing but generous with his body when they had made love before. He could do nothing less now. "Philip," he moaned his surrender.

The sound of his name in that soft, desperate voice only augmented the passion driving Philip. He tore open his trousers, baring his own throbbing erection. His lips closed over Nicolas's again, stealing his breath, leaving the older man trembling.

Desperate now, he urged Nicolas to turn and brace himself against the wall. Sucking on his fingers swiftly, he slid them into the tight seam of his lover's buttocks, probing eagerly. Nicolas pushed back against him, encouraging him to do more than tease.

"God, you're so tight," Philip gasped, his finger caught in the vise of Nicolas's body.

"It's been awhile," the older man admitted, squirming against the discomfort of the barely damp digit. He tried to spread his legs to ease the way, but his trousers still around his knees prohibited such movement.

"Fuck," Philip muttered, knowing he was too worked up to prepare Nicolas the way he would need for this to be anything other than painful. Grabbing his lover's hand, he pulled the older man into the main room, bearing them down onto the rug in front of the fireplace. Spitting in his palm again, he ran it up the length of Nicolas's cock.

"Philip?" Nicolas asked hesitantly even as his body arched into the determined caress.

"I won't hurt you that way," Philip insisted as he straddled Nicolas's hips and impaled himself roughly on the hot flesh. It burned, but that was part of what he needed, that proof of being alive, of loving and being loved. Perhaps it did not have the same significance for Nicolas as it had for him, but his brush with death had crystallized his feelings. He groaned as he bit back the words, knowing it was not the time, with Shawn summoned, probably already on his way. Later, when the sheriff had left, they would have time to talk and make plans. For now, more pressing matters demanded his attention.

He rocked fitfully on the hard cock spearing him, Nicolas's hips lifting in time with each of his downward thrusts, their bodies slapping together desperately as they strained to reach the goal, the moment of release, of communion, that even now, even like this – half-undressed and wild with lust – would take them.

They could not maintain the frenzy that took them for long, their bodies seizing up in climax almost as quickly as they had begun, catapulting them into the forge of passion, the heat melting away their reserve, their strength, even their consciousness, so that they collapsed back to the floor.

HEAVY pounding on the door roused them from their dozing. Nicolas dropped a quick kiss on Philip's lips, straightening his clothes as he walked toward the door. Philip stirred and rose as well, much more slowly, though he had managed to dress again by the time the overseer came back into the room with Shawn behind him.

"What happened?" the sheriff asked, his eyes raking Philip's body for signs of harm.

"He caught me at the forge," Philip began simply.

"Who was it?"

"I don't know," Philip admitted. "He was behind me and I couldn't see him. Nicolas scared him off."

"I couldn't tell who it was either," Nicolas chimed in before Parnell could ask. "He ran off when he heard me call Philip's name. All I saw was his retreating back."

"But it wasn't someone you recognized from that view?"

"No. He was a little taller than Philip, about as broad in the shoulders. He was dressed roughly, thick coat, homespun trousers, heavy boots, dusty and non-descript, but that's all I could really see. And that description could fit any man here, just about, including me."

Shawn frowned, having hoped one of the two men could give him enough detail to narrow his suspects. While Wells's information was better than nothing, it could easily have applied to at least half the men on the island. Philip was not short, by any means, but neither was he especially tall. His shoulders were broadened by his work, but beyond that, he was not particularly large. "I'll need to determine the whereabouts of the entire crew around the time Philip was attacked."

Nicolas nodded. "The crew bosses should be able to speak for the majority of them, unless someone went to the privy at that exact moment. The only ones who wouldn't have been at the manor itself, besides Philip, were the men on guard."

"We have to suspect anyone who wasn't at the manor when the attack occurred," Shawn insisted. "Anyone with the right build, that is."

"I'll go get West, Sullivan, and Malone, then," Nicolas said. "They'll be able to narrow the list down for us."

Shawn nodded as the overseer strode out of the cabin, careful to lock the door behind him. "Anything you want to tell me?" he asked Philip, pointedly staring at the disarranged rug by the fireplace.

"No." Philip had plenty to say, but he wanted to tell Nicolas first. It hardly seemed fair to confide in Shawn without sharing his feelings with his lover first.

Shawn cocked an eyebrow. "You're playing a dangerous game," he warned.

"I'm not playing games," Philip retorted. "I'm trying to live my life and find some happiness in it."

The sound of the lock opening again ended their conversation. "They were waiting for me," Nicolas explained as he came back inside with the other three men in tow.

"Mr. Wells said you wanted to know where everyone was when Philip was attacked," Eric commented. "Everyone in my crew was there. I'd given them a break about an hour before, so nobody even needed the privy or anything."

"I sent two men to get more brick," Carl added, "but they came back, with the brick, far too quickly for them to have done anything else except run the errand I sent them on."

Shawn nodded. "And you, Mr. West?"

"I can't think of anyone who was missing either," Johnny said. "I'd gone to the privy myself when I saw Mr. Wells with

Philip, right after the attack, but I don't think I left long enough for any of them to have slipped away and attacked Philip."

"I can get one of West's crew and ask if you'd like," Nicolas offered.

Shawn shook his head. "No, I think it's the guards we need to talk to."

"We can round them up for you," Eric offered, incensed that all their efforts to protect Philip had still almost failed. Despite his initial hesitations, he had come to enjoy the blacksmith's company.

"Rough them up a little, too, if you want," Carl added, the threat to Philip hitting far too close to home for comfort.

"Not too much," Shawn replied. "I want them willing to talk to me."

The three crew bosses rose as one, an air of hard determination marking their faces as they left the cabin in search of the guards.

"Have you learned anything else since we last talked?" Philip asked, not wanting to revisit the subject of his future.

"I spoke with Martin," Shawn replied, "but I can't actually accuse him of anything except making threats, and while that's irritating, it isn't a crime. The best I can do is try to trick him into letting me search his property, but even that might not lead to anything. I know he hates you – that's no secret – but as far as I know, he never exchanged a word with Reed and had no particular quarrel with Leonard. So while it might explain the attacks on you, it doesn't explain the murders. I'll talk to him again, make sure he has an alibi for today – besides his cronies since I don't particularly trust them either, especially where you're concerned – but even if he doesn't, that isn't proof."

Nicolas concentrated for a minute on the two memories he had of the man in question: from the day in town and the day on the coast. "Yes, it could have been him," he decided after a moment. "He's about the right height and build, though I'd have to see him next to Philip to be sure."

Shawn's mouth twisted. "Again, suspicion, not proof. Short of tricking him into confessing or finding a bloody weapon on his property, all I can do is keep an eye on him for now." His face tightened. "And make a few no-so-casual threats."

A tap on the door signaled the crew bosses' return. Nicolas rose and let them in, along with the four men who had been assigned to guard duty that day. His artist's eye catalogued each of them appraisingly, trying to determine if any could have been the man he saw attacking Philip. The clothes he had seen, non-descript, dusty, bland in color, could have described what all of them were wearing, but only one of them struck him as tall enough. A nod of his head as he walked behind him signaled his suspicion to the sheriff.

Shawn saw Nicolas's gesture and interpreted it correctly, but his own quick study of the man in question left him doubting whether that guard was guilty. He could not have said exactly what made him doubt he was looking at the killer, but years of dealing with criminals had given him instincts he could not explain but which rarely let him down. His gaze shifted to the other three as he stood. He motioned for Philip to do the same. "Have a seat, gentlemen," he ordered, his voice one step away from menacing. "I have some questions for you."

All four men sat down quickly, expressions varying from curiosity to nervousness on their faces. "I'm sure Mr. Wells explained to you why he set a guard this summer," the sheriff began, his gaze studying each face closely as he spoke.

Three pairs of eyes met his confidently. One pair did not.

"Mr. Hall was attacked today," Shawn told them gravely, "while you were supposed to be ensuring no one got onto the construction site, and we have accounted for everyone other than you."

He dropped his bombshell and waited as, with utter predictability, the four men reacted. The three pairs of confident eyes faltered, then grew angry as they realized the implication. They alternately protested and sought Philip with their gazes as if checking to see if he was unharmed. The fourth pair of eyes fell even farther into the man's lap, his face flushing.

Shawn moved to stand right behind the fourth man. "Do you have something you want to tell me, Mr....?"

"Cox," Nicolas supplied, coming to stand at the guard's side. The one sitting next to Cox scooted back obligingly, giving the overseer space.

"Mr. Cox?" Shawn prompted when the man remained silent.

"I got nothing to say," the heavy-set man mumbled defensively as he pushed to his feet, jostling against both the sheriff and the overseer.

"Really?" Shawn challenged, slamming the man against the wall. A loud clatter drew everyone's attention, the cheap metal hip flask falling from the man's jacket. Nicolas scooped it up and sniffed at it.

"Whisky," he snarled. "You know my policy about alcohol on the site, Cox."

"Not exactly inspiring confidence here, Cox," Shawn drawled. "What else are you hiding in your pockets?"

Before the man could protest again, the sheriff started turning out the other man's pockets. All he found in the coat were a pocket knife and ball of twine. A search of the man's trouser pockets, though, revealed a wad of money. "I didn't realize Mr. Wells was such a generous employer," he drawled as he counted out the bills. "Twenty dollars already and so early in the season."

Nicolas's frown deepened. "Where did you get the money, Cox? It certainly wasn't from me."

Philip and the three crew bosses joined Nicolas and Shawn in crowding around Cox. "I could have died today," the blacksmith ground out, his face hard. "Where did you get the money?"

"I don't know his name," Cox protested. "He gave me money to let him onto the site. That's all I know, I swear. He always met me at night. I could barely even see his face."

"Get your things and get out," Nicolas spat in disgust.

"And get off the island," Shawn added. "There's a ship sailing tomorrow. If I see you after that, I'll throw you in jail for impeding my investigation. You can use your ill-gotten gains to get the hell out of my territory."

Cox nodded vehemently, his eyes darting toward the door. Shawn stepped back and let him go. "Gentlemen," he said to the other three, "thank you for your time and I apologize for the accusations."

The three guards nodded and left the cabin, followed by Johnny, Carl, and Eric. Shawn turned back to Nicolas and Philip. "I'd hoped having you here would be enough to keep you safe," he sighed, sitting down at the table again, "but it seems that isn't enough. Are you sure you won't reconsider leaving until I catch this bastard? My sister in Birch Harbor would gladly let you stay with her until this is over and you can come back safely."

Philip started shaking his head even before Shawn finished, moving closer to Nicolas as if the older man could somehow prevent the sheriff from making him leave. "This is my home," he replied, "my life. If I let him make me leave, he wins."

"No, he only wins if you die," Shawn retorted.

Nicolas listened to them argue back and forth, listened to Philip protest his desire to stay on the island, on the site. With him. Philip did not say it, but Nicolas understood. His lover was endangering himself because he wanted to stay here, and that was something the overseer simply could not allow. "You should go," he interrupted.

The words, quiet but firm, stopped Philip mid-rant. "What?" he asked, turning to Nicolas in surprise. "But I thought…"

"You thought the fact that we spent a couple of nights together meant something?" the overseer challenged cruelly, his heart breaking as he said the words intended to drive his lover to safety. "You thought the fact that you're a good lay would make me endanger myself and my crew for you? Sorry to disillusion you, Mr. Hall, but you're not that good."

Philip's face fell, the words hitting him hard. "Why are you saying these things?" he demanded, completely ignoring Shawn who watched with the morbid fascination of someone captivated by a train wreck, cringing yet unable to look away. "I thought…"

"It doesn't matter what you thought," Nicolas finished, keeping his face stern. "You're not worth the danger you bring to my camp and my men. Go to Birch Harbor where you'll be safe."

Philip stumbled backward as if struck. "Go to hell."

Nicolas's eyes shut on the sight of his lover leaving, unable to bear it even knowing it was the fruit of his own labor. Opening them again, he saw the sheriff still standing there. "I hope to hell you know what you're doing because you just destroyed a man who deserves far better than the way you treated him."

"I know," Nicolas replied softly, gesturing for the sheriff to leave as well. Parnell was almost at the door when the overseer called him back. "Let me know when he's safe with your sister. Please?"

"Why the hell should I?"

"Because this'll be worth it then."

Chapter 19

A knock on the door drew Philip's attention from his blind contemplation of his table. He looked toward the entrance, trying to make his blurry gaze focus on the lock. Seeing the key was turned, he heaved a sigh and rose from his seat, walking slowly toward the door. "Who is it?" he called, his sense of self-preservation still strong enough to keep him from opening the door without checking first.

"It's Eric, Johnny, and Carl," a familiar voice came through the heavy wood.

Philip grimaced, not wanting any reminder of Cleftstone Manor or its infuriating overseer, but the crew bosses had become his friends while he was there and he could hardly send them away simply because they reminded him of Nicolas. Opening the door and pasting a smile on his face, he invited them inside.

"Are you all right?" Johnny asked when they had all settled at the table. "We asked Mr. Wells where you were when you didn't show up for breakfast yesterday, but he just said you'd left. Nearly bit my head off, too. I don't think I've ever seen him so out of sorts."

"Sure," Philip lied. "I'm fine. I just… I just needed to be at home."

"There's no place like home and that's for sure," Eric agreed, thoughts of the little house he was building for Rachel flashing through his mind, "but what about the murderer, the vandal? What if either of them comes after you here?"

"You three are the first visitors I've had besides Shawn, who brought me home, since I got here two days ago," Philip assured them. "No one else knows I'm here, so there's no reason for anyone to come looking for me. And if they do, I just won't open the door."

"And if he succeeds in burning the house down around you this time?" Carl insisted, remembering the charred wood they had torn from the house and replaced with new. "It's been a dry summer. It wouldn't take much to get a fire started now."

Philip shrugged, thinking that at least then he would not have to suffer as he was now. "I'll be fine," he promised, knowing he lied.

The three crew bosses looked at each other in silence for a moment, trying to find a way to draw out their new friend, to convince him to trust them again. They could tell something was wrong, but unless Philip confided in them, they had no way of knowing what it was.

"Shall we come here to play poker on Wednesday, then?" Eric asked, thinking perhaps the presence of Philip's friends would draw him out and lead him to open up some.

Memories of the last poker game, of Nicolas, assailed him. "No," Philip said softly. "I don't think I'll play on Wednesday. I'm sure my friends from town will come out to the site, though, and you should enjoy yourselves. I'll just stay here and…"

"And what?" Johnny prompted.

"Look," Philip said, sidestepping the question, "I appreciate you coming here to check on me, but there's nothing you can do, nothing anybody can do. I just need some time alone to think, to move on. I'll be fine in a few days."

"You're not coming back to the site, are you?" Johnny asked softly.

Philip shook his head. He might eventually move on, but nothing could persuade him to return to Cleftstone. "If you bring me the designs, though, I'll try to finish the hinges and the like at least here at home. After all, I did agree to do them and I know I've left everyone in a lurch."

Johnny wanted to ask again why that had happened, knew his two friends felt the same, but it was clear that Philip was not going to answer their questions and forcing the issue would not help. At the moment, the blacksmith was still talking to them, sort of. If they alienated him completely, they could lose even that, and despite his sudden defection, they did not want to give up that friendship entirely. "If you need anything, just let us know," he said finally, rising from the table and clearly expecting the others to do the same. Eric stood immediately, but Carl gestured for them to go on without him. He had one more thing he wanted to say, best added just between him and Philip.

Johnny looked surprised but he shrugged and went outside, Eric behind him.

When they were alone, Carl said softly, "I don't know what happened between you and Mr. Wells that made you leave. He won't talk any more than you will, but I don't like seeing either of you this way."

"It wasn't..." Philip protested automatically, his promise not to let anyone know of their affair still fresh on his mind.

"You don't have to pretend with me," Carl interrupted. "I'm not going to say anything to anyone else, and I'm certainly not going to judge when I know exactly what you're going through, exactly what he makes you feel. I just wanted you to know that he's suffering, too."

Philip snorted disbelievingly at the thought. "Ask him," he said coldly. "Ask him why I'm alone here in my house instead of snug in his cabin. It wasn't my idea to leave." Realizing what he had said, he turned away. "Please, Carl. I appreciate that you came, really I do, but I can't talk about this. It's hard enough already, trying to forget. Remembering just makes it worse."

"We'll come back..."

"No, don't," Philip insisted. "I don't want to see anyone right now. If I'm ready to be around people from the site again, I'll let you know. For now, it just makes things worse."

SHAWN was pretty sure it had already been the worst week of his life, and it looked like it had just gotten worse. Even after the scene with Wells, Philip had still refused to leave the island, refused any kind of protection other than the locks on his own house. Shawn might have been worried about that if Philip had left the house, but as far as he could tell, Philip had not moved from his spot at the kitchen table since he got home. His bed was still neatly made, never appearing to have been slept in, no matter how early Shawn arrived to check on his friend. No dishes had appeared in the sink, no matter what Shawn had brought to try to tempt the blacksmith into eating. Stubble covered his friend's face, not merely his goatee, but all along his cheeks and jaw. Anger had grown steadily in the sheriff as he watched the young man collapse in on himself. When Reed's infidelity was revealed, Philip had been angry, confronting the banker and ending their relationship. He had been unhappy, but not like this. It had all been outward, rather than this in-turned self-destructive pain.

Another scene kept playing in Shawn's mind, though; the look on the overseer's face after Philip left haunted him. Wells's words had been cruel, driving Philip away and into the depression that now haunted him, but there had been no cruelty on the overseer's face after Philip had gone, only the same pain Shawn now read in Philip's eyes. He knew his young friend. Philip would never have left his lover willingly, especially since both men knew the murderer was targeting homosexuals. Wells had made sure Philip was free to leave the island, to go to safety. Unfortunately, the blacksmith was too stubborn to do it, even without the incentive of the overseer in his bed.

He had encountered the overseer again in town, the blue eyes begging him for assurance of Philip's safety. He had seen how Wells reacted to the news that Philip had not left the island, seen the hurt, anger and frustration on the other man's face. "I did all I could," he had said in reply when the blond's outburst had finished.

"So did I," the overseer had murmured sadly.

Shawn shook his head. It was far easier just to admire Widow Taylor from afar and dream than to risk the kind of heartache the two men were suffering.

He had expected the killer to go for Philip as soon as he realized the blacksmith was at home and alone, but there had not been any attempt to get to him, at least not that the sheriff could tell. He still believed it would only be a matter of time. The proof lay on the ground in front of him, as battered and bruised as Leonard had been. He recognized the young man, the barkeep from Eden who had come asking for news of Leonard after his disappearance. As far as he knew, the victim had no connection to Philip, since the blacksmith rarely traveled to the neighboring town and was not a habitué of bars in any case. Questions about Reed's and Leonard's habits, though, had revealed that the two men had occasionally visited the bar in Eden. It seemed a small enough connection, but he had nothing else to go on for the moment.

He had no doubt, though, that it was the same murderer, the same motivation. Goddard's throat was sliced wide open, his face and torso bruised and battered, a broken broomstick protruding obscenely from his body. It could have been any of the other victims from the presentation. Cursing volubly, he scanned the clearing for any indication of the murderer's identity, any clue that had been absent from the previous crime scenes, but the pine needles concealed any footprints. He could find no sign of a horse or wagon used to transport the body, yet the murder had not occurred in the clearing for there was no blood, either from the gash across the victim's neck or from his abused anus.

Removing the broomstick and covering the body with a blanket, he transferred it to his wagon and headed back to town.

"PHILIP! Let us in!"

"It's open," Philip muttered, bracing himself to deal with his friends. Working up the energy to stand, though, was beyond him.

"What's going on?" Matthew demanded as the three men came inside. The cabin was as spotless as usual, but the sense of desolation was far too strong for them to imagine the situation was normal. Philip sat at the table, shoulders slumped in defeat, cheeks hollow and unshaven, rumpled, as if he had not moved in days, only the light of a guttering fire illuminating the room. "We went to Cleftstone for our game, but Johnny said you'd left the construction site. We'd have heard if Shawn caught the murderer, so that isn't it. Why are you here instead of there where you're safe?"

"I couldn't stay," Philip said simply, still staring at his clasped hands.

The three friends looked at each other and frowned. They had only seen the blacksmith looking this defeated once before, when he discovered Reed's infidelity, before righteous anger kicked in. Sitting down at the table, William clasped Philip's shoulder firmly. "Talk to us," he ordered gently. "Tell us what happened. Maybe we can help."

Philip laughed, a sharp, derisive sound. A month ago, he might have hesitated to confide even in his three best friends for fear of their reaction to the identity of his lover, but they had not judged him, had not abandoned him over James. If anything, they had been his staunchest defenders. Now, broad shoulders sagging, he gave in to his despair and told them the truth, sharing finally with them in his misery the kinds of confidences they had shared with him since they first started noticing the girls on the island. His face twisted in pained need as he whispered, "Unless you've got a cure for a broken heart, there's not a damn thing you can do."

"Who?" Joseph demanded, rising to his feet. Philip's posture when they first came in had reminded him of finding the blacksmith after his fight with Reed, but his friend had never before evinced this kind of wretched melancholy. Anger swelled in him at the thought that anyone could treat his friend so badly.

"Sit down, Joseph," Matthew chided, though he understood the impulse driving the youngest of the group. A time could well come when Joseph's reaction would be appropriate, but for the moment, it was counterproductive. "It's Wells, isn't it?"

The anguish on Philip's face was all the answer they needed. Joseph still looked angry enough to go after the overseer himself, but Matthew's and William's glances kept him from offering.

"What happened?" William prompted.

"I fell in love with him," Philip replied hollowly. "Not like with James – I see the difference now. James was... attractive, exciting, different from everyone else in town. He dazzled me with his city polish and I believed him when he told me he cared about me, but I didn't see how he looked down on me, how he was always wanting me to change."

"He was different, all right," Joseph muttered, thinking back to the flamboyant banker. "I'm not sure that was a good thing."

"I thought... I thought Nicolas was different," Philip went on as if Joseph had not spoken. "He seemed to want me exactly as I was. He wasn't any more polished than I was, never harping at me to clean up after a day in the forge or anything like that. He seemed like someone I could trust, someone I could look up to. Someone who would be honest with me. I should have known he didn't feel the same way when he insisted on pretending in public that we just worked together. He made it sound so reasonable, though, for my protection as much as his, given the mood of the town and the crew."

"The town's properly horrified," Matthew interrupted, surprised at Philip's sudden loquaciousness but willing to listen to whatever confidences his friend chose to share, "but on your behalf, not because of you. You should have heard the tirade Widow Taylor went on when she found out about the attempt on your life."

Philip mustered a smile at the thought of the spirited woman who had first taken him in when he arrived on the island. "Widow Taylor is more than a little biased in my favor," he pointed out dully.

"That may be, but by the time she was done, everyone in the mercantile was nodding and agreeing with her," William amended, wanting to encourage Philip to keep talking. It hurt to listen to the blacksmith's pain, but talking about it was definitely preferable to keeping it all bottled up inside.

"It doesn't matter," Philip sighed, giving in to the depression that dragged at him, body, mind and soul. "Nicolas doesn't love me. I was just a convenient body to fuck when he needed release." His eyes filled with pain, he looked from one friend to another. "I might have even been satisfied with that if he'd been honest with me instead of making me think I meant something to him."

The three men looked at each other in helpless silence, not sure how to respond to such a statement. They had come planning to cajole Philip out of whatever black mood had taken him, but that was clearly beyond their power. They remained where they were, though, hoping their presence would somehow be a balm to their friend's clearly battered soul.

PHILIP looked up when he heard another knock at the door, but he did not move from his seat. "It's open," he mumbled, not even caring any longer who it was. At this point, he would have even welcomed the murderer if it meant an end to the pain he could not shake from his chest.

"I know you're upset, but that's no reason to be stupid," Shawn harangued as he walked into the room. "The killer struck again, a barkeep from Eden who was apparently good friends with Leonard. The man, whoever he is, is losing it, Philip. There isn't even any evidence that Leonard and Goddard were lovers, just friends. They spent their evenings together sometimes, playing poker or just drinking. Leonard sat at the bar, talking to Goddard when he wasn't working. But there was nothing overtly sexual about any of it. That doesn't seem to have mattered to the killer, though. Given the way he's been acting, if he can't get to you, he'll seek some other target." When even the news of another murder failed to rouse the blacksmith from his despondency, Shawn's voice sharpened. "He could decide that William or Matthew or Joseph are more than just your friends. He could decide to go after Wells."

Philip's head jerked up at the overseer's name. "No," he whispered. "He can't."

"He can, if we don't stop him."

Philip's face hardened when he heard the calculation in Shawn's voice. "You have a plan."

Shawn nodded. "We know he wants you. So why not give him what he wants?"

Philip frowned. "What?"

"He hasn't tried to get back into your house, but you working alone in the forge would surely be a temptation he wouldn't be able to resist," Shawn explained. "He doesn't need to know that I'm hiding inside, waiting for him."

"So what, we bruit it around town that I'm back at home and working again?" Philip asked.

"It should be easy enough to get the gossips to take notice," Shawn pointed out. "I don't think they've lost interest in you since your fight with Reed."

Philip shrugged. "Let them talk. I don't even care anymore."

"But you'll help?" Shawn verified.

Philip nodded again.

"Good. I'll talk around town today and be here in the morning, but for God's sake, lock the door behind me. The plan won't do us any good if he gets to you tonight."

Only the thought of his friends at the mercy of the madman roused him from his stupor enough to lock the door, but while he had no care for himself, he did want to live long enough to help Shawn stop the killer.

Returning to his seat again, he let his thoughts spiral downward once more. How could he have misjudged Nicolas so completely? He had not known the older man long, but he had thought he knew him well. The overseer was firm but kind. Philip had rarely even heard him raise his voice, yet the words that had poured from his lips, the filth he had covered Philip with, had made a lie of every tender touch, every gentle kiss. His heart screamed at him to believe the silent promises their bodies had made, but his mind could not dismiss the cruel words. And so he stayed where he was, torn between his heart and mind, unable to do anything other than sit there and give in to the despair that wracked him. His shoulders sagged as he lost his hold on optimism. No matter what he thought had passed between them in silence as their bodies joined, he could not find any way to reconcile the overseer's casual dismissal. A sob tore from his throat and he buried his face in his hands, defeated.

ANOTHER one gone, another one who begged and pleaded and protested his innocence. The sheriff thinks he's making progress, but he has no proof, just empty suspicions. The blacksmith is out of my reach for the moment, having disappeared from the construction site. I suspect he has returned home, but I cannot reach him at the moment. The sheriff is watching the homestead too closely. His vigilance will falter eventually, though. And when it does, I will be ready. In the meantime, there are others for me to punish.

DOOR locked at Shawn's behest, Philip still sat in the same slumped pose an hour later when pounding at his door startled him. He glared at the interruption and returned to staring at his hands. Shawn would not have to work hard to spread the news that he was back at his cabin – half the island seemed to know he was here already.

"Philip! Let me in!"

Philip's heart leapt when he heard Nicolas's voice, but he did not move. "Why?" he demanded, loudly enough the overseer could hear him through the door. "So you can heap more abuse on my head?"

"So I can shake some sense into you."

Growing angry again, Philip rose from his seat, throwing the door open and glaring at Nicolas there in the doorway. His eyes drank in the sight that sent his pulse racing, the familiar, angular face that had haunted his dreams in his few minutes of fitful sleep, the strong, muscular body that had commanded his for such a short time. His breath caught in his throat as he forcibly kept his hands at his side when all he wanted to do was throw himself in the other man's arms and beg him to deny all the things he had said before. "Why the hell do you care what happens to me? You sent me away, not the other way around."

"I sent you to safety," Nicolas retorted, "not to do some stupid half-assed stunt like deliberately setting yourself up as bait for a madman."

Philip looked gaunt, Nicolas realized with a lurch to his stomach. He looked… as bad as Nicolas felt, his eyes heavy and underlined with dark circles, his face unshaven, his shoulders slumped in a defeat Nicolas had never seen. His heart broke again in his chest as he realized how badly he had hurt this beautiful man, the man his heart wanted only to love.

"I'm an adult," Philip reminded him belligerently, insulted that the overseer would even try to make such decisions for him. "I don't need your permission. And I say again, what the hell do you care?"

"I love you, you idiot!" Nicolas shouted, mere inches from Philip's face. He had suffered the tortures of the damned over the past week, unable to sleep at night because he had already grown used to Philip's presence, short-tempered with the men because he was tired from tossing alone in his empty bed and because he could not stop thinking about the look on Philip's face as he drove him away.

He had almost relented when the sheriff told him Philip had refused to leave the island, but he had stayed away. He wanted Philip to go somewhere safe, but he did not know what else he could do to push the blacksmith to leave. Already, uttering the words once had been almost enough to break him. Telling those cruel lies again, when all he wanted was to pull the younger man in his arms and kiss him, hold him, love him, would have been impossible.

He had considered apologizing as well, begging Philip to come back – to the site and to his bed – but that would surely have drawn the murderer's attention even more, a perceived lover's assignation even if Philip denied him. Either way, broken heart or increased threat, it was not a risk Nicolas had been willing to take. Until now. Until the sheriff came to him and asked for his help in protecting the blacksmith one more time.

"Love me?" Philip challenged, remembering all too clearly the cruel words his lover – ex-lover – had spoken. "If you treat everyone you love the way you treated me, I'd hate to see the way you treat people you hate."

Nicolas's heart clenched at the painfully true accusation. "Let me explain, Philip. Please."

"Philip," Shawn said from behind the overseer. "Let's go inside so you can talk."

The sight of Shawn stepping out from behind the man who had so betrayed him, so insulted him, was the final straw for Philip. It had been bad enough when Nicolas hurt him. To have Shawn now side with the overseer was more than he could bear.

"*Et tu, Brute?*" Philip asked, turning his back on both men and walking back to his place at the kitchen table, hands clasped in front of him on the worn wood, head bowed in defeat and despair.

Shawn's face showed his confusion, but Nicolas caught the reference. "No, Philip," he insisted, taking the seat next to the blacksmith and closing his hand around the clasped fists. "Neither one of us has betrayed you, despite what you think. I should never have said those things. Every one of them was a lie, intended to make you leave me and go somewhere safe. I thought you were refusing to leave because of me and I couldn't bear the thought of anything happening to you, not if I could protect you. I shouldn't have said what I did. I should have talked to you rationally, tried to persuade you to go to safety instead of trying to drive you away. I'm sorry."

"Did you know about this?" Philip asked Shawn softly, looking at his friend but pointedly avoiding Nicolas's gaze.

Shawn shook his head. "I wondered, but I wasn't sure, but if we're going to risk your life to catch this bastard, I want all the help I can get to keep you safe. I figured Wells here was my best bet, if I was right about him. And if I was wrong, at least I would have known for sure and could have kicked your ass for wasting away over a man who wasn't worth your time and energy."

"Wasting away?" Nicolas repeated sharply, his eyes returning again to Philip's disheveled form. "What do you mean?"

"When was the last time you ate?" Shawn challenged Philip. "Or slept?"

Philip looked away, not wanting to admit to his lovelorn behavior.

"Philip?" Nicolas prompted, pulling the blacksmith's hands toward him, angling his head to try to meet his lover's eyes.

"I don't know," the young man answered finally. "I think I ate the day I came home. Maybe I slept yesterday. I can't remember because it didn't matter."

Nicolas's eyes closed against the pain into those words. Looking up at the sheriff after a moment, he said, "Why don't you go spread the rumors about Philip being home and alone? I'll stay with him tonight and take care of him, and we can bait our trap in the morning."

Shawn rose, his hand settling on Philip's shoulder. "Will you be all right if I leave you two here?"

Philip nodded slowly, not trusting himself to speak. So much had been revealed in the past few minutes that he had trouble fathoming it all. Could he have been so completely wrong? Could he have misjudged the situation so comprehensively?

Shawn left them alone with a final admonishment to lock the door. Nicolas heard him, but did not acknowledge it. He simply kept holding Philip's hands, waiting patiently for some sign from his lover.

"You really love me?" the blacksmith said finally. His voice wavered with the contrasting emotions swirling through him: disbelief, shyness, wonder, hope. They assaulted him from every direction, his entire future riding on the answer to this one single question. He looked up desperately, needing to see the truth of any answer in Nicolas's eyes.

"I do, heaven help me," Nicolas admitted, unsure how his declaration, made in the heat of the moment, would be viewed now in the calm.

"Heaven help us both," Philip agreed, his heart pounding with the joy slowly coursing through his system. Nicolas loved him. Slowly, he unclenched his fists beneath Nicolas's hand, turning his hand over so their palms met. He lifted his other hand to cup his lover's cheek, feeling the stubble that had always been absent when he had touched the overseer before. "You've suffered as much this week as I have, haven't you?" he murmured.

"It hasn't been my best week ever," Nicolas agreed ruefully, leaning into Philip's longed-for touch. "But I deserved it. You didn't."

Philip frowned. "You were trying to keep me safe," he verified, his hand on Nicolas's tightening. "You didn't mean what you said."

"Not a word," Nicolas swore, lifting their clasped hands to his chest. "I would have done anything, given anything to protect you. I still would."

Philip traced Nicolas's lips with the tips of his fingers before pulling his lover to him for a tender kiss. Their mouths touched softly at first, testing the waters, the fear and pain of the past week holding them back. Then Philip's reserve shattered, his love for the other man stronger than any constraint, and he deepened the kiss, his tongue plundering Nicolas's mouth, much as he had the week before. Much as he had the week before, Nicolas consented, giving Philip control of the kiss, head tipping back as he offered himself to his lover, body and soul.

Gasping, Philip lifted his head. "Then stand at my side and protect me."

Chapter 20

"CAN we go to bed now?"

Nicolas set down the razor Philip had handed him a few minutes earlier and let his eyes rake over his lover's body. The blacksmith had shaved even before Nicolas did, trimming his beard back to its usual neat shape along the line of his jaw, and had then taken a rag to his body, washing away a week's worth of grime. Philip had wanted to go straight to bed after their declarations to celebrate their love, but the overseer had insisted on "taking care" of him first. So Philip had let the other man hover, eating the hearty stew Nicolas had prepared. When they had finished eating, Nicolas had insisted they both shave and clean up from their week of misery.

They danced around each other as Philip shaved and then washed, eyes heated and hungry as their ablutions led to a slow functional strip tease that tantalized their senses. Finally, Philip could stand it no longer. With a final sweep of the cloth over his chest, he moved to the doorway into his bedroom. "Come to bed with me."

Smiling at the echo of their first night together, Nicolas followed Philip into his bedroom. He glanced around the room quickly, his eyes taking in the carefully crafted furniture, the hand-woven rug on the floor, the Irish chain quilt on the bed.

Seeing where Nicolas's eyes landed, Philip smiled. "Mrs. Gibson made that for me when her husband took me on as an apprentice. I arrived on the island with the clothes on my back and my mother's necklace. When she died a few years ago, all Mr. Gibson's interest in smithing went, too. That's when he left the island. Their son kept their house in town but let me have all the equipment since he had no interest in the craft."

It struck Nicolas again how rooted Philip truly was on the island, despite the current situation, and he felt his hopes for a future plummet again. What could he offer his lover as inducement to leave his home? Lodgings in Boston, little more than a temporary home since he had moved around so much with his work? A life hidden from all those around them? He loved Philip and he believed the blacksmith loved him, but he still saw no way to extend their relationship beyond the summer even if they managed to catch the murderer. His hand traced the pattern on the quilt reverently. "I don't know what you see in an old man like me."

Philip's face broke into a grin as he considered all the ways to answer that. Folding the quilt and setting it aside, he urged Nicolas onto the bed. "Lie back and let me show you," he murmured, his lips already tracing the lines of his lover's face.

Nicolas gazed up into the dark eyes, love shining in their tender depths, and nodded slowly. He was not, had never been, completely comfortable giving up control, but this was not about control. This was about love. And for the man he loved, he would take this step deliberately rather than overcome by the heat of passion later. Taking a deep breath, he lay back, his hands falling to his sides as he gave himself over to Philip's care.

Philip stared down at the feast spread out before him, his heart pounding as he realized the magnitude of Nicolas's acceptance. The overseer had already shown himself to be a tender, but dominant lover. To have that same strong man now surrendering sent sparks of passion dancing down his spine. This would bear no resemblance to any of his past encounters with

James or anyone else, not when Philip knew Nicolas had the strength of body and will to change their dynamic at any moment.

No, this would be something completely new.

Philip skimmed his fingers down Nicolas's chest, enjoying the rasp of hair beneath the pads. James had been as smooth as a baby, much as Philip's own chest was, the lack of friction allowing them to brush skin to skin with nothing between them. While that had its advantages, Philip was quickly coming to appreciate the sensations evoked by Nicolas's hair against his smooth skin, the way it teased his nerves, heightening his awareness of every point of contact until his entire body tingled, even where they were not touching, purely from the anticipation of feeling such a touch in the near future.

Something completely titillating.

He did not speak, not sure he would be able to match the tribute Nicolas had offered their first night together. Instead, in silence penetrated only by the sighs and gasps of their mounting passion, he lavished attention on his lover's body, lingering, worshipping, using every trick in his repertoire to show the older man how loved and desired he was. He started with Nicolas's chest, kneading at the heavy muscle, plucking at the taut nipples, bending his head and tasting the traces of soap and sweat that the quick sponge bath had not totally erased, savoring the scent of the man.

Something completely voluptuous.

Nicolas tensed beneath the amorous onslaught, gasping as Philip's lips closed over one peaked nub, sucking and nibbling at it firmly. His fingers tangled in his lover's dark hair, letting his hands encourage the younger man since the firm caresses had robbed him of speech. Philip's lips trailed across his chest to capture the other pebbled peak, teasing it as well until Nicolas could hold himself still no longer. He shifted restlessly on the bed, seeking friction for his now-leaking cock.

Something completely lascivious.

Feeling Nicolas's movement beneath him, Philip scooted closer to his lover, letting the weight of his body press against the overseer. Nicolas turned immediately into him, his erection jabbing against Philip's thigh. Lifting his head, the blacksmith looked down at his lover with glittering eyes as he boldly encircled the straining flesh with his callused palm. Holding Nicolas's gaze, he stroked up the thick shaft, then back down again, deliberately baiting his lover, challenging him. When the overseer made no move to take control, Philip lowered his head so his lips met Nicolas's ear. "I'm going to make you scream before the night is over," he promised, his voice a husky, lustful purr. "I'm going to make you beg to come and when you do, it will be harder than you ever have before, driven over the edge by my cock buried inside your ass."

Something completely carnal.

Nicolas swallowed around the moan that escaped him. "Keep talking like that and I won't last long enough for you to keep your promises," he admitted.

Philip smiled lecherously. "I like the sound of that."

Something completely raw.

His hand never stilling, Philip's lips moved lower, coasting across the planes of Nicolas's belly, enjoying the way his lover's skin jumped and his breath hitched with each brush of his mustache over sensitive flesh. Nicolas's erection leaked steadily, easing the passage of skin against skin.

Something completely incendiary.

He swooped down and captured the tip between his lips, needing to taste, to prove to himself that they were there together again, as they were meant to be, as he had feared they would never be again.

Something completely genuine.

His hands did not leave Nicolas's body, but the tenor of his touch changed, gentled as he met Nicolas's eyes again and saw the trust that outshone even the desire. His throat tightening at the magnitude of the emotions that assailed him, he lapped at the bulbous head, licking away the fluid that had gathered there.

Something completely reverent.

Keeping one hand on his lover's thigh so Nicolas would know he was not pulling away, Philip sat up and reached for the bottle of oil he kept by the bed. He had not used it since James was killed, but now he was glad he had kept it.

Something completely tender.

His hands trembled as he uncorked the container, oil splashing on his hands and onto Nicolas's thighs.

"Easy," Nicolas soothed, a crooked smile on his face as he took in the nervousness on the younger man's face. "I want this as much as you do, but there isn't any rush."

Something completely profound.

Nicolas was right. There was no reason to rush. Sealing his lips over his lover's, he tangled their tongues together, letting them intimate what their bodies would soon be doing. His fingers slid between Nicolas's parted thighs, seeking the tight entrance, but his mind was more caught up with the promises they were making silently in this primal dance, the joining of their hearts and lives in a way nothing would be able to put asunder. He had taken lovers to his bed before, but this was the first time he had ever truly made love with anyone.

Something completely fulfilling.

Nicolas's hips lifted to meet Philip's hand, straining for the almost forgotten touch, the caress that he knew would drive him wild. His self-doubts had driven him to ask for reassurance.

He had gotten it.

Philip's every touch, every caress shouted his devotion, his love, and Nicolas basked in it, letting it warm his heart and soul, letting it fill the empty places inside him until he felt whole for the first time in his adult life. All that remained was to seal the promises they were making in the joining of their bodies. He had told Philip there was no hurry, but his own eagerness belied his words. He needed Philip inside him, needed to be one with the other man.

Something completely unifying.

Philip's fingers probed the tight portal, seeking ingress, seeking entrance. He had focused so completely on Nicolas, on lavishing love and pleasure on the other man, that he had ignored his own throbbing desire. His control was starting to wear thin, though. Fortunately, Nicolas's body opened to him with surprising ease, a testament to his lover's eagerness. With delicate precision, he stretched and prepared the snug channel until the overseer's begging gasps convinced him to join their bodies at last.

Something completely rapturous.

They moved together, bodies striving in rhythm to find the peak of pleasure that would leave them breathless and broken, reborn in each other's arms, each other's love. Frail flesh ceased to exist for them, their lovemaking a merging of souls even more than of bodies. Passion pushing them to greater and greater lengths, their lips met and clashed, broke apart on a gasp, and met again, forging another link in the chain that bound them, body, mind and heart. With a single cry, they shattered, their desire overtaking their senses.

Something completely obliterating.

Neither knew, later, how long they lay there, hovering between consciousness and darkness, panting for breath, bodies trembling with the force of their mutual release.

When they came to themselves once more, they found themselves loath to part, moving only enough to settle comfortably on the bed before twining around each other again. They spoke no words, none being necessary, their eyes meeting and holding for a long moment, then closing in sleep.

Something complete.

Chapter 21

SLIPPING from his hiding place, Nicolas strode up the road to Philip's house as if he were coming from town. As he had done every night for the last week, he feigned arriving just as the blacksmith was finishing his work. He had no idea if the murderer was watching, but he hoped with this ruse to at least keep anyone from finding out their plan. Shawn was still hiding in the bushes and would stay there until after he and Philip were safely inside before returning to town. If the murderer was watching the house, Nicolas knew he had become a target as well, but he almost welcomed it. He would gladly go head to head with the other man, whoever he was, if it would keep Philip safe.

He called a greeting to Philip as he arrived at the forge, as if he had not watched his lover's every move for the entire day.

Turning, his smile radiant at seeing Nicolas rather than simply being aware of the other man's presence in the bushes, Philip returned the greeting. They chatted for a few minutes as the blacksmith finished ordering his forge, leaving everything in readiness for the next day's work. The urge to touch, to kiss, worked in them both, but they kept a respectable distance, aware that Shawn would not leave until they were safely inside the cabin.

The sheriff had heard their declarations a week ago and surely knew how they spent their nights, but they had enough respect for his sensibilities not to make him watch them.   Side by side, they walked into the cabin, the door shutting behind them for the night.

THEY think they can fool me, the blacksmith and the overseer. They think because they never touch outside that they are safe from my eyes. They should think again.

For a week now, he has come to this filthy den of iniquity, just as the sun begins to set and the blacksmith finishes his tasks for the day.   They talk and act like good friends while they are outside. Then they go inside. They think they can fool me, but I know what they're doing once the door is shut. I have seen their shadows through the windows, seen them in their obscene embrace.

Their corruption cannot be allowed to spread.   I had wondered if Reed was the source of this canker on our island, outlander that he was, especially since he further revealed his immorality by taking more than one lover, but I begin to doubt that now.   In all the years he has been coming here, the overseer showed no sign of this affliction, yet after only a few weeks in Hall's company, he has succumbed to the blacksmith's sick lure.

I have watched long enough. I do not need the spectacle of their silhouettes entwined to know what they are hiding. It will be the same tonight as it has been every night since I started watching. They will embrace as soon as they get inside, beginning to strip away their clothes to reveal their unnatural desires. Their lips will meet in twisted passion, their hands moving over each other's bodies.   Then they disappear from my sight, but I know what perversions they undertake. I do not need – nor want – to see it.

Tomorrow.   Tomorrow I will finish what I have begun. During the day, when the blacksmith works alone, I will take him and finish him off. Then, in the evening, when the overseer comes for his aberrant pleasures, I will take him as well.

I have never done the Lord's work this way twice in one day. Always before, I had to wait days to chastise my next victim. Not tomorrow, though.   If I wait, the overseer will change his habits and I will lose the chance. No one will know Hall is missing until Wells arrives to fornicate with him in defiance of the Lord's natural order. If I let him raise a hue and cry, the outlander could well leave, spreading this pestilence wherever he calls home. My primary duty is to protect the island, yet I would be remiss in letting him escape punishment, not when I know without a doubt that he is as perverted as the rest.

I will rest tonight and pray that the Lord strengthen me for my dual task tomorrow. He has given me the strength each time before to resist their sickness, to prove myself above their temptation. He will give me the strength once again. Then, when morning comes, I will wait for the opportune moment and seize my prey, showing him the error of his ways. And when I am done with the overseer, I will leave them together as an additional warning that deviants will not be tolerated on my island.

SHAWN tensed when he heard hoof beats on the road leading to the forge. Philip often had customers arrive in the morning before the locals started work. Occasionally, someone besides Nicolas would come in the evening, but the days were usually undisturbed. His hand fell to his gun as he waited to see who approached.

The noise drew Philip's attention as well, as he paused between hammer strokes to reheat the ingot between his tongs. Casually setting the metal in the coals to heat, he turned to greet his visitor. Every muscle in his body went on alert when he saw Martin Thomas dismount in his yard, revolver riding low at his hip. His own gun was conspicuously absent from the forge, everything arranged to give the murderer no reason to hesitate should he take the bait. Philip did not know whether he now faced merely a childhood adversary or the madman who had killed three times already, but either way, he remained on his guard.

"All alone?" Thomas asked as he swung down to the ground.

"I don't need guard dogs," Philip retorted, resisting the urge to pick his hammer back up for protection. He had to let this play out however it would and trust that Nicolas and Shawn would protect him. "That's more your style."

"And hiding behind words is yours," Thomas challenged, walking into the forge.

In the woods, Nicolas tensed, seeing the tall man advance on Philip. He had not been sure, when he had seen the killer before, if it was Thomas, though he knew it could have been. Now, seeing the way the other man moved, he knew. Every fiber of his being urged him to break cover now, to defend his love from the murderer, but he knew he had to wait, to allow Philip to draw the other man out or for the other man to make a move that would be incontrovertible proof of his guilt. Otherwise, they would give away their hand for nothing.

Turning away to check the heating metal, Philip demanded, "What do you want, Martin? If you want something, tell me what it is. Otherwise, get the hell out so I can get my work done."

"Oh, I want something all right," Thomas replied, grabbing Philip's arm and spinning him around. He pushed hard, forcing Philip to his knees. "I want some of what Reed got, some of what you're giving the overseer." Grabbing the blacksmith's head, he ground the younger man's face against his crotch. "Open up, whore. Convince me you're worth leaving alive."

Philip pulled his head back, jerking his head out of Thomas's hands and scrambling backward. "You killed them, didn't you?" he asked, getting to his feet and reaching for one of his tools to defend himself. "You killed James and Jason."

"And Goddard," Thomas boasted. "They were worthless sluts, perverted freaks of nature who didn't deserve to live."

"You're the freak," Philip retorted, circling Thomas at a distance, trying to get out of the forge and into the open yard so Nicolas or Shawn would have a clear shot at the taller man. "Why did you do it? What gave you the right to decide if they should live or die?"

"They were – you are abominations!" Thomas roared. "You defile the Lord's pure and holy love with your unnatural desires, and He will wreak justice upon your heads for it!"

"That may be," Philip replied, backing into the yard finally, "but the Lord also said, 'Thou shalt not kill.' I will not be the only one facing His justice on the last day." He swung the heavy hammer toward Thomas's stomach, making him jump back. Philip turned and ran, but Thomas lunged after him, catching him around the waist and bearing him to the ground.

"You'll beg and plead just like they did," Thomas ground out, his body pinning Philip to the dirt. He pulled the gun from his belt and pressed it hard against Philip's temple. "And I'll show you just as much mercy as I showed them, as soon as I'm done with your ass. Will you sing as sweetly before I kill you? Reed certainly seemed to like being roughed up."

"And you call us sick," Philip protested, his struggles dying as he felt the muzzle of the gun against his head. "You're no different than we are."

"Oh, but I am," Thomas drawled, sure now that he had the upper hand. "Each time, I prove that I have the strength to resist your perversions. They tried to tempt me, to bargain with me, promising me whatever I wanted in exchange for their lives. I let them give it to me, just to prove that it could not sway me from my mission. And then, when they were done, I killed them."

"That's enough!"

Unable to watch any longer, Nicolas stepped from his hiding place, gun cocked and aimed at the men on the ground. "Get up and let him go."

Cursing under his breath, Shawn, too, moved from the shadows. "It's over, Thomas," he called, his own gun trained on the killer as well. "We all heard you admit to the murder of three men. You're under arrest."

Thomas's maniacal laughter rang across the clearing as he rose to his feet, pulling Philip with him, keeping the blacksmith firmly between himself and the other men. "You won't take the chance at shooting me," he pointed out, "because you can't be sure I won't kill him first, and the little freak is too precious to you to risk it. Let's go."

Philip looked at Nicolas with pleading eyes. If he had to die, he preferred to do so with a bullet in his head rather than raped and strangled like the others had been. He hoped his lover understood, but Nicolas made no move to fire as Thomas forced him across the yard toward his horse.

Helplessly, Nicolas and Shawn watched the two men's progress, neither sure enough of his shot to take out Thomas without either killing Philip themselves or giving Thomas the chance. Yet if Thomas succeeded in getting away on horseback, they would lose Philip for sure, both of them having arrived on foot so there would be nothing to give them away to the murderer.

"Don't do this, Martin!" Shawn called. "Even if you manage to get away with this, we know it was you. I'll still come after you and when I do, you'll hang for what you've done. This is pointless."

"No, it isn't," Thomas insisted. "There will be one less sodomite on the island, and that will make everything, even my death, worthwhile."

Reaching his horse, he forced Philip to mount.

As soon as his lover straddled the horse, Nicolas took a chance, firing into the air, drawing Thomas's attention firmly his way and startling the animal into motion. He knew it was a risk, but he had seen Philip ride. His lover had far more chance of living on a runaway horse than he did at the hands of a madman.

As quickly as he could, he cocked the gun again, shooting at Thomas as soon as Philip was clear. The killer jerked backward with the force of the bullet, only to fall sideways as another slug slammed into him.

"This isn't over," Thomas coughed as blood filled his lungs.

Shawn and Nicolas approached cautiously, guns still trained on the downed man. "It is for you," Shawn insisted.

Whatever Thomas might have said was lost in his death rattle as reddish spittle covered his lips and his breathing ground to a halt. "Good riddance," Shawn spat.

The whinnying of a horse drew their attention as Philip guided his mount back into the yard. "Is he dead?"

Shawn nodded in confirmation.

"Good. Now get him the hell off my property," the blacksmith demanded.

"If you'll give me back his horse, I'll do so gladly," Shawn retorted, but with no heat in his words. "I'm happy you're safe," he added, his face softening as he looked up and met Philip's eyes. "You handled yourself well."

Philip could not stop the swell of pride at Shawn's words. He swung down from the horse, tossing the reins to the sheriff as he walked to Nicolas's side.

The overseer was deaf and blind to anything other than the sight of his lover returned to him safely. Heedless of their audience, he pulled Philip into his arms, kissing him fervently, his hands flying over the blacksmith's body to check for injuries.

Beside them, Shawn coughed discreetly. "I'll just take this offal and leave then, shall I?"

Neither man looked up.

Shaking his head, he nudged them in the direction of the cabin before turning his attention to the corpse in front of him. Four dead, he mused as he hefted the body onto the back of the skittish horse. At least it was finished, though, and peace could return to his island once more. Glancing back as he started down the road to town, he could not stop the smile that crossed his face as he watched the door close behind the other two men. He did not claim to understand their desire for each other, but he could not deny its strength. He only hoped it would be strong enough to weather whatever else came their way. Thomas was gone, but Shawn knew the dead man was not the only one to hold the beliefs that had driven him to kill. Their life together would never be easy, even without the shadow of murder hanging over them.

INSIDE the cabin, Nicolas and Philip had no such concerns. Adrenaline had focused their minds on one thing alone: release. Nicolas's heart pounded in his chest as linsgering fear for Philip's safety warred with his revulsion at the way Thomas had treated his lover. His hands were rough as they tore at the younger man's clothes, needing Philip naked and writhing beneath him immediately, needing to prove they had weathered together the challenges of the past two weeks and the past hour, needing to prove the strength of their love.

Philip gasped as Nicolas took charge, his heart and loins thrilling as they always did when faced with the dominant side of his lover. He pulled his shirt over his head, uncaring for the buttons down the front, needing to offer himself the way Nicolas needed to take. With any other man, he would have been fighting for control, but with Nicolas, he seemed made to give. Bare to the waist, his head fell back, offering his neck to his lover. Nicolas's lips swooped down immediately, latching onto the sensitive skin just behind his ear, sucking hard enough to mark him.

Philip cried out, his hips arching forward to pulse demandingly against the overseer's, the unexpected mixture of pain and pleasure weakening his knees, leaving him aching for more.

The sound drew Nicolas up short. He raised his head and looked down at Philip's face, features contorted with pain or pleasure, he could not tell. Panting, he struggled for control of his body and his emotions. His hands clutched at Philip's biceps, whitening the skin around his fists. Already, a livid mark stained the blacksmith's neck. Horrified that he could be hurting his lover, he took a step back.

Of all the possible reactions Philip might have predicted, he would never have expected Nicolas to pull away. Opening his eyes, he met his lover's troubled gaze. "Nicolas?"

Even as the overseer started to shake his head, Philip closed the distance between them. He could see the sudden unease on Nicolas's face and guessed at what caused it. If he was right, it was easy enough to set his lover straight. If he was wrong, then they could discuss the real problem, whatever it was. "You're not him," he insisted. "Nothing you could do to me could ever resemble what he would have done. Take me to bed and prove we're still alive. Help me prove he didn't win."

Nicolas's head still argued with his body as Philip drew them toward the bedroom, pulling the overseer's shirt free from his trousers, hands sliding beneath it to coast over sweat-drenched skin. Nicolas's reluctance faded as his passion soared again, Philip's touch a lure he could not resist. Even so, his earlier fears kept his touch lighter than it had been as his fingers ghosted over his lover's back.

"I'm not fragile, Nicolas," Philip reminded the overseer, stripping the shirt away from Nicolas's torso, leaving them both bare to the waist. "You're not going to break me." His hands slid up the older man's chest, kneading at the strong muscles, tweaking the rosy disks.

"I don't want him to taint what we're doing," Nicolas protested, even as he arched into the caress. "If I can't love you the way you deserve..." He never got the chance to finish his sentence. Philip stopped the words with his mouth, bringing their lips together in a passionate clash of teeth and tongues.

As he had once before, Nicolas gave in to the blacksmith's unleashed power. Immediately, he felt the hatred and revulsion he had felt toward Thomas begin to fade in the face of the love he felt for Philip. Consciously, he relaxed into his lover's embrace, ceding all control to the other man.

Feeling Nicolas's resistance end, Philip lifted his head. "A few love bites, a bit of rough sex aren't going to hurt me," he reiterated. Flushing a little, his voice trembling with suppressed desire and lingering fear, he admitted, "Right now, honestly, they're what I need. *You're* what I need. Hard and fast and now."

Turning so they fell backward on to the bed, Philip fully on top of him, Nicolas cupped his lover's buttocks, grinding their bodies together. Their lips clashed as the demands of their bodies made themselves known. Needing to feel his lover's skin beneath his hands again, Nicolas worked his fingers under Philip's waistband. Immediately, Philip reared up on his knees, ripping at the buttons on his trousers and pushing them out of the way.

Nicolas's hands slid possessively over the smooth skin and hard muscle, drawing Philip back down to him, lips seeking contact again. Philip's lips were right there, seeking his as well, lifting the passion between them to a fever pitch. The blacksmith's hips moved demandingly against his cloth-covered erection, reminding the blond he had still not fully undressed. Breaking the kiss, he gasped, "Get these off of me."

"With pleasure," Philip growled, his voice husky with unsated desire. Kneeling up again, he stripped away the fabric of Nicolas's trousers. His mouth watered at the sight of his lover's fully erect cock bouncing against his belly, but as tempting as it was, he did not have the patience to love the older man that way. Not tonight.

Aligning their bodies again, Philip gasped as their cocks brushed. Nicolas immediately slid a hand between them, circling both lengths, stroking them in concert.

"Shit," Philip muttered. "You'll make me come too soon."

"Then I'd just have to get you worked up again," Nicolas taunted huskily.

"Or you can stop teasing me," Philip retorted, nipping at Nicolas's jaw. "Come on, lover, fuck me like you mean it. Let me feel your strength within me, around me, protecting me."

Worded any other way, Nicolas might have hesitated again, might have considered trying to put Philip in charge, but having heard the slight tremor in his lover's voice, he put such thoughts aside. Philip had not let any fear show when Thomas had attacked him, had dragged him away, had held a gun to his head. Realizing that his veneer of control was fading, the overseer gave his lover what he had requested, rolling them so that Philip lay on his back. Reaching for the oil they kept now by the bed, he coated his fingers thoroughly.

Letting go of everything else except the love and lust he felt for the man above him, Philip raised his knees, planting his feet firmly on the bed as he raised his hips in invitation. "Hard and fast and now," he repeated.

Taking Philip at his word, Nicolas prepared him quickly, only making sure his lover's entrance and passage were slick before replacing his fingers with the head of his cock. "Tell me if it's too much."

Grabbing Nicolas's hips and using that leverage to drive the hard shaft deeper into his tight channel, Philip demanded, "Stop coddling and fuck me already."

The clinging heat clasping his cock overcame any lingering reservations Nicolas might have had. His hips snapped forward, burying himself completely in his lover's responsive flesh. Philip's groan might have worried him had not the blacksmith clung to him so desperately, kissed him so passionately.

Striving frantically for release, they moved in perfect concert, their bodies in tune. Far sooner than they would have liked, their climaxes drew them near to the precipice. Together, they flew, the moment of communion strong enough to rock the foundations of their world, leaving them clinging to one another, adrift on a changing landscape of needs and emotions as the realization that they were free of Thomas's threat sank in finally.

Where that would lead them, what they would do with this newfound liberty remained to be seen, but in that moment of perfect unity, all things seemed easily within their grasp.

Chapter 22

"SHERIFF?"

The widow's soft voice pulled Shawn from his bleak thoughts. He had returned home over an hour ago, exhausted from the tension of the day and the furor caused by Thomas's death and all that had been revealed in its explaining. He had wanted nothing more than to retreat to the boarding house and curl into the widow's embrace, letting her touch, her affection, ease the strain of the day, of the last months. That was not an option for him, though, and never would be now. Instead, he had retreated to the stone bench in the back of the garden he had helped the widow tend since he had first moved into the boarding house. He would miss that when he left, almost as much as he would miss her. "They say you caught the killer."

He looked up into her gentle brown eyes, the shadows from the overhanging trees making her expression hard to read, and knew that in saving his friend, he had surely lost any hope of winning this woman's heart. "I killed him," he said bluntly, wanting to end the doubt as quickly as possible, wanting to know exactly what his sentence would be.

She flinched, exactly as he had expected. Sighing, he looked down again. "The caretaker's cabin at Cleftstone is empty," he added dully, accepting his banishment as fact. He could not expect the tender-hearted widow to feel anything but disgust for a killer. "I'll stay there until I can find other, more permanent lodgings."

Widow Taylor frowned. She had watched the sheriff for most of the past hour, working up her courage to come and speak to him, to offer what comfort she could. This was not the reception she had come to expect from him. "What on earth are you talking about?"

"I killed a man today," he repeated. "You can't possibly want me to stay here."

"You didn't kill a man," the widow declared, hands planted firmly on her hips, beginning to understand. "You put down a rabid dog, one who had already killed three men and had tried to kill another. Tell me this, sheriff," she went on, refusing to let him succumb to his self-pity. "Did you try to arrest him before you killed him?"

"Of course," Shawn protested. "What kind of man do you think I am?"

A kind, generous, loving one, she thought, remembering all the instances of his kindness to her, to Philip, to anyone in need. "An honorable one," she said aloud, not quite ready to speak of her feelings. She would wait until he was in a better frame of mind. She just hoped she could cajole him into it quickly. "So you tried to arrest him, but he resisted."

"He tried to flee, using Philip as a shield. It was kill him or – " he shuddered even to think of that moment when Philip's fate hung in the balance, when one wrong move could have ended the blacksmith's life " – let him kill the boy."

He was such a protector, she knew, one of the many traits she admired about him. Sitting down next to him on the bench, she took his hand boldly in hers. "That man has haunted you for weeks, ever since Mr. Reed was killed," she began. "I've sat by and watched you suffer each time you found another body. I watched your resolve harden with each passing day, your determination to stop him, to keep him from hurting Philip, keeping you up at night as you tried to figure out who he was."

She had kept vigil with him, though he had not realized it, sitting in her darkened bedroom, listening to him pace the halls. She had seen the dark circles under his eyes as the days went by with no end in sight. More than once, she had started to go to him, to offer to share the dark hours at his side rather than in spirit alone, but modesty and the habit of years had held her back. Seeing him come in from town, though, defeat written on his face and in his posture, she would not leave him to suffer alone anymore. Perhaps he did not share her feelings, did not return her interest, but at least he would know he was not alone.

"I couldn't let him win," Shawn insisted. "I only wish I could have caught him sooner. Even if I couldn't have stopped Reed's death, I should have been able to prevent Leonard's and Goddard's. They died because I wasn't fast enough or smart enough to stop him sooner."

Widow Taylor tightened her grip on the sheriff's hand. "They died because he was a sick man." She hesitated. "That is why he killed them, isn't it?"

Shawn nodded. "You don't need to know how sick he was," he murmured, thinking of all he had seen, all Thomas had revealed at Philip's that afternoon.

"No, I don't," she agreed. "It's enough to know he's dead and the town is safe again, because he wouldn't have stopped. He would have kept going until Philip was dead and perhaps his friends as well, and then he might have moved on to others he considered immoral. There was no wrong in what you did today."

Shawn looked deeply into the velvety brown eyes, seeing a depth of compassion that eased his guilt. "Do you truly believe that?" he asked.

"You have always been a good man, a strong man, but today you're a hero, Shawn," she insisted.

Shawn's eyes widened as she called him by name rather than by his title. "Alicia," he murmured, reaching for her other hand, lifting them both to his lips. For ten years, he had watched her from afar, loved her in silence. It seemed the day for change, for revelations. "Alicia," he murmured again.

"About time," Alicia muttered, leaning forward. She drew her hands away from his lips, using them to steady his face as she kissed him, taking what she had wanted since long before her husband died. She had not admitted it to anyone, was not even sure she would admit it to Shawn in the years to come, but she had lain in her marriage bed, unloved and unloving, and dreamed of him. Now, finally, her chance had come and she had every intention of seizing the moment with both hands.

Shawn gasped in surprise at the tender onslaught, never having imagined Alicia's soft smile sheltered such passion. His own rose immediately in response, but he kept himself in check, not wanting to startle her or offend her sensibilities. He could not stop himself from returning the gentle kiss, though, tilting his head slightly to improve the angle. Her lips moved softly, encouragingly beneath his, inviting him to linger. "How long?" he murmured, skating his mouth across her ivory skin, over the elegant cheekbones, the smooth whorl of her ear.

"Too long," she replied breathlessly, sliding her hands from his face and over his broad shoulders. Her eyes had memorized every line of his body years ago, summoning them in her thoughts whenever her late husband insisted on his conjugal rights. Since his death, she had let thoughts of the sheriff warm her on even the coldest winter nights. Finally, she dared hope he, not thoughts of him, would be keeping her company through the night hours.

The idea that she might have been waiting for this moment, wanting it, for as long as he had released Shawn from the constraints that had held him back. He sealed their mouths together in a passionate kiss that spoke volumes of his pent-up longing, his lingering fear, even his dissipating guilt. Their arms went around one another, bringing her softness into contact with his steely strength.

The breeze that never completely died in the summer danced around them, pulling tendrils of her long hair loose from the chignon that bound it away from her face to brush against his stubble-roughened cheeks. His hands lifted to her nape, burrowing into the thick bundle, sending pins scattering as her hair tumbled down her back. He pulled back to look at her in the early evening light, the setting sun behind them casting her features in a golden glow. Her eyes sparkled in a way he had not seen since her father had arranged her marriage, her lips parted and glistening with the evidence of their kiss. With her hair unbound, she was once again the girl he had fallen in love with from a distance and pined for the entire time she was married to the good-for-nothing Taylor. He wanted to speak, to tell her how he felt, but words had never been his strong point, especially not with her. Instead, he leaned forward and kissed her again, his hands cradling her head gently, stroking her scalp tenderly.

The shackles that had held her back fell away with the pins in her hair, with the adoring look on the sheriff's face. She had always known she had such passion within her; she had simply never had the opportunity to experience it before, her clod of a husband inspiring nothing but disgust. Now that she had the chance within her grasp, she swore she would never let it, let him go. Breaking away with a gasp, cheeks flushed a delicate shade of rose from their kiss and from her own daring, Alicia smiled. Rising to her feet, she offered him her hand. "Come inside."

"YOU really need to make up your mind where we're going to play," Joseph teased as he and the others made themselves comfortable around Philip's table. It was close quarters with eight of them, but no worse than it had been the night they played in the caretaker's cabin at Cleftstone Manor. At least here, Philip had built the house with the idea of occasionally having guests. The caretaker's cabin was purely functional in design. "First it's your tent, then Nicolas's cabin, now back here. Where next?"

Philip's eyes met Nicolas's with a cheeky grin. "I think we'll be staying here for the foreseeable future," he replied. No one in the room imagined for a moment he was just speaking of poker.

The crew bosses and three townspeople smiled delightedly, beyond relieved at seeing an end to the tension between the other two men. Johnny, Carl, and Eric had been shocked at the transformation in their employer after Philip had left the construction site, the usually affable, reasonable man replaced by a short-tempered fury who had no patience with anything. With the murderer dispatched and harmony restored between the lovers, the overseer was back to his old self, often even more easy-going than before, a smile always sneaking around the corners of his lips.

Joseph, Matthew, and William had been even more concerned after they had visited Philip a few days before Thomas was killed. They had seen their friend in many, many moods over the time he had been on the island, but never had they seen him so desolate. If Shawn had not caught them in town and expressly forbade them from visiting – for their own safety, he had explained – they would have taken turns keeping watch, so greatly did they fear Philip would do something rash. To see him now, a transformed man, reassured them immensely. They had not even needed to discuss it. Anyone who could make Philip so obviously happy deserved their friendship and support.

Nicolas's lips formed a smile at Philip's comment, but the expression did not quite reach his eyes. He had tried once to explain to his lover the reasons he had to return south for the winter. To no avail. Philip seemed blithely determined to ignore that reality. For the moment, Nicolas had let it go. They had two months still before he would have to sail for home, two months in which to convince the blacksmith to go with him.

"Let's get this game started," he said roughly, hiding the emotions that wracked him at the thought of failure. He had known from the beginning that any relationship with Philip would be nothing more than a summer fling, yet he had allowed it to start anyway. He had no one but himself to blame for his current predicament.

Carl dealt the first hand, having let Eric examine the cards as always, and the game progressed quickly around the table, the conversation desultory as they all concentrated on the play of the hand.

"Have you ridden into town since Shawn killed Thomas?" William asked Philip after placing his bet and drawing new cards.

"No," Philip replied idly, keeping an eye on who kept and discarded what. "Why?"

William shrugged. "Just wondered what you'd heard. You know, since it came out why he killed those men."

Honestly, Philip did not care what they were saying. He would never be completely accepted in town again, a fact he was still trying to live with. Hearing it from William would only cement what he already suspected.

"What are they saying?" Nicolas asked in Philip's place, wondering if the town's reaction would give him an additional argument to persuade his lover to join him in Boston.

"That Martin Thomas was a twisted bastard who deserved what he got," Matthew inserted vehemently before William could reply. "You should have heard Mr. Waring when he got going. He lambasted Thomas and his narrow minded views for a good fifteen minutes when somebody suggested that Thomas might have had his reasons."

Philip tensed. "He had his reasons, all right," he spat, remembering his last conversation with the deceased killer, "and you really don't want to know how twisted he was."

Nicolas shuddered as the memory of those tense few minutes assailed him again. He had not admitted it to anyone, even to Philip, but he often awoke during the night trembling with terror, imagining the man beside him broken and bleeding, at the killer's mercy.

"But that's my point," William insisted. "He was twisted and the town agrees with that. Nobody's sorry he's gone, except maybe his three cronies, but given the mood of the rest of the town, I don't see them opening their mouths any time soon."

"And they never do anything but talk anyway," Matthew reminded everyone. "Without Thomas around to incite them to do anything at all, they're just blowhards."

"Mr. Waring was also very pointed in his reminder of what would happen to us all without a blacksmith," Joseph added. "Thomas is the villain in this story, Philip. Not you."

"Until the next time I do something to scandalize them," Philip replied wryly. "They're glad I survived, but will they still want me around when they remember why Thomas started all of this in the first place? Will they still want me around when they remember I'm not likely to settle down and take a wife?"

"When they realize Nicolas isn't sleeping at Cleftstone anymore, you mean?" Matthew asked bluntly. "I'm pretty sure that isn't a secret now, no matter how much you'd like it to be one. Nobody cares, Philip. They might have before, but they saw what that kind of intolerance leads to, and it's scared them enough to make them reconsider their prejudices."

"Lots of people've been reconsidering their prejudices this summer," Eric added softly, thinking of his own initial reaction to Philip. He had come to admire and accept the blacksmith on his own merits, but the real change in his perception had come in the realization that the overseer he so respected shared those predilections. To his surprise, it had changed nothing. Wells was still the man he had always known, only... more. Complete, maybe. The two men were discreet in public, but every once in a while, Eric would catch them looking at each other when they thought no one else was watching, and he saw on their faces the same emotion he was sure showed on his every time he thought of Rachel. "It's easy to condemn something on principle. It's a whole lot harder when it's real people, people you know and care about."

"So you're saying the islanders would just turn a blind eye to Philip living here openly with another man, a man who was clearly his lover," Nicolas pressed, feeling himself losing ground in his reasons for Philip to go with him.

"Maybe not completely," William allowed. "It's a lot for them to take in, for all of us to take in, but we're here, aren't we? We've figured out that he's the same man we've known for years. Everybody else is coming to that conclusion, too, just maybe not quite so quickly. But they will, given time."

"Either that or the horror of Thomas's bigotry will fade, and they'll go back to hating us for being different," Nicolas pointed out, finally letting himself admit to these men who had become his friends what he had not admitted to any but his past lovers.

"If they do, they're as big a fool as that idiot Hayden who we caught last week vandalizing the forge work," Eric replied vehemently.

Johnny and Carl shook their heads. "I still can't believe he thought we wouldn't catch him," Johnny mused. "After the first time, he should have known we'd be watching for another attempt."

Eric shrugged, having given up trying to understand the kind of intolerance that had led Thomas and Hayden to act. Turning back to the overseer, he finished, "Your life's your own to live as you please. I don't care what anybody says, you're still the best damn overseer in the business, at least in my experience."

"Amen to that," Carl and Johnny echoed immediately.

Nobody seemed to have a response to that, and the poker game resumed, the conversation returning to its usual pattern of jeers and taunts about how badly the other men played.

Chapter 23

"**THERE** was ice in the harbor this morning," Nicolas commented softly as they sat down to dinner.

They had completed Cleftstone Manor three weeks ago, the crew dispersing to their respective homes almost immediately. Even the crew bosses had only stayed long enough to assure themselves that Nicolas would be back the next summer, with another crew.

Nicolas had lingered, having no deadline for his return to Boston and every reason to want to stay as long as he could. He and Philip had avoided mention of the sword of Damocles hanging over their heads, living each day in isolation, pretending the summer would never end. The flurry of conversation at each of his stops in town that morning, though, discussing the rime that had coated the still waters of the harbor, had forced him to consider his return home.

"You could stay."

Nicolas flinched.   He did not want to have this conversation, had avoided it all summer, but it seemed they could put it off no longer. "I can't. My job's in Boston. You know that."

"So go to Boston as soon as the harbor thaws in the spring, get the new plans from Emerson, and come back. You know no ships sail north until at least one has made it south from here, so at the most you'll lose a couple of weeks. Surely that would be all right."

"You could come with me," Nicolas suggested.

"After all I went through not to have to leave?" Philip asked incredulously. "That would be letting him win!"

"No, it would be living your life on your terms," Nicolas countered. "Think about it, Philip. In Boston, nobody would know us. Nobody would think anything of us sharing lodgings. It wouldn't be like here where everybody stares at us all the time."

Philip was not convinced things would be all that different in Boston, but he did not argue the point. "This is my home," he reminded his lover. "I have a life here, a job. I'm needed here. What would I even do in Boston?"

"What do you do here in the winter?" Nicolas challenged.

"Fix everything that didn't make it through the summer," Philip retorted. "Replace any tools that can't be repaired. Forge work happens year-round and I'm the only smith in Bar Harbor. You're not just asking me to leave my home. You're asking me to abandon my responsibilities to my town, my friends!"

The sheriff had told him the same thing, Nicolas remembered, explaining when he first proposed to move Philip to the job site that the island could not survive without its blacksmith. "There isn't someone in Eden or Tremont, or even Southwest Harbor who could do the smith work for the winter?"

"That isn't the point," Philip insisted. "Look around you. Do you see this house? I built it with my own hands. Do you have some place as nice in Boston?"

Nicolas had to admit that he did not, living in a rented apartment during the winters and in the caretaker's cabins of the cottages he was building in the summers. "We could still stay here in the summers," he suggested. "Emerson already sent a telegraph saying he had a commission for another house."

"So you'd make this as temporary a dwelling as the one you have in Boston," Philip replied bitterly with a shake of his head. "I love you, Nicolas, but I can't do what you're asking. I can't just leave."

"So you'd turn this into just a summer fling?"

Philip pushed to his feet, slamming his hands on the table as he glared at his lover. "If either of us is making this a casual affair, it's you. I'm not the one leaving, the one walking away."

"No, you're just the one refusing to come with me when I asked."

"To be what?" Philip challenged. "Your kept man? I can't do it, Nicolas. I can't give up everything I have here to go to Boston with nothing to do but be your lover. I can't just live on your generosity with nothing to contribute but my body. Not even for you will I make myself a whore."

"It's not like that," Nicolas insisted. "It won't be like that."

"How?" Philip demanded. "How can it not be like that? You have a job, a life in Boston. I understand that, but I don't, and I don't see anybody local being willing to hire me for the winter, knowing I'll be leaving again in the spring. Which leaves me totally dependent on you for everything: my food, my lodging. Sorry, Nicolas, but that just isn't my style."

"The last thing I want is for you to be dependent on me," Nicolas retorted. "One of the things I love about you is your fierce independence. I'm not trying to turn you into some male version of a mistress. I want you as my partner."

"That implies some degree of equality," Philip pointed out, somewhat mollified by Nicolas's comment, "but there's no equality in what you're proposing."

They fell into silence, neither knowing what else to say.

"So what do we do?" Nicolas asked finally.

Philip slumped back into his chair. "Honestly, I don't know. I don't want this to end, but you say you can't stay and I know I can't leave." His head bowed in defeat, cradled in his hands. "I'll be here next summer if you come back."

Anger at the unfairness of the situation surged through Nicolas. Pushing back his chair, he moved to Philip's side, catching the blacksmith's hands and pulling him to his feet. "When," he swore, tipping Philip's chin up so their eyes met. "When I come back, and you damn well better be here. If you won't come with me, at least give me the consolation of knowing you'll be waiting for me when I come back."

Philip nodded, feeling suddenly like the mariners' wives who paced their widow's walks, watching for the ships to come in, hoping each was the one that would bring their husbands home from sea. He already hated the feeling and Nicolas had not even left yet. "If you won't stay with me, then I'll look for you in the spring."

Nicolas touched their foreheads together, his arms wrapping around Philip's waist to hold his lover tight. "There's a ship sailing at the end of the week. I spoke to the captain today and he has a cabin aboard for me. I'll leave for Boston on Saturday."

The dreadful finality of those words struck them both hard and their lips met desperately, the thought that they only had three more days and nights to spend together making their hands frantic as they pulled away the barriers that separated them.

Seeing Philip fighting with the buttons on his shirt, Nicolas paused, then caught his lover's hands. "Let me," he requested, drawing Philip toward the hearth.

Philip acquiesced, the weight of the moment settling over him. Three days. He had three days left with his lover, with the man he loved. He believed Nicolas loved him, believed Nicolas would do everything he could to come back to Bar Harbor in the spring, but the world was a vagarious place and anything could happen between now and then. These three days could well be the last he ever had with Nicolas and he intended to store up every precious memory he could. They might have to last a lifetime, for he knew he could never let another touch him.

Tenderly, Nicolas released the buttons on Philip's shirt, his knuckles stroking the smooth skin, worshipping each inch as it was revealed. The summer spent outdoors had darkened the olive skin of his upper body, adding to his allure in Nicolas's eyes. "Beautiful," he murmured, slipping the fabric from the blacksmith's shoulders.

Philip had given up trying to tell Nicolas that he was not beautiful, that the overseer was the beautiful one. It was an argument neither of them would ever win. Instead, he let Nicolas guide him down to the hand-woven rug, his own hands exploring again the now familiar planes of his lover's chest.

Kneeling next to Philip's recumbent form, studiously ignoring the fingers that would have incited his nerves to riot if he had given them leave, the blond lovingly traced every line of muscle, working his way from strong shoulders across the broad chest. He circled each nipple slowly, watching them pucker in anticipation, but he avoided them for the moment, determined not to be distracted by their temptation.

"Tease," Philip muttered.

"Only if I don't deliver in the end," Nicolas riposted.

Philip could not argue with that, especially not when he knew how well Nicolas could deliver on that promise. His lover seemed never to tire of touching him, a fact that excited the blacksmith immeasurably. Nicolas's obvious delight in Philip's pleasure only increased it, leaving him a trembling mass of incoherence in his lover's arms at the end of each bout of lovemaking.

Nicolas's fingers slid down Philip's abdomen following the dips and curves of his stomach, pausing to tangle in the short, fine hairs that arrowed down into his waistband. They did not delve beneath the fabric, though, instead working their way around the blacksmith's narrow waist and then back up his sides to his arms. "So strong. So responsive."

Only with you, Philip thought breathlessly as the questing fingers brushed his sides almost lightly enough to tickle. Then they moved on, down one brawny arm to the crook of his elbow, the inside of his wrist, his callused palm, his long fingers.

Nicolas lifted Philip's hand to his lips, not wanting any moment of separation between them now. As miserable as the thought made him, their parting in three days was inevitable. He refused to have it come a moment sooner.

Each finger received attention in turn, sucked into the hot cavern of Nicolas's mouth, licked from end to end, teeth scraping just enough to raise goose flesh on Philip's arms. When he had finished with the long digits, he kissed the hard palm, tongue teasing over the calluses that were a tribute to his lover's dedication. As much as it tore at him to know this was part of the reason Philip refused to go with him, Nicolas still admired the trait.

"Nicolas," Philip gasped, caught off guard by the tender onslaught.

Nicolas looked up and met Philip's eyes. "I have to store up enough memories to last through the winter," he explained hoarsely.

Philip's eyes shut against the pain. "Then don't go."

"Don't, Philip," Nicolas pleaded. "Don't make this harder than it already is."

Philip rolled to the side, curling around himself. "I can't do this," he said softly. He rose to his feet and moved to the window, staring out at the frost covered landscape.

Nicolas stood as well, coming to stand behind his lover, wrapping his arms around the blacksmith's waist. "It's not forever," he reminded Philip. "It'll just be a few months, and then I'll be back."

"For a few months, only to leave me again," Philip pointed out bitterly, his hand coming to rest on Nicolas's arms. "Is that really the way you want to live?"

"No," the overseer admitted, "but I don't see any other option. I can't stay and you won't leave. Unless you don't want me to come back."

Philip's grip tightened. "Don't say that. Don't even think it." He turned in his lover's arms, looking up into the smoky eyes. "I don't want you to leave. I don't want to only have six months at the most with you before you leave me again, but if the other alternative is living without you, then I'll find a way to endure. Just promise me you'll come back."

The despair in Philip's voice tore at Nicolas's soul. He crushed his lover to him, sealing their lips in a ferocious kiss. Philip responded with equal urgency, hands gripping desperately at Nicolas's back as they held tightly to one another.

They backed toward the bedroom of one accord, pushing at clothes until nothing separated them but their own flesh. Falling onto the bed in a tangle of limbs, they writhed together, needing that contact, needing to know that they were together still, even if only for a few more days. Nicolas's fingers swiped through the fluid leaking from Philip's cock, not even bothering to fumble with the bottle of oil on the table by the bed. Preparing his lover swiftly, he watched Philip's expression, not wanting to cause the blacksmith any pain. Only pleasure showed on the younger man's face, though, as the long fingers stretched his entrance. They had made love often enough that his body reacted instinctively, loosening of its own accord with barely any prompting from Nicolas's fingers. "Now," he urged, lifting his hips.

Nicolas did not hesitate, pressing deeply into his partner's body, wanting the joining as much as Philip clearly did. Life would tear them apart far too soon; he needed this affirmation of their love.

Philip cried out at the sense of completion that rocked through him as Nicolas thrust home, locking their bodies together, a last haven against the inevitable separation. The sound changed to a keening moan of protest when Nicolas began to withdraw. He knew it was not rational, that Nicolas had to pull back in order to thrust again, but the thought of even that much distance between them tore at him. He grabbed the overseer's buttocks, stopping the outward movement.

As if reading his mind, Nicolas thrust forward again, their loins meeting as he closed the gap that had grown between them, no more accepting of the separation than Philip. Instead, he circled his hips against his lover's, staying as deeply joined as possible, letting the tiny movements nudge their desires closer and closer to the breaking point.

Their orgasms, when they came, were long and slow and deep, rolling through them with all the power of the tides that would soon carry them apart. They clave to one another, not wanting the moment of unity to end. Nicolas buried his neck in Philip's shoulder, ignoring the stickiness between their bodies, the chill on his back. The thought of moving, of anything separating them right now was anathema to him.

Finally, though, his shaft softened and slipped free of Philip's body, eliciting a soft sob from both men. "Don't go."

NICOLAS'S feet felt as heavy as his heart as he walked through the chilly morning. Philip had refused to accompany him into town, declaring he had no interest in seeing the ship that would carry his lover away from him. For three days, Nicolas had wracked his mind for a solution to their impasse, but none had presented itself. And so he found himself alone as he made his way from the livery where he had returned his rented horse toward the harbor where the schooner awaited.

"Leaving us, Mr. Wells?"

Nicolas looked up at the sound of his name and mustered a smile for the shopkeeper. "In an hour or so, yes."

"And will you be back in the spring?" Mr. Waring asked.

"Emerson has another commission that will take at least one season to build," Nicolas replied.

"We'll look for you in the spring, then," the shopkeeper declared. "We've gotten used to having you on our island in the summers."

"I wasn't sure..." Nicolas began. "Under the circumstances..."

"Martin Thomas was a sick, narrow-minded man," Mr. Waring interrupted, voice and face hardening as he thought of the dead killer. "Don't judge the whole town by his prejudices."

"Thank you," Nicolas said softly.

"We'll look for you in the spring."

Nicolas smiled and walked on, passing in front of Parnell's office.

"You're really going to leave."

Nicolas looked up to the porch where the sheriff stood. "I don't have any choice."

"There's always a choice," Parnell retorted.

"He has one, too," Nicolas replied defensively.

"He does," Shawn agreed. "He just has far more to lose."

"Take care of him for me?" Nicolas asked softly.

Shawn harrumphed. "I'll pick up the pieces and try to hold him together through the winter, but if you don't come back in the spring, I'll hunt you down myself. He doesn't deserve to suffer this way."

"At least he has his friends to help him through the winter. I'll be alone."

"So will he," Shawn corrected. "Don't think for a moment that any of us can replace you." He turned and started back into his office. "Take your ship. I can't look at you anymore."

Nicolas felt the dismissal like a slap in the face. He knew Philip's friends were loyal to him, but it hurt that they saw only his pain and not Nicolas's. He was not sure how he had become the villain in this story. Yes, he was leaving, but he had no other choice. His job on the island and starting a new cottage in the spring meant spending the winter in Boston, in consultation with the architect, their suppliers, the clients themselves in some cases. Philip protested being dependent on Nicolas for his well-being in Boston, but the same would be true for Nicolas in the winter if he stayed in Bar Harbor.

Sighing, he left his portmanteau with the porter at the pier and walked up the gangplank to the deck of the schooner that would take him south, his satchel holding his sketchbook gathered tightly to his chest. His garments, his gear, could be replaced if anything happened to him, but he would take no chances with the precious sketches inside, all he was taking with him of the man who had stolen his heart.

"Welcome aboard, Mr. Wells," the first mate greeted him as he stepped on board. "Would you like to put your satchel in your cabin?"

"No," Nicolas replied, clutching it tightly. "I'll take it down after we've sailed."

The first mate nodded. "We've about fifteen minutes until the tides are right. You're welcome to stay on deck. Just mind the crew."

Nicolas leaned on the rail, desolation leaving him hollow as he stared blindly out over the town, the white-washed buildings glowing in the weak sun, the grass on the common glistening from the melting frost. The trees were bare now, the leaves scattered across the cobblestone streets blown here and there by the fitful wind. The sight called to him, beckoning him to stay, but duty called the hollow man home. Perhaps... perhaps this winter he could make arrangements...

He shook his head, locking away the pipe dream. Even if Emerson was amenable – and there was no guarantee he would be

– Nicolas was not convinced he could move to Bar Harbor permanently as Philip believed. The town had been suitably horrified at Thomas's murders to have left Philip alone for the rest of the summer, but that tolerance would certainly not last as time passed and the horror wore off. Then they would remember all their reasons for condemning Philip after his fight with Reed. No, as tempting as the idyllic town seemed from the shelter of the ship, it could not be home to Nicolas's dreams.

He heard the call to cast off ties and closed his eyes, unable to watch their departure as it took him away from the man he loved.

"Wait!"

Nicolas's eyes flew open to see Philip running across the green, a bag over his shoulder.

"Wait!" Nicolas echoed the call, turning to the crew. "Please, just wait a minute."

Two burly sailors grabbed hold of the last line still connected to the pier, tugging with all their strength to hold the ship against the tide. Nicolas rushed to their side to add his weight to theirs, his eyes glued on the figure that had reached the entrance of the pier. The rope burned as it slid through his ungloved hands, but he held on. A few seconds more… if they could just hold on a few seconds more, Philip would be aboard.

Philip ran down the pier, jumping the gap the gangplank had crossed, landing on the deck as the rope tore free from the sailors' hands, leaving their gloves shredded.

"Thank you!" Nicolas called over his shoulder as he ran to Philip's side.

"I couldn't do it," Philip gasped, heart pounding with his exertions. "I couldn't let you leave without me."

Nicolas fell to his knees next to his panting lover. "What about…?"

"There's a blacksmith in Eden, another in Southwest Harbor. They can get the town through the winter, but nothing would have stopped me," Philip interrupted. "Everything else is unimportant."

"Mr. Wells?" the captain asked, joining the two men.

Philip reached into his pocket and pulled out a sheaf of bills. "Fare for passage to Boston," he said.

"I don't have an extra cabin," the captain protested.

"He can share mine," Nicolas offered immediately.

The captain took the money. "Highly unusual," he observed, "but I suppose if Mr. Wells doesn't mind…"

"I insist," Nicolas assured, eyes meeting Philip's as he struggled to believe this was real. "In fact, it will be my pleasure."

Philip's smile broadened invitingly. "Let's go below."

Epilogue

LULLED by the gentle rocking of the ship, Philip woke slowly to the sensation of Nicolas nuzzling his neck, morning stubble rasping enticingly against his skin. His eyes fluttered open to the sight of his lover bathed in the pre-dawn light that filtered through the small portal in their cabin. The silence that enveloped them was marred only by the occasional shout of the crew on deck, assuring him that they had as much privacy as the ship could afford them.

"Morning, love," he mumbled, his voice hoarse from sleep.

"Morning," Nicolas replied, his lips moving lower to tease Philip's shoulder.

Philip stretched, trying to shake off the lingering effects of the night's slumber, wanting to be completely awake for whatever his lover had planned for them. "Last day on the boat," he commented as his movement rubbed his body against the other man's equally naked form.

Nicolas hummed in agreement. "Tonight we'll be home."

"No regrets?" Philip verified, though they had gone over this subject often enough that he was confident of the answer.

"None at all," Nicolas insisted, lapping gently at a cold-peaked nipple. The flesh warmed immediately but, to his delight, did not soften at all. "I had enough of nosy neighbors this winter to last a lifetime."

Philip gasped in surprised delight, his back arching into the caress. "I don't know that the people of Bar Harbor will be any less nosy," he felt obliged to point out, his fingers burrowing into Nicolas's hair to keep his head in place.

"Maybe not," Nicolas conceded, "but at least they're more than one thin wall away. I'll be glad not to have to worry about every moan and groan you make when we make love." To illustrate his point, he bit down gently on the pebbled skin in his mouth, smiling at Philip's sigh.

"My moans and groans?" Philip forced himself to say, pushing Nicolas onto his back and moving over him. "What about yours?"

"You're definitely louder than I am," Nicolas retorted playfully.

"Oh, really?" Philip teased. "We'll see about that." He lowered his head and rubbed his beard back and forth across the rosy disks on his lover's chest, knowing exactly how Nicolas would respond to such a caress.

As expected, a hoarse shout tore from Nicolas's lips, his hand lifting to his mouth to silence it. "Too late," Philip quipped proudly, snuggling back against the overseer's side and pulling the blanket back over their shoulders.

"In a few hours, it won't matter anyway," Nicolas declared, refusing to admit defeat. "Mrs. Crenshaw is still in Boston and we'll be off the ship and in the complete privacy of your house."

"Our house," Philip insisted, knowing he would not win that argument either until Nicolas had time to settle in and begin to feel truly at home in what had always been Philip's domain.

"Our house," Nicolas conceded because he knew it bothered his lover to think that he was less than committed to their new adventure. It had not been a question of commitment but of practicalities that had held him back, until he realized that Boston was not the haven of anonymity he had imagined it to be. Every time he touched Philip in even the most innocuous of ways, he had felt eyes on them, assessing them. He told himself he was being ridiculous, but it had inhibited him until he no longer dared to have any physical contact with his lover outside their apartment.

Philip had been saddened by the change but had accepted it. Then one night, as they lay in bed, they heard the sounds of the couple in the apartment below them making love. They had stared at each other in horrified shock as they realized that if they could hear others, then those same people could hear them. Suddenly, the haven they had imagined for themselves had become a prison, keeping them from expressing their feelings for each other except in the most hushed, repressed tones possible.

Nicolas had taken one look at Philip's face after harshly telling him to stay quiet as they made love and realized what he had said. He had apologized immediately, but the damage was done.

"We didn't have to be this careful in Bar Harbor," Philip complained the next morning as they ate their breakfast.

Those simple words awoke in Nicolas the same desire he could see in Philip – the desire to be home again. They had talked for hours that day, considering possibilities. The next morning, Nicolas had gone to Emerson to determine how he could effectuate a permanent move to Bar Harbor. Once his mind was made up, everything had fallen into place with remarkable ease. Nicolas's experience with Emerson's blueprints and his familiarity with the suppliers meant he could handle most of his winter business by telegraph as long as the plans arrived before the harbor froze for the winter, leaving him free of the necessity of returning to Boston for the season. If an occasional trip became necessary, he could arrange it for early spring or late fall when it would not interfere with his duties but would still allow him to spend the winter at home.

Guessing the direction of Nicolas's thoughts, Philip kissed his lover gently. "It'll be fine. You'll see."

"I know it will be," Nicolas agreed. "It can't be any worse than it was in Boston."

"It'll be far better than that," Philip insisted. "Like the end of last summer without having to worry about being separated at the end of the season."

"You know I had to go back for the winter," Nicolas protested, still feeling guilty for having dragged Philip to Boston.

"I know, love," Philip assured him. "You couldn't have made all those arrangements unless you were there. I'm not sorry we went, not at all. I'm just glad we're going home."

"So am I."

Philip's smile turned seductive. "Why don't you show me just how glad?" he teased, his hand sliding between their bodies to cup Nicolas's morning erection.

The overseer yelped at the sensation of Philip's cold hand on his skin. "Bastard," he hissed, though there was no heat in his words. "Don't complain that I'm not any good to you later if you're going to freeze me now."

Philip snickered, ducking beneath the covers. "Let's see if I can make it up to you."

Before the older man could react, Philip had sucked his cock into the hot cavern of his mouth, reviving the wilting erection immediately.

Nicolas's moan was as loud and uninhibited as Philip could have asked for, encouraging him to take his time and lavish as much pleasure as possible on his lover.

"Turn around," Nicolas gasped, hips arching toward Philip's mouth. "Let me taste you, too."

Philip shifted on the bunk, angling his hips so Nicolas could reach them. He shivered slightly at the sensation of the cold air biting his skin, but then Nicolas was licking at his eager erection and everything else faded to nothing.

Feeling Philip's reaction, Nicolas spread his large hands over the muscles of his lover's buttocks, covering the smooth flesh with the heat of his palms. He felt the other man relax almost immediately, his attention returning to the overseer's erection.

Licking in long strokes, Nicolas wetted every inch of Philip's cock, enjoying the musky flavor that lingered from last night and the sharp, fresh tang of this morning's secretions. His lover was so responsive, a fact that never ceased to amaze and arouse Nicolas. That Philip was as generous in giving pleasure as he was delighted in receiving it was an added bonus that had led to long hours spent exploring each other's bodies during the long, cold nights they had spent tucked together in his bed in Boston.

He looked forward to a lifetime of such explorations.

Hands kneading the strong muscles they encompassed, Nicolas closed his mouth around the tip of Philip's cock, teasing his lover every way he knew how. Hearing – and feeling – the heartfelt groan from beneath the blankets, he started working his way down the silky shaft, his fingers sliding inward toward the tight portal that always opened for him so eagerly. To his delight, the muscle was still relaxed from the night before, letting a long finger inside without any resistance.

Philip shivered convulsively when he felt Nicolas's finger slipping inside him again, unerringly stroking his gland, leaving his legs trembling with the effort of supporting his weight. He told himself to focus on what he was doing to Nicolas, to concentrate on giving his lover pleasure, but each pass of the edge of the older man's fingernail over his sweet spot sent another bolt of mind-numbing lust through him. "Keep that up and I'll come too soon," he husked, lifting his head from Nicolas's cock long enough to speak.

Releasing Philip's erection in turn, Nicolas shrugged and replied, "So come. We have the rest of our lives to love each other."

The words alone almost shattered Philip's control, but he held back a little longer, not quite ready for their morning interlude to end. Not that he thought it would truly be the end. The long days on the ship with nothing to occupy their time but each other had led to lazy, languid hours full of making love, one climax building slowly to the next and the next, a heated surfeit of pleasure that left them at the same time sated and hungry for more. He dipped his head again, taking Nicolas back into his mouth, determined not to neglect his lover despite the passion swamping his senses.

Knowing he could not add another finger without something to ease his way but wanting to add to his lover's desire, Nicolas angled his head, parting the tight muscles and running his tongue along the point where his finger met Philip's flesh. The convulsive shudder that went through the younger man brought a smile to his face. "More?" he asked, nipping at the curve of Philip's buttock.

An inchoate jumble of sounds was Philip's only reply, but it was all the encouragement Nicolas needed to slip his finger from its snug sheath and replace it with his agile tongue.

Philip tried to wait a little longer, to take Nicolas with him, but the combined provocation of his lover's tongue inside him and the sensation of a firm fist closing around his cock was more than his lust-driven senses could withstand. His muscles spasmed reflexively, his entire body trembling as his cock disgorged its creamy load all over his lover's broad chest. His legs wanted to collapse beneath him, but Nicolas's hands kept him upright, his tongue moving down the still twitching shaft to lick the tip clean.

Finally convinced he had wrung all from his lover that Philip had to give, Nicolas rolled them gently to their sides, his hands stroking his lover's flanks slowly, gentling him as he would a spooked horse. He could feel the aftershocks that still shuddered through the younger man's body, prolonging his pleasure. Philip always reacted this way to a particularly intense orgasm. Nicolas's cock throbbed with unassuaged desire, but he reminded himself to be patient, that Philip would see to him thoroughly as soon as he recovered.

Eventually, the blackness around the edges of his vision eased and Philip angled his head, seeking Nicolas's cock in the darkness beneath the blankets. He longed for the hot days of summer when he could lay his lover bare and enjoy the sight of him as well as the scent and taste, but the chilly air of the cabin made that impossible for now. He would just have to rely on touch to guide him. Sliding his hands over Nicolas's strong thighs, he made his way back to their juncture, seeking the hard flesh between them. When he found it, he drew it into his mouth, sucking forcefully, knowing that his lover would be too far gone now for gentle caresses.

It took mere moments for Nicolas to come explosively, his seed shooting down Philip's throat, his body trembling with the force of his release. The blacksmith stroked his lover's hips through his climax, enjoying the fact that he had turned the tables on his controlled lover, making him thrash and cry out as loudly as

Philip had done earlier. Releasing the softening shaft, he turned back around so that his head rested against Nicolas' shoulder again. "I love you," he murmured softly, letting the post-coital lassitude wash through him, leaving him boneless against his lover's side.

Nicolas kissed the top of Philip's head softly, not having the energy to move more than that, even after hearing his favorite words fall from his lover's lips. Closing his eyes, he drifted off to dreams of what would await them when they reached Bar Harbor.

THE spring sun glistened on the gentle waves in the harbor as the schooner docked at the pier. The two men standing by the rail exchanged meaningful smiles.

"Home at last," Philip murmured, taking a deep breath of the crisp air, relishing the smell of land so different from the city stench of Boston.

"Home to stay," Nicolas agreed.

"We'll have to stay at Widow Taylor's for a few days," Philip mused as the crew lowered the gangplank. "I have no idea what condition our house will be in after the winter storms."

"With this being a new site, we won't be able to start until all the materials arrive anyway," Nicolas reminded him. "We should have a few weeks of peace at least to get settled back in."

"It'll save time, too, not having to start with the caretaker's cabin," Philip said with a grin. "You aren't going to insist on that ridiculous pretense, are you?"

"What would be the point?" Nicolas retorted. "I hardly used it last summer and the crew didn't desert me then. I may lose a few more this year over it, but it's like you kept telling me all winter. We're old news here. The scandal's come and gone and now we'll just be an oddity."

They walked down the gangplank and into town side by side, hands not touching but close enough they could feel each other's warmth. They had discussed at length how their lives would play out if they moved back and both of them had agreed they would not in any way flaunt their relationship.

"Philip! Nicolas! Welcome back!"

"Hello, Shawn," Philip called when the sheriff hailed them. "It's good to be here."

"Will you be staying then?"

Both men nodded. "For good. We're headed to Widow Taylor's now until we can open my house and repair any damage from the winter."

"It's not Widow Taylor's house anymore," Shawn told them, stifling a smile.

"What? Is Alicia all right?"

"Oh, she's fine," Shawn assured him, his grin breaking free. "It's Mrs. Parnell's boarding house now."

"About time!" Philip exclaimed, hugging his friend. "So, do you think she has room?"

"For you? Always. Welcome home."